THE SECOND CHANCE

MORGAN UTLEY

ACKNOWLEDGMENTS

Writing a book is a lot harder than it looks. I've dreamed of writing a book since I was sixteen years old, and I never thought I would finish one. However, through persistence and lots of revisions, ten years later I finally completed my first novel. Due to this accomplishment, I have a lot of people to be thankful for.

First off, I have to thank my wonderful husband, John. He constantly encourages me, listens to my endless thoughts and ideas, and helps with the kids, so I can have some peaceful writing time. His level of support is something I could never repay, and I am eternally grateful that I have him by my side. He truly is the love of my life.

To my teacher Lisa Lowell, who was always willing to lend an ear, offer advice, or point me in the right direction. If it weren't for her, I never would have finished this book or found Next Chapter, so thank you so much.

To my family for encouraging me and being my lifelong friends. To my wonderful parents, Jeff and Susie, who have loved and supported me through my many ups and downs. They have been the best cheerleaders anyone could ask for and have loved me no matter what. To my in-laws, Wendy and Chad, who welcomed me into their family and love me as if I was one of their own.

Finally, to all those who played a part in helping me finish this book: Mary Clark, Kirstin Glenn, Hailey Harris, Jenna Lumb, Rachel McClellan, Lynn McFarland, Vivian Rogers, Sarah Villarreal, Kylee Wilcox, and Douhet Wilcox. Thank you for everything you have done.

For my husband John, who gave me my own second chance. I love you, sweetheart.

CHAPTER 1

"Hello, Peyton. How are you doing today?" Dr. Schoenborn asked.

Peyton walked into the room, sat down in the chair across from the doctor, and answered his question.

"I'm fine, and you?" She looked at Dr. Schoenborn and tried to give him a smile that didn't look as fake as it felt.

"I'm well. Thank you for asking." He looked down into a file folder she assumed was hers and briefly read over the notes written in it. "So," he said slowly, "last week we talked about you communicating with Derek's parents again..." Peyton flinched at the sound of Derek's name. "Did you by any chance do that?"

He looked up at her with big brown, curious

eyes. They reminded her of the cows back at home that would follow her wherever she went, waiting with subtle anticipation. Peyton looked down to avoid eye contact to try and get the image of Dr. Schoenborn with a cow's head out of her mind. He wasn't the best-looking man and, at times, made her uncomfortable when he would look at her. She knew the moment she spoke, he would start writing down notes on his notepad as if his life depended on it.

"Actually, I did," Peyton stated. Dr. Schoenborn's head shot up and looked at her in amazement.

"You did?" he gasped and leaned forward with eagerness. "How did it go? What did they say? How did you feel?" He clearly couldn't stop the questions from spewing out his mouth.

"Uh…" She didn't know where to begin and was overwhelmed with all the questions he had asked her.

"I'm sorry. I don't mean to jump at you. I'm just very shocked. We've been talking about doing this for months, so why now? Answer me that first." Dr. Schoenborn was practically on the edge of his seat now, waiting for my response.

"It just felt like the right time. I woke up and felt —different. I can't explain it. I had been thinking a lot about Derek the day prior and wondered how his parents were doing. So, I thought I would give them a call." Peyton didn't know what answer the man was looking for or what he would get out of her answer, but she couldn't explain it any better.

"Oh, Miss Peyton! At last, I think we are seeing progress!" he exclaimed.

Despite his comment being a bit brash, she couldn't help but smile at the little party he was throwing himself, while scribbling away on his notepad.

The past few months hadn't been easy, and no one expected them to be any easier after what she had been through. After the accident, she was assigned a therapist and was forced to go by her parents after weeks locked in her room, refusing to come out or do anything. Every week on Thursday, at eleven o'clock, her mom would drive her to her therapy session, drop her off to go run errands, and pick her up afterwards. The first few sessions, her mom would walk in with her and wait for the doctor to walk her back to his office. As the weeks went on, she began to trust Peyton a little more and would start dropping her off instead.

To begin with, Peyton had absolutely no desire to ever step foot into a therapist's office. She thought she was just fine and could cope without it since only crazy people needed to go see a therapist. However, when she had to see a primary care doctor for routine check-ups following the accident, they were under the impression that she was depressed. The moment they mentioned a therapist, her parents agreed right away and set up an appointment. Naturally, she fought and argued about it and was adamant about not going, but when the doctor had mentioned antidepressants, she conceded.

"Well Peyton, I'm glad to hear you called them! How were they? Were they surprised by your call?" Dr. Schoenborn asked again.

"Yeah, I guess. They were definitely surprised, tears were shed," she said and shrugged her shoulders. "I don't know, but we didn't talk about the actual accident. We just asked how we were and what we were up to. It wasn't a very long conversation. It honestly felt kinda awkward." She made her sentences short and abrupt, hoping he wouldn't ask any more questions because, honestly, the whole phone conversation with her late husband's parents was awkward. They didn't speak much and didn't know what to say. They mostly spoke about the weather, asked how her parents were doing, and inquired whether or not she was still working at her old job. Unfortunately, she had to answer no to that one and told them that she had quit her job and was helping her dad out instead. After that they didn't push for anymore answers, because they knew why she chose to quit.

"Good, good." He nodded and began writing again. Thankfully he took the hint and didn't ask any more questions on the subject. "How has your anxiety been?"

Shoot. She hoped he wouldn't ask this one. She thought about lying, but she had made a promise to her parents and the doctor that she would tell the truth to the best of her abilities and wouldn't sugar-coat anything.

"It's been okay. I have my panic attacks now and again. I think it's getting better..." she trailed off. She knew he wouldn't buy it. It didn't help that she had recurring nightmares of the accident and then woke up in full-blown panic attacks. Then her mother would rush in to hug her and wipe away the tears.

"You know, we can solve that problem and pre-scribe you something that can help with those," he said with concern in his eyes.

"No," she said abruptly. "No, I think it's getting better. Truly, I'm just fine."

The doctor wrote on his notepad, looked up at her, and smiled. "Well, if you ever think it could help, please don't hesitate to let me know, and I can help you. I want to congratulate you on finally reaching out to Derek's"—Peyton flinched again —"parents..." He trailed off and jotted a note down. He had noticed Peyton flinching at the sound of Derek's name again. "Now that we have completed that goal, I want to give you another one. It has to do with trust."

Oh boy, Peyton thought to herself.

"I want you to find a friend. Whether it be an old one or a new one. I want you to find a buddy you can hang out with, go shopping with, go out to eat with, or just simply be able to lend an ear to someone. No one deserves to be alone, and Peyton, I know you have been alone."

Peyton looked down and felt tears begin to well up in her eyes. She tried to hide it, but nothing got past the man. She looked up to see a tissue being held out to her. She smiled and nodded in gratitude, gently wiping her tears away.

"It's okay to cry, Peyton. It's okay for people to see it. You've been through a lot, and it's so hard to watch you struggle because you're so young. You have the whole world laid out at your feet. I just don't want you to see it pass by and regret it someday. But you have done so well since you've started coming to see me! Don't disregard all the growth and progress you've made over these last few months. You're doing quite well. So, Peyton, what's the new goal?" The doctor looked at her and smiled encouragingly.

She exhaled and said, "To find a friend." Now that she had said it, she began to get worried. Where was she going to find a friend? All her old friends were married and had moved away. She was spotty at going to church, and she didn't go out very often. Her opportunities to find a friend were pretty limited, so she had a feeling she was going to be stuck with this goal for a while.

"Perfect! And on that note, we will end for today." He stood up and waited for her to do the same. They shook hands, and he followed her out of his office.

Once they were in the reception area, he called out to the front desk, "Noah, care for a lunch break?"

Peyton looked toward the front desk and saw a man rise from behind it. He was tall, with dark brown hair and blue eyes that twinkled. He was obviously athletic and had laugh lines by his eyes that she noticed when he smiled.

"That sounds great, thank you," he said and began to put on his jacket. He had a deep voice, and she noticed a bit of a twang in his speech. She didn't realize she had been staring until he looked at her once his jacket was zipped and smiled. She smiled back and sped up her walking pace.

"Oh, Peyton," Dr. Schoenborn called after her. She wasn't fast enough. "Allow me to introduce my nephew. This is Noah. Noah, this is Peyton. He will be filling in for Nancy while she is on maternity leave.

Suddenly a million thoughts began to flood her mind. First of all, she didn't even know the receptionist's name, let alone that Nancy was pregnant. She tried to keep to herself as much as possible. Obviously, Dr. Schoenborn wasn't going to let that happen. Second, she was upset that he had even bothered to introduce her to Noah in the first place. She was already embarrassed enough coming here and didn't want people to know. Third, Noah didn't look anything like Dr. Schoenborn, who was a plump man in his late forties with blonde curly hair to match with his big brown cow eyes. He had absolutely no resemblance to Noah, and clearly, Noah was blessed with the looks.

In the midst of her thoughts, Noah had walked up to her and was holding out a hand without her realizing it. Once she noticed Noah in front of her extending his hand, she jumped and, without hesitation, grabbed his hand, unsure how long he had been standing there.

"Hi." It was all she could spit out.

"Nice to meet you," Noah said and smiled at her.

She could feel her cheeks flushing red and managed to say, "Nice to meet you too." Peyton was looking at Noah, and he was looking at her in return real intently. It was as if they had all the time in the world to stand there, still shaking hands, look at each other, and memorize as much of each other as they could.

The sound of someone clearing their throat made Peyton jump, again, and she dropped Noah's hand. "Well, Noah. Let's get going. I have an appointment in an hour, and my tummy is wanting some Mexican food," Dr. Schoenborn said while patting his stomach.

"Sounds good," Noah replied, still looking at Peyton. "Peyton, I'll see you around."

"See you," she said and half ran out the front doors to her mom waiting in the car.

CHAPTER 2

*B*y the time Peyton got into the car, she was breathing heavy and caused the windows on her side of the car to fog up.

"Peyton?" her mother asked. "Peyton, are you alright? What happened?"

The only word that she could muster was, "Drive."

"What?" her mom questioned.

"Drive! Drive, drive, drive! Hurry, before they come out!" she said a little clearer, and her mom pulled away from the curb and in the direction of home.

As her mom drove away, Peyton looked back and watched Noah and Dr. Schoenborn walk out of the office. She turned around to breathe a sigh of relief and closed her eyes.

"Excuse me." Peyton's eyes opened to see her mother looking back and forth between her and the road. "Why did I just do that? What just happened? Are you okay?" She'd successfully scared her mother.

"Yes, I'm fine." She was hoping she could get away with not answering the other questions.

"Then why did I have to drive away so fast? I felt like we just got done robbing a bank, and the cops were coming after us!" her mom dramatized.

"Well, I didn't want them to see us and have to make another awkward conversation," Peyton admitted.

"Us? Who?" She wasn't going to let it go.

"Dr. Schoenborn… and his nephew, Noah."

She tried to look in her rearview mirror to see if she could see him, but they were too far down the road by now.

"Why didn't you let me see him?" her mother asked with concern.

"Because I was a complete idiot in there, with my mouth practically hanging open and staring at the poor guy like I was crazy!" Peyton cried and put her head in her hands.

"Ah, so he must have been cute." Her mom smiled.

Peyton whipped her head around to look at her mother. "Don't go there," she said coldly.

11

It was as if a cool breeze had just blown into the car.

Her mom took a deep breath as if to brace herself for what she was going to say next.

"Honey, it's been eight months. Don't you think it would be alright if…"

"No," she interrupted, "I don't think it would be."

"Okay. Okay. I guess so." Her mom decided to change the subject for the moment. "I made roast and potatoes with brown gravy. You know, your favorite." She tried to win her daughter back and get her talking again.

"Sounds good. Thanks, Mom," Peyton said with a smile.

"How was Dr. Schoenborn today?"

"As weird as ever. He gave me a new goal today."

"Oh yeah? That's good. What is it?" her mom asked.

Peyton sighed, "To make a new friend."

All her mom said was, "Interesting."

Peyton figured she was thinking more like it was a mere coincidence that she had met Noah but wasn't going to dare say that. Peyton had absolutely no desire to even think about making a new friend, let alone dating or thinking about boys. That ship had sailed and ended up crashing and sinking to the bottom of the ocean.

The rest of the car ride was quiet, which Peyton appreciated. She enjoyed watching the trees become closer together as they drove farther away from the city. Pretty soon, it looked like they were driving through a forest, not seeing any houses nearby. Their driveway was hidden, and unless you were looking for it, it was easy to drive right by. It was a gravel road with many potholes, and it stretched about a mile. Every day, Peyton would wake up and run up and down the driveway, sometimes multiple times to get a good run in. She enjoyed running quite a bit and had even been on the cross-country team when she was in high school. After the accident, she spent lots of time walking and running up and down the driveway to cry and get away from the constant questions of, *"Are you okay?"* or *"Do you need anything?"*

Once they arrived at the house and climbed out of the car, she could smell the pot roast her mom had promised. Eager to be inside, she rushed in and headed straight for the kitchen. She had expected her dad to be in there but found someone else standing in there instead.

"Hey, Sis!" It was her younger brother, Chris.

"Hi, Chris"—she forced a smile—"How are you doing?"

"I'm doing great! I just got back from hiking and canyoneering in Zion National Park," her brother replied. "It was amazing! I wish you could have come! It was a complete blast, and I met someone! Her name is Gloria. She's amazing! In fact, I brought her here to meet you all! She's in the living room talking to Dad." Chris was practically jumping up and down. He looked like Peyton. He had dirty blonde hair, which honestly looked a little longer than his usual haircut. He liked to travel a lot and was a big outdoors guy, so if he felt like going somewhere, he did it. He had gray-blue eyes that could easily reflect what he was feeling, like Peyton's, and his eyes right now were full of energy and excitement. He was a pretty good-looking and overall fun-loving and charismatic guy. If anyone felt like going on an adventure, he was the guy to call up and do it with.

"That's great," Peyton stammered. "Let me talk to Mom really fast." She turned around to look at her mom, and she looked just as concerned as Peyton felt.

Peyton walked toward her mom and pulled her into the pantry, shutting the door. "Don't make me go in there," she pleaded.

"Peyton, he's very excited," her mom said. "Please, put on a welcoming face for just five minutes, and then you can make your excuse and leave."

"Ouch," Peyton mumbled, and tears started forming in her eyes.

"Peyton, he would have wanted you to be happy." Peyton started to look down, but her mother's hand caught her chin. She knew now that she wasn't talking about Chris. "He wouldn't want you feeling this kind of pain after all this time. He would have wanted you to move on as I'm sure you would have wanted the same for him. Don't let your past keep you from progressing to your future. That's why it's called the past. Derek loved you, and there's no doubt about that." Hearing his name caused her to wince, and her mom didn't miss it, but she kept talking regardless of Peyton's reaction. "But can you imagine if he were here right now? He would tell you to wipe those tears from your eyes and to start doing something for yourself! He would want you to be happy and enjoy the moments, even the little ones. Am I right?"

Peyton nodded her head and began to cry. She was heartbroken, and it wasn't a secret. For months she had spent her time at home, helping with the farm, working on her dad's paperwork for his butchering company, cleaning as much as she could, and only going out when she had her therapy appointments. She would only run errands with her mom every once in a while because she was always afraid of seeing someone she knew. She usually wore a hat whenever she went out in public now. She hadn't even gone to church, which was something she had always done every Sunday. But now she couldn't bring herself to do it. Every time someone asked if she was okay, she was reminded that she actually wasn't. That the accident really did happen, and Derek was gone because of it. Whenever that happened, it was as if the accident happened over and over again, and it was heart-wrenching.

However, what her mother was saying to her was true. Derek wouldn't have wanted her to still be moping around at home avoiding people. She should also be happy for her little brother even if it meant stretching herself out of her comfort zone.

"Okay, I can do it. I'll go out there." Peyton nodded, wiping away her tears.

"That's my girl," her mom said. "Now let's go. I want to check out this girl."

They walked out of the pantry and found Chris eating the roast that her mom had made for dinner.

"Christopher Neal, you get your grubby fingers out of that roast right now! That is for dinner," her mom said sternly.

Chris put his hands up in the air, "Okay, okay. Sorry, Mom. Now that you're done talking, can we go in there now? I think Dad is boring her to death."

"Yes, we can, but on your way out, grab another plate setting for your little friend." It was obvious that Peyton's mom wasn't happy, but if there's anything that boy had lacked in learning, it's that no one messes with mom's pot roast.

They all started walking in the direction of the living room. Peyton took a glance in the mirror to make sure she didn't look like a mess. To her dismay, she did. She had makeup under her eyes that she quickly wiped off, and her dark brown braid was coming undone. She pulled her hair out and put it up in a high ponytail, and quickly smoothed out her clothes.

In the living room sat her father, who was a tall man with gray hair that was thinning on the top of his head. He was a man who looked as if he was always happy and having a good time. In the chair next to him sat a little Latina woman who was absolutely gorgeous. She had long dark black hair that went all the way down her back, brown eyes that matched with her incredibly long eyelashes, and a big white beautiful smile with red lipstick to compliment it.

"Hey! You guys are home!" her dad said and walked over to stand by his wife while Chris walked over to stand by Gloria, putting his arm around her.

"Guys, this is Gloria! Gloria, this is my mom, Cheryl, and my sister, Peyton," Chris gestured back and forth between the ladies.

"Hi! It's very nice to meet you!" she said with an accent Peyton assumed was from Mexico.

"Nice to meet you," Peyton's mom said and

reached out to shake Gloria's hand, and Peyton followed suit.

"You have a beautiful home!" Peyton got the impression she was very happy and excited about everything all of the time. This reminded her of Chris, which was probably why they got along so well.

"Thank you," Peyton's mom said. "I have dinner all ready to go. Are you guys ready to eat? I know someone is." She peered over at Chris and gave him a look.

"That sounds great, Mom!" Chris replied to his mom's jab, and everyone headed to the dining room table.

The roast and mashed potatoes were just as good as Peyton expected them to be. Her mom was a natural at making it, and Peyton never got sick of it. Luckily, she didn't have to do a lot of talking because her parents wanted to know all about Chis and his new girl, Gloria, from El Salvador. Where they met and all those things that conveniently took up the majority of the conversation at dinner. She tried to ask Peyton questions, but Peyton kept the answers short to try and prevent her from wanting to ask more questions and delve into subjects she had absolutely no desire to talk about. To Peyton's relief, Chris and Gloria had made plans with another couple for the evening and left shortly after dinner.

After they left, Peyton helped her parents clean up dinner, kissed them goodnight, and headed to bed. The moment she reached her pillow, she cried. She was angry, frustrated, and disappointed. She didn't understand why Chris could be happy but not her. She didn't understand how he could find love, but she couldn't have it. She was upset because he came all the way home to rub his happiness in her face. She was upset because she didn't want any negative feelings towards her fun-loving, carefree brother. She wanted to be happy for him and congratulate him on doing one of the hardest things a person ever had to do—find love.

Nevertheless, Peyton knew that she really wasn't upset with her brother, and that she knew already all the answers to her questions. Deep down, Peyton knew that she was jealous. That's what frustrated her most.

CHAPTER 3

*P*eyton woke up Saturday morning with a terrible headache. Her conflicting emotions and stress had given her vivid nightmares that caused her to toss and turn all night. It's not that it wasn't normal for her, but last night was just so much worse, and she briefly remembered her mom coming in to console her. She sat up to look at the clock to see that it was ten o'clock in the morning. She bolted straight up from her bed and started scrambling around looking for some running clothes. By now, she should have had her run in, been showered, dressed, and ready for the day. Granted, it wasn't like she did much during the day.

Her mornings consisted of waking up around seven, going for a run, feeding the cows and the goats she had out back, showering off the stench she had accumulated throughout the morning, and then hanging with her mom or working with her dad. Sometimes she would help her in the garden or help with dinner. Other times, they would run errands or read together. Most of the time, since Peyton hadn't been going to church, they would study the scriptures together and read past conference talks.

It wasn't that Peyton didn't believe in the church, she did. Admittedly, the first few weeks after the accident, she was angry and repeatedly questioned in her prayers why Derek had to be taken away from her. She felt like she was being punished and didn't deserve it. Time passed, and she slowly began to understand that everyone has their time, and to her dismay, everything happens for a reason. She still didn't understand what the reason was, but she hoped one day she would.

Peyton finished her run, only doing a couple of miles due to the accidental sleep in, cleaned herself up, and entered the kitchen. Her dad—Peyton assumed he was out working on the fence—had left his homemade waffles for her with some eggs and bacon. Every Saturday, her dad made a big breakfast for the family, usually involving his homemade waffles. Since he would go to work so early during the week, he hardly had any chances to make them then. So, Saturday became the day for waffles. It was a tradition that even Chris would make an effort to not miss, but she hadn't seen him anywhere around the house.

"Hello!" As if right on cue. "Hello? Anyone in here?" Chris called.

"Always," Peyton said.

"Peyton! Oh, sweet. I'm glad you're here. I was dying to ask you if you liked Gloria!" he said ecstatically.

"Yeah, I thought she was very nice." Peyton smiled at him for encouragement.

"Awesome! Where's Mom?" he asked, looking around in an attempt to find her.

"I don't know. I just got down here," Peyton admitted.

Chris raised his eyebrows. "Isn't it a little late for you?" he teased.

"I thought the same thing when I woke up. I didn't even realize."

"Well, sleepyhead." He picked up a waffle and took a bite of it. "I'm going to go find Mom," he said with a mouth full of food.

"Sounds good. I'm going to go find Dad." Peyton didn't know she had any intention of finding her dad, but it had just slipped out. However, she figured it was a good idea since she bailed on him with the chores this morning.

She grabbed a piece of waffle and headed outside to the field. Her dad was hunched over, dripping in sweat and trying to fix part of a fence that a dumb cow had run into.

Her dad was a man who never liked to sit still. He always had to be doing something, especially on Saturdays. He liked to find projects to do and make the most of his time. Sometimes, it drove her mom nuts because she liked to have her dad home, but whenever he was home, he was trying to get something done.

"Hey, Dad," Peyton said.

Her dad spun around and chuckled to himself, "Did the Sandman get you last night?"

Everybody had noticed she had slept in longer than usual.

"Apparently. He didn't let me know he was coming, but, yes, he visited." She decided to play along with the joke.

"Are you doing alright today?" he asked with concern on his face.

"I think so. I don't know. Thursday was a very off day for me, I guess, and my sleep clearly reflected it. I feel completely jumbled this morning."

"Yeah, I never thought I'd see your brother settle down or even attempt to. But adventures are better when you have someone by your side enjoying them with ya." He looked up at Peyton, and tears starting to well up in her eyes. "Oh, I'm sorry, sweetheart. Sometimes I say the wrong things at the wrong times."

"It's okay," she sniffed and wiped her eyes. "You're right. It is better to have someone by your side. To tackle the world with, to laugh with, to enjoy it. He should want that, who doesn't." She knelt in the tall grass and sobbed.

She heard her dad walk over and wrap his arms around her. "Oh, Peyton, my little bumblebee. Someone took your sting."

"I don't want to cry anymore, Dad. I don't. I really don't. I feel pathetic every time I do, but I still cry. It still happens, and it makes me so frustrated."

"Listen, Sis. You have been through a tough time. Most people go through life not understanding the amount of loss you have gone through. It's okay to cry. Your mother and I understand. I can't imagine what I would do if I lost your mother."

"It sucks. I know there's a time to mourn, and Mom was telling me that Derek wouldn't want me to still be sad and crying, but I'm having such a hard time moving past this. And then seeing Chris with his new girlfriend and how happy he was. I had that, and it was taken from me. I had complete happiness. I did everything right, but it was short-lived." Peyton was blubbering now and could hardly utter any words.

"At least he got to finish out his life with you! He couldn't have been any happier than what he was," her father said soothingly. "He married you, and he left this world knowing he was going to be a dad. What better way to end this life. If there's any advice I could give you, it's to count your blessings and think of all the people who love you and will always love you for eternities to come. Including Derek. Also, keep in mind that you were left here for a reason. We almost lost you in the accident, but you miraculously recovered. Make the most of this life that you have been blessed with even if you think you're being punished."

Peyton nodded her head and leaned into her dad's hug. She knew he was right. It was time to make the most out of life. "Thanks, Daddy, I'll do my best. I'm going to try and take your advice. I really am. And you're right, Derek was happy, and I thank heaven that he left this world feeling nothing less." She had her breathing under control now and wasn't crying as hard.

Her dad kissed her on the forehead and hugged her. "You can do it. I know you can. Now I'm going to get back to this stupid fence. If that cow runs into the fence again, I just might shoot it," her dad teased and winked at her.

"Do you want any help?" Peyton asked.

"No, you head back to the house. I think your mom wanted to see if you wanted to go shopping with her," her dad informed her.

"Ah, I guess I should probably go, huh?" Peyton hated shopping. Not only because her mom took "shop 'til you drop" literally, but every time they went out shopping, they ran into people, and the questions began.

"I think you know the answer to that, sweetheart. Go have fun!" He turned away from her and headed back toward the warped fence.

She stood up and walked back toward the house. She was surprised to hear her dad mention that she had been pregnant when the accident had happened. It was as if there was an unspoken rule throughout the house to not mention that she had, in fact, lost the baby. Peyton wasn't sure if it was because of the actual accident or the emotional toll it took on her body once she realized Derek was never going to wake up that had caused her miscarriage. She had concluded that it was probably a good mix of both.

During her walk back to the house, Peyton remembered the day that she had found out she was pregnant…

She had been throwing up for the past week out of nowhere. She thought it was food poisoning because they had tried out a new Mexican restaurant the night before. Then nausea and the puking had continued, and she thought she had a bug. So, she went to the doctor concerned since she had been throwing up so much over the week. He decided to take some blood samples and sent her home to wait for the results.

Not an hour later, she received a call back from the doctor. "Miss Peyton, I got your lab results back, and you show no sign of infection or anything. You're just pregnant."

"Excuse me?" It was all she could say.

"You're pregnant, just barely though. It's been about five weeks. Have you noticed whether or not you've had a period yet?"

"Uh…" As she was thinking about her cycle, she ran into the bathroom where she kept a calendar to track her cycle, and her jaw dropped. She hadn't even realized that she was a week late. She had been so distracted that she didn't even think about the timing of her period.

"Peyton?" The doctor snapped her out of her daze, "Are you okay?"

"Yes, sorry. I guess I didn't even notice that I was late. Um, should I be making an appointment or doing anything at all?" She could hardly get the words out. She was in shock.

"You should think about getting some prenatal vitamins, and when you're eight weeks pregnant, then you should come to see us. Do you have any other questions for me?" the doctor asked.

"No. No, I think that clears up everything for me. Thank you so much, Dr. Peterson."

"No problem. See you in a few weeks." Then he hung up the phone.

Peyton started jumping up and down with excitement and running around the house squealing like a little girl. Then she started becoming dizzy and ran to the bathroom to throw up. After that, she wanted to tell her husband so badly that she picked the phone back up and started dialing. Once the phone started ringing, she quickly hung up before he could get the chance to answer.

She didn't want to tell him over the phone since he would be distracted at work, and she wanted to see his face. She looked at the clock and realized he would be home in three hours. She had three hours to prepare.

Peyton zoomed around her apartment like a tornado. She cleaned the entire house, did the laundry, made the bed, and even made his favorite dinner—lasagna with garlic bread and a green salad. Luckily, lasagna was a long process, and it kept her busy to help the time pass quickly. She kept looking at the clock and expected him to be home within the next fifteen minutes. She quickly set the table, lit a few candles, and then turned some music on in the background. She looked at the clock again and saw that now it was ten minutes. She wasn't the most patient person in the world, so she sat at the table and waited as best as she could.

As time ticked on, she became more and more

irritated and aggravated. This was the best possible news she could ever tell him, and he was taking forever to get home. She couldn't stand it. Peyton stood up from the table to finish the dishes and clean off the counters. When those were done, she started looking at the floors and decided to grab the broom, sweeping the entire floor. She was starting to become so meticulous in her sweeping, she would brush the same corner over and over again to get every last crumb off the floor.

Then, of course, she noticed a smudge on the floor, so after the pile was swept up, she grabbed a rag and started mopping on her hands and knees.

She was so distracted with her cleaning that she didn't even hear the door open.

"Peyton? Peyton, where are you? I'm home!" he called.

She jumped right up, threw the rag into the sink, and straightened out her clothes before replying, "I'm in the kitchen!"

He walked in and was covered in grime from head to foot. He was a mechanic and worked on cars all day long at his shop. He always had a faint oily smell to him that she always loved, and it had become a homey smell. Peyton looked at him and just admired him, thinking how lucky she was and how he took her breath every time he was in her presence. He was pretty tall, about six feet, which was good, because she was not very tall at all. He had piercing blue eyes and messy blonde hair. It was always messy, but she didn't mind. She couldn't expect it to be perfect when he was under cars all day. He had a smile that could wake a whole room up with laugh lines all around his eyes. He was always laughing or smiling, because he was just happy, and it was contagious. He was her little sunspot, her shooting star. He lightened up her world every day and reminded her of how blessed she genuinely was to have a man like him in her life.

"Boy, does it smell good in here! I'm hungry! I haven't eaten since this morning. I've been so busy." He looked over at the table, and his face lit up, "Lasagna! Oh no, what did you do?" She couldn't fool him.

"Oh, you shut up. Do you want to eat now or wait until you shower?" she asked.

"What, you think I need to shower, huh?" He started coming closer to her. She knew what was coming.

"Don't you dare," she started to back up slowly. A playful grin spread across his face. Then he darted into a sprint towards her, and before she could escape, he grabbed her and started hugging her tightly.

"Aw, come on. You're going to make me smell too!" Peyton whined.

"I guess you're going to need a shower too." He

winked and smiled. He thought he was so funny. Before she should reply, he started talking again, "Let's eat though. I'm so hungry."

"Okay, that's fine with me." They sat down at the dinner table, said a prayer, and started dishing out the food.

"Man, this looks so good. Thank you for making this, sweetheart," he said.

Her heart started thumping harder in her chest; should she tell him now or later? She had been waiting for what felt like forever, and anticipation was practically bubbling up to her lips from excitement. Instead of spoiling his dinner, she decided to at least let him finish his plate.

Peyton sat there and tried not to eat fast but couldn't help it. She was so excited. There were a few times she almost just blurted it out, but she didn't want to. She just listened to him talk and tried to enjoy the nice dinner as much as she could.

He finally finished the last bite of his lasagna and started reaching for the spoon for seconds.

"Honey, do you mind waiting? I wanted to tell you something," she said abruptly.

"Aha! I knew there was something!" he exclaimed.

"It's not what you think. I have some news to tell you…" she started trailing off.

"Oh, so you didn't break anything or spend lots of money?"

"No." She took a deep breath and contemplated how she was going to tell him. Then she started freaking out about whether or not he was going to be happy or upset.

"Peyton, whatever it is you can tell me. Sorry, I was just teasing you." He grabbed my hand, looked right at me, and smiled.

"I know, I know. It's okay." She took a minute to collect herself and looked at him. She slowly started to calm down and get her breathing back to normal. The look of reassurance in his eyes helped her believe that no matter what, he was going to love her and take care of her little family for the rest of her life.

"Derek, I'm pregnant," she whispered.

"What? Really?" Derek whispered back.

"Yes, I went to the doctor this morning because I was so sick. They took a blood sample, and well, they found out I was pregnant. It explains why I've been sick." She looked into his eyes, and she could see the wheels turning in his head. "Are you okay, honey?"

He picked her up, spun her around, and kissed her forehead. "I have never been so happy in my life. I love you."

It had been one of the happiest days of her life and a treasured memory that she liked to look back on and remember. Pure joy emulated throughout both of them, and they couldn't stop smiling for days. It was a good reminder to her that true happiness was possible, and it could be found. Even though, at times, it felt like a sad memory because of the tragedy that followed weeks later. It was still a memory that brought her a little hope. Hope that she could find that kind of true happiness again.

CHAPTER 4

*P*eyton walked inside the house and found her mom sitting there with Chris in the living room. It wasn't a big house, but it had enough room for everyone. Her mother had spent a lot of time working on this room after the accident in an attempt to keep her mind occupied, and she had turned it into a beautiful room. The room was color coordinated with navy couches accompanied by white and orange pillows, white end tables, and a white TV stand. The walls were a light grey color decorated with many family pictures and artwork that her mom had collected throughout the years. Each picture was placed perfectly on the wall, in a way that didn't look cluttered, but it kept your eyes flowing easily from picture to picture.

"Hi, sweetheart," her mom said, looking up

from her conversation with Chris. "Would you like to go shopping with me? I want to look for a new top, and I thought we could look for some new running shoes for you. I noticed yours were pretty worn, and I can imagine your feet are starting to hurt."

"Yeah, that sounds like fun. And you're right, my feet are starting to hurt when I run. Are we leaving right now?" Peyton asked.

Her eyes widened. Peyton hadn't agreed to go shopping with her in a while. "Yep, I just need to go grab my purse. Chris is going to go have lunch with Gloria anyway. Right?" Her mom looked over at him.

"Well, if you're going to buy me new shoes, I'll cancel my lunch date." He started smiling widely and blinking his eyelashes.

"I took you shopping not too long ago and helped pay for some new repelling gear, so I think you're just fine," she said and patted him on the leg.

"Only joking, Mom. Thank you, by the way." He kissed her on the cheek and stood up from the couch. "I better head out or else I'm going to be late for my date. Love you guys."

"Love you too," Peyton and her mom said in unison and watched him walk out.

Peyton's mom waited to make sure her brother had left and said, "That boy is head over heels for La Señorita."

"Yeah, I could tell. Do you think she feels the same way?"

"Hard to say. I guess we will know with time. Ready to go?"

"Just about. Let me go change into some jeans and grab my purse. And maybe I'll put a little mascara on." Peyton shrugged her shoulders and started walking away to her room.

"You look exhausted," her mom pointed out.

"I feel exhausted. Last night was a bad night, so maybe I'll put some concealer on too. I'm sure the bags under my eyes are horrendous," Peyton admitted.

"Okay. Well, I'm going to go tell your father goodbye, and then I'll be waiting out in the car."

"Sounds good."

Peyton climbed the stairs two at a time and quickly changed into jeans, a zippy hoodie, and some Converse tennis shoes. She looked in the mirror but resembled a zombie. She pulled out her makeup and began applying it to the dark bags under her eyes and to the pimples that had popped up.

She finished the rest of her makeup routine, which included a little foundation, blush, and mascara, then threw her hair into a high ponytail, and grabbed her purse. When she stepped outside to head to the car, her mom was in the car just as she said she would be. She climbed into the passenger seat and buckled up.

"Ready?" her mom asked.

"Yep, let's go!" Peyton tried to act enthusiastically, but she certainly wasn't. She just hoped her mom wouldn't try to shop the entire day.

The drive back into town was just as beautiful as usual with all the greenery surrounding them, except the closer they got, the more houses that interrupted the natural beauty the earth provided. Sometimes, Peyton wished she lived in a cabin out in the forest, where she could live on her own and enjoy the beauty of nature. However, she knew that this earth life was never meant to be lived through alone. It was meant to enjoy being surrounded by people who love each other, and Peyton was having to constantly remind herself of that. Some days, the idea of becoming a hermit sounded amazing, but that would only lead her down a dark and lonely path.

Her mom pulled into the mall parking lot and parked the car in the closest stall possible.

"Brace yourself," her mom teased.

"Don't worry. I am," Peyton said in a serious tone.

They climbed out of the car and half ran to the entrance nearest them because there was a crazy wind storm going on. Once they entered the mall, they went into a store that was obviously intended for her mom because it had a bunch of clothes that were not meant for Peyton's age group. Not at all Peyton's style. Although, Peyton didn't really have a style. Her wardrobe consisted of sweatpants, jeans, t-shirts, sweatshirts, and workout clothes. She also had a few dresses that she would wear to church, but she hadn't worn them in a while. So, they stayed in the back of her closet for the time being.

They shopped around the store for a little bit, and her mom grabbed a few new blouses to try on in the fitting rooms. She would come out occasionally, and Peyton would give her an opinion of the shirt. Then she would go back in to try another shirt on.

"What do you think of this?" Her mom came out of the dressing room in a beautiful royal blue blouse that brought out her blue eyes perfectly.

"I love it, Mom! I really do, and it looks stunning on you!" Peyton sincerely tried to sell it because the sooner her mom found a blouse, the sooner they could go. Not only that, but she truly did love the shirt, and her mom was an indecisive woman.

"Are you sure? You don't think it accentuates the wrong places?" Her mom was gesturing toward her stomach and kept turning around to look at her backside. Her mom wasn't a large woman, but she was definitely curvy and was self-conscious about showing them.

"No, I actually don't. I love it, and that blue could go with anything. You could also either dress it down and wear it as an everyday shirt, or you could dress it up and wear it to church or on a date with Dad," Peyton explained to her mom as she was still looking at herself in the shirt and fussing with it.

"Alright, if you say so, I'll get it." Her mom had been convinced, and Peyton was elated.

"Mom, the important thing is, do you feel pretty in it?" Peyton looked at her mom and waited for her to answer.

Her mother smiled and said, "Yes, I do. I really like the color and it flows just enough for it to not show too much, ya know?"

"Yep, I thought the same thing." Peyton smiled.

"Great. Well, I think I'm going to buy this, and then let's get something to eat. It's been too long since I've eaten, and if I'm going to keep going, I need fuel," her mom admitted.

They left the dressing room to stand in line at the cashier to buy her mom's new blouse. Once they reached the front of the line, her mom became excited when the cashier mentioned that her shirt was on clearance, so she ran back to get the same blouse in a different color.

Her mom looked at Peyton and shrugged her

shoulders. "Can't hurt, right? It was cute, and I love this maroon color."

Peyton chuckled and nodded in agreement, watching her mom complete the transaction. The other people in line were a little annoyed because her mom ran out of line to grab another shirt, but she didn't care. Peyton was surprised she bought a shirt in the first place because most of the time she would just get frustrated and walk out empty-handed.

"Ready?" her mom asked after grabbing her bag of new shirts.

"Yes, I'm hungry too. I didn't get to eat much before we left. I was talking to dad, and then I got ready to go," Peyton answered as they walked out of the store toward the food courts.

"Did you guys have a good conversation?" she asked.

"I think so," Peyton replied. "Although, I'm sure he told you about it." She looked at her sideways, and her mom smiled.

"Nothing gets past you, does it?" Her mom chuckled.

"Nope. Not much. Plus, I know how that works. You tell each other everything, I get it. I'm not upset by it either. I wish I still had that…" Peyton trailed off and became quiet. She started looking in the shop windows to try and distract herself.

"You will again. Someday."

Peyton gave her a look that made her mom put her hands up in a defensive manner. "I'm not saying right now. But eventually, you will. That's all I'm going to say."

The funny thing was that her mom always said, "that's all I'm going to say," but she always ended up saying something else.

"Anyway, what do you want to eat? What sounds good?" her mom asked in an attempt to change the subject.

"I'll eat anything, you know that. You just pick what you want, and I'll find something I like on the menu."

"Alright, then it's going to be Chinese. Your dad doesn't like Chinese, so I might as well take advantage of the opportunity while he isn't here." She headed towards the Chinese line, and Peyton followed. Once they ordered the food, they sat down at a nearby table to eat while they people-watched around the food court.

"Dad doesn't like Chinese?" Peyton asked in disbelief.

Her mom shook her head, "Nope, never has. He's given it an honest try, too, but he just doesn't like it. It's sad."

"I love Chinese food. I can't believe he doesn't. I guess that makes sense though, now that I think about it, we've never eaten it at home." Peyton said in between bites of her orange chicken.

"Yep. It's a shame too. But you know your dad is more of a hamburger-and-fries guy anyway. He doesn't like any of those crazy spices. Don't even get me started on the first time he tried Thai food. He acted as if someone had just insulted him when he put the curry in his mouth." She started laughing to herself as she recalled the memory.

"I can't blame him there, I..." Peyton stopped talking immediately when she noticed someone else in the food court. He was standing in line for food with his back slightly turned away from her, but she could still recognize him from the distance.

"Peyton, are you okay?" She turned to her mother and realized she had been staring with a worried look on her face. Peyton started blinking her eyes as if she had been in a trance.

"Mom, we need to go," she said urgently.

"What! Whoa, why? You mean leave? We haven't looked for your shoes yet." Her mom sounded upset. She had obviously been enjoying herself with her daughter, so Peyton tried to relax and hide her face.

"We can go anywhere, anywhere else. Just not here," she whispered. She didn't know why she was whispering because Noah was a few yards away from her table. She figured it helped her stay inconspicuous and less likely to be heard.

"Peyton, who are you hiding from?" her mother demanded.

"The guy from Dr. Schoenborn's office. His nephew Noah," she tried to explain quickly.

"Oh, that guy!" Her mother turned around to look behind her. "Which one is he?" Peyton thought her mom sounded too excited.

"No, Mom, please don't try to look for him. I don't want him to see me," she pleaded.

Her mom sat up straight, trying to act casual, "Okay, fine. Will you please explain to me which one he is, and I will very casually look around to find him. I want to see what this boy looks like."

"But mom…"

"Now," her mom interrupted. She was looking serious now, but Peyton knew her curiosity had just peaked, and she wasn't going to let it go.

"Okay, he's in the sandwich line over there," Peyton gestured with her head. "He's the tall one with jeans and a grey pullover sweater."

Her mom very slowly—and in Peyton's opinion quite obviously—turned around to look for the man matching Peyton's description.

She turned back around and leaned forward across the table, "Honey, you know you just about described every man in this food court?"

"Look, it's not my fault every guy has the same wardrobe!" Peyton said sarcastically.

"Okay, okay. Just try to tell me something else, so I can spot him easier," she said.

"Fine, let me look." Peyton looked over at the

line where she had seen Noah standing and then scanned the line to find him. After a brief moment, she found him ordering his food.

"Mom, if you look right now, you can see him in front of the cashier ordering his sandwich," Peyton whispered again.

Her mom turned around a little faster this time, not trying to be as subtle, and looked in the direction Peyton told her to. After a couple of seconds, she turned around and smiled at Peyton.

"That guy taking out his wallet?" she snickered.

Peyton nodded her head and started blushing for what reason she didn't know. "Yes," she mumbled.

Her mom took another glance and smiled even bigger. "Peyton, he's a doll!"

"I know," Peyton admitted and blushed.

"You do?" If her mom smiled any bigger, Peyton was afraid she may be stuck like that.

"Mom, don't go there," Peyton said coolly.

"I won't, but you can't deny that he's a cutie," her mom said.

"Well, I didn't. He is cute, but he's..." Peyton glanced over at the sandwich line and realized he was gone. Quickly scanning the food court, she searched for him until she realized he was walking in the direction of their table, only a few yards away.

"Oh crap. Oh crap, Mom. He's coming!" Peyton

hissed. "Do you think we can make a quick escape?"

"No, but you do need to compose yourself!" her mother said quickly and started wiping her mouth with a napkin and smoothing her hair.

Peyton did the same and looked to see where Noah was at now, and sure enough, he was walking towards them. She knew there was a panicked look in her eyes when she looked at her mom, and her mom motioned for her to inhale and exhale. She took a deep breath and picked up her fork, looking down at her plate of food to try and act as normal as she could.

While she was looking down, she heard a male voice say, "Hi. You're Peyton, right?"

Peyton looked up and could feel her face blushing, "Yeah, that's right, and you're Noah."

"Yeah, we met at my uncle's office. I'm the temporary receptionist," Noah clarified.

"That's right. This is my mom," she pointed across the table, thankful to get the attention off her for a second.

"Hi," her mom said and held out her hand. "Nice to meet you."

Noah took her hand and shook it, "Nice to meet you too."

"Are you here with anyone or would you like to sit down?" her mom asked. Peyton looked at her mom, and her mom smiled at her. But it wasn't a nice smile. It was the kind of smile that told her she was up to no good.

"I can sit down for a minute." He sat down and put his sandwich on the table.

"So, you work as a receptionist? Temporarily?" her mom asked nosily.

"Yes, I'm actually just wrapping up my last few weeks of dental school, and my uncle called in dire need of help while his receptionist was on maternity leave," Noah informed her.

"That's so exciting. Congratulations! A dentist is a great job." Her mom sounded excited, and Peyton knew she was over the moon elated that this happened.

"I think so, and I'm definitely excited to be done with school and move forward in my life," Noah admitted to the ladies.

"I bet you are. Peyton never liked going to the dentist. At one point, she was convinced they liked to watch her squirm in pain when they would scrape her teeth. Once, she got so upset, that she bit the dentist's finger!" Her mom chuckled to herself, and Peyton was less than amused she had mentioned that fact.

"Thanks, Mom," Peyton said sarcastically.

"No, it's all good. I know a lot of people aren't fans of the dentist, but I hope to change some people's minds about going to the dentist." Noah turned to her and smiled.

"Well, if you can clean my teeth without putting me in pain, then I will definitely change my opinion about going to the dentist," she said back to him.

"Deal," he said and smiled.

"Fine. Deal," she said and smiled back at him and felt her face blush even more.

"Well, I had better get going. I promised my uncle I would run some errands, including delivering this sandwich," he teased and held it up.

"That's okay," her mom said. "Peyton and I are on the hunt for running shoes next."

"Oh, cool. You ladies like to run?" Noah inquired.

"No, not me. But Peyton runs every day." She motioned toward her daughter.

"You run every day? That's awesome. I run a lot too. I used to run track in high school actually, and now, I try to run a few times a week. Maybe we should run together sometime," Noah mentioned quickly.

Peyton didn't actually believe her ears. She felt as if her mind had completely drawn a blank until she quickly realized that she wasn't speaking or doing anything. "Yeah, we could definitely do that. Just let me know when."

"What about Monday?" he asked.

Peyton was taken aback at how soon he wanted to get together. "Um, yeah. I think that should work."

"What time do you usually like to run?" he asked her.

"I like to run at about seven in the morning," she informed him.

"Cool. That would be perfect. I have to be at work at nine, so I should have plenty of time. Where do you run?"

By now Peyton was shaking, she could feel her armpits sweating, and she knew her face was absolutely red. She could hardly believe that this boy was interested in running with her or doing anything with her. It was obvious he knew she was going to a grievance counselor and wondered why on earth he would want to date someone in therapy. It was completely embarrassing. The funny thing was that he was completely calm and asked these questions as if they were no big deal. Not to mention, Peyton thought he looked gorgeous today. His hair was a little messy but still looked good like it had been tousled in the wind. He had a strong jawline and rosy cheeks that were most likely caused by the cold outside. It also looked as if his eyes were a little stormy today, yet alert and playful.

"Peyton usually runs around our house," her mom interrupted. She must have noticed Peyton had become tongue-tied and answered the question for her. "She runs around a couple of trails we have around our property, or she runs up and down our driveway."

"That sounds cool. I like trail running. It's a lot of fun. I don't do it often enough. If you want, we can always run there if you like." He looked over at Peyton and waited for an answer.

"Uh, sure. Yeah."

"Sweet. Well, I guess I'll see you on Monday," Noah said and smiled crookedly at her. It made her heart skip a beat.

Of course, this caused Peyton to forget that she could speak and, her mom had to talk for her, again.

"Here, let me write down our address, so you know where we are." Her mom dug into her purse and pulled out a pen and paper to write down our address. Then she handed him the piece of paper with the very valuable information and smiled.

"There you go," she said.

"Okay. Thank you, Mrs..." Noah trailed off..

"Sheffield. Mrs. Sheffield," her mom clarified.

"Great. Well, Mrs. Sheffield, it was good to meet you, and Peyton, do you mind if we exchange numbers too? Just in case I get lost or something?" he asked shyly

"Oh yea, no problem!" she sputtered.

"Great, here's my phone if you don't mind," he offered.

"Here, you can input yours into mine while I use yours," I handed over my phone and he smiled.

"Okay sweet!" After a couple seconds, we gave

each other's phone back. "Alright, well I guess I'll see you Monday. Bye," he waved and started backing away.

"See you then," she said and smiled.

He smiled back a crooked smile, stood up, and walked away from the table.

As Peyton was watching him walk away, her mom spoke. "That was the best thing that has happened in months!" she exclaimed.

"Or the worst thing," Peyton mumbled. "I cannot believe you practically invited him over to the house. And what was up with telling him I hated the dentist? That's a great thing to tell him as he's just finishing up dental school," she said sarcastically and realized her voice was becoming louder and louder with every word she said.

"Honey, I was just trying to help the conversation. You kept wandering off into space and not answering the poor man's questions, so I had to give a little nudge," she said innocently.

"That was more than a little nudge, Mom. That was humiliating. Not only for me, because I acted like a complete idiot once again, but also because of you. And now he has our address. What if he's a stalker? What if he's just taking some bet, and he's out to mess with me?" Peyton questioned.

"Peyton. You and I both know that he did not seem like that at all. He was a very sweet guy, especially since he came out of his way to talk to you.

He was the one that spotted you out of the crowd and decided to talk to you. All I was doing was trying to help. I didn't mean to embarrass you or do anything that made you uncomfortable. And for Pete's sake, it's not my fault the man asked you to go running with him. It's not my fault that a guy other than Derek"—Peyton flinched again at her husband's name—wants to spend time with you. I only have your best interests at heart. Now, before I get too upset to shop anymore, let's get you some new shoes. You are definitely not running in those old things at home when he comes." Her mother stood up, grabbed the trays, and dumped the left-over food in the garbage can, then waited for Peyton to stand up.

At this point, Peyton was fuming. She had no desire to go and look for new shoes for this up-coming running date she had not planned. Quite frankly, she had half a mind to walk away from her mother and call a taxi to drive her home. However, she figured enough damage had been done and de-cided to finish the shopping trip she agreed to be on with her mom.

She stood up and followed her mom in the di-rection of the running store. Her mom was walking at a faster pace than usual, but Peyton knew that was because she was upset. They stepped into the store, and her mom started looking at outfits while Peyton looked at and tried on running shoes. It didn't take her long to find a new pair because she liked to keep to the same brand and type of shoe. When she found the shoes, she showed her mom, and her mom took the shoebox and started matching the shoes to different outfits that she had put together. Apparently, her mother was buying her a brand new outfit as well. The only questions she asked were what size she preferred. Other than that, she picked everything out and bought it without consulting with Peyton or asking if she liked it. Peyton didn't even see what her mother had gotten because she picked it out so fast and stalked off to the cashier to buy everything.

Once the new outfit with matching shoes was paid for, her mom walked out of the store and into the direction of the car. Evidently, they were going home now, and she wasn't going to speak to Peyton at all.

CHAPTER 5

The ride home was quiet. Her mother didn't say a word to her the whole time. When they arrived home, she took the bags out of the car and walked into the house, not bothering to wait for Peyton. Once Peyton entered the house, she was nowhere to be seen. She assumed that her mom went straight up to her room and locked herself in.

Peyton knew she had some apologizing to do. She felt sorry for telling her mom that she had embarrassed her, and that she was out of line. No matter how bad she felt, she knew all her mom wanted was to see her happy again, and that she was just excited that some guy came up to Peyton and asked her on a running date. Not only that, but she was there to witness it, and even if she got ahead of herself, she was over the moon and eager to get whatever ball rolling she could.

Before Peyton could go and face her mom, she went into her room to drop off her purse and take off her shoes. In her room, she found a shopping bag on her bed. The one her mom carried out of the running store in the mall. She took the clothes out of the bag and pulled out a new pair of dark grey running capris with a hot pink sports bra and a lightweight black zip-up jacket with pink accents on it to match her black shoes that happened to have pink laces on them. She had even gotten pink socks to complete the look. After seeing what her mom had bought, she felt really bad and started getting a stomachache. She had been completely unfair to her mom, and she had, in fact, saved Peyton's carcass out there. Her mom was the perfect wingman, and Peyton had thrown her under the bus and told her that she did a horrible job.

Peyton pulled the tags off all her clothes and put the complete outfit on that her mom had thoughtfully picked for her. She even put the new shoes on and walked out of her room towards her mom's.

She knocked on the door, but no one answered.

"Mom?" Peyton called.

Again, no one answered.

"Mom, it's me, Peyton. Can I talk to you?" she asked.

No sound came from behind the door.

"Please, Mom! I'm sorry. I was out of line. Please, open the door," Peyton pleaded.

She waited there for a minute, and when she still heard no sound coming from behind the door, she gave up and started walking back toward her room.

Halfway across the hall, she heard the sound of a lock clicking and the door open. She turned around and saw her mom standing in the doorway, with tears running down her face.

Peyton walked toward her mom and hugged her.

They stood in the doorway hugging for a couple of minutes, and then her mom pulled away to look at her.

"What do you think?" she asked.

"I really like it a lot. I like the subtle hints of pink, and the pants are easy to move around in and not too tight. My shoes are super comfortable too. I'm going to need to walk around in these today to break them in," Peyton told her.

"I'm glad. I think you look cute and ready to run!"

"I feel like I should go run now, but I just don't have the energy," Peyton told her mom. "I didn't know you were going to buy me an entire outfit too. Thank you so much for getting me all this." She gestured to the outfit.

"Well, I wanted to make sure you were all set

and ready to go on Monday, with Noah…" Her voice became quieter at the end, and she started staring at the floor.

"Mom," Peyton began, "I shouldn't have said you humiliated me. I did that all on my own. You were the perfect wingman, and I was too overwhelmed and upset to see that. And I'm truly sorry I hurt you and embarrassed you."

Her mom looked up from the floor with tears in her eyes and tried to speak but was getting choked up. Once she composed herself a little bit, she told Peyton, "I was just trying to help you. That's all I wanted, and I was so excited to see this sweet, handsome guy have the guts to come up to you with me there and ask you on a date."

Peyton wasn't sure if going on a run around her parent's property would qualify as a date, but she decided to not argue about it.

Her mom continued, "I know I may have embarrassed you a little bit, and maybe I did encourage it, but I only had your best interests at heart. And if I do say so myself, I think he still liked you even though you couldn't form a sentence to save your life." She teased and started laughing.

Peyton began laughing too. "Yeah, I felt like a little school girl today. You saved me. I'd be surprised if he even showed up on Monday."

"Oh, I think he will." Her mom sounded all too confident.

"Well, even if he does, it won't mean anything. He's probably just trying to be nice. Besides that, I don't think I'm ready to think of another man like that," Peyton stated to her mom.

"You might be surprised," her mom replied to Peyton's comment.

Peyton looked at her mom and smiled, "I know you want what's best for me and for me to move past this grief, but I don't think it's time for me to move on yet. I miss Derek so much." Peyton's voice cracked as tears began to form in her eyes. "I already feel like I got my happily ever after. I got my prince charming. My ending just came a lot sooner than I ever wanted it to come. I know it could never happen, but sometimes I just wish he could come back. I wish I could go back in time and change what happened. And in those moments, the worst part is realizing that I can't. I'm stuck with a consequence from somebody else's actions. If it weren't for that stupid drunk driver, my life would be completely different. I just have had a hard time moving past that aspect." Peyton had never admitted this to anyone. Not even her parents or her therapist. She had been doing her mourning in silence and struggled to admit her true feelings to anyone.

"Peyton. His life ended, but yours didn't!" her mom said. "You are a strong, independent, amazing woman who deserves to have the best life possible. You deserve to wake up every morning and be excited to be alive. I know you think you don't get a second chance. I know you miss him. I'm sure he misses you. But please take advantage of the life you have. Take advantage of the opportunities that you will have and don't let them pass by. You know what, honey? Moving on doesn't mean forgetting, it means you chose happiness over hurt. It's time to stop hurting, my darling. And honey, it's also time to start forgiving. Forgiving yourself, forgiving that drunk driver, and forgiving God."

"It's so hard, Mom! All of it! I'm having this mental battle with myself about getting out there, hanging with friends. Meeting new people, but it makes me sick. But as I told Dad, I will try my best to make the most with what I have. I'm trying, and I will work on my forgiveness. Although that one may take time."

"And you have time to do it! As long as you're working on it, take all the time you need. Just do your best. Be your best you, and find her again. Find my happy Peyton." Peyton thought it sounded as if her mom was pleading.

"I will, Mom. You know, I've been thinking, and I think it's about time I started going back to church," Peyton informed her mom.

"Peyton, that's great. I'm so happy about this." Tears started forming in her mom's eyes, and she gave Peyton a big hug.

"Mom," Peyton said sheepishly, "just take it

easy tomorrow. I know everyone is going to have questions, and I really don't want to get bombarded. So, can you please do your best to shield me just a little bit? If I have to recount these last few months over and over again, I'll break down."

"Yes, I'll make sure people are aware and sensitive to anything they may ask you and answer them myself if that will help you. We will take things one step at a time." She looked at her and smiled.

"Thanks, Mom. I'm going to take these clothes off now and put them away, so they're ready to go on Monday." Peyton turned and started walking toward her room.

"Oh yes, I'm so excited about that!" her mom shrieked.

Peyton turned her head back towards her mom, "Remember, one step at a time—baby steps."

Her mom gave Peyton two thumbs up with a cheesy smile, "That's right, sweetheart, baby steps."

CHAPTER 6

Sunday morning, Peyton dug through the back of her closet and pulled out her church dresses. Part of her was regretting she had told her mom she wanted to go to church, but she knew that part of it was the nerves getting to her. Peyton and her parents were a little late for church, so, gratefully, they were able to sneak in and sit down while the meeting was going.

The meeting went fast, and she received many hugs from people she had known previously or had grown up with. A lot of people tried to ask questions about how she was doing and if she had any plans, but her mom would quickly interrupt and say things were good. People got the hint that questions weren't welcome. Peyton appreciated the people who would talk to her and pretend as if nothing happened.

The two-block hours passed, and Peyton had never been so relieved in her life. She felt a lot better about going to church, but the number of tears she saw and the hugs she got just about put her over the edge.

"I'm proud of you, Peyton," her mom said on the way home. "I can't imagine that was easy for you to do, but I'm so impressed that you did it."

"Thanks, Mom, but don't be mad if I say I'm glad it's over. Not because of the church part because I really did miss it. But, I didn't miss all the hugs with lingering perfume and smiles with tear-stained faces."

"I don't blame you."

The rest of her day was quiet. Sundays were a time when she enjoyed reading a book and helping her mom cook dinner. Her brother and Gloria came back for Sunday dinner and kept the conversation going. Chris talked the most and was very animated the whole time. Peyton mostly sat and listened to Chris talk about their recent experience of trying a new Peruvian restaurant that resulted in them having food poisoning. Peyton had kept thinking about the next morning and was constantly looking at the clock. Every hour that passed, she knew Noah was going to be coming that much sooner.

When bedtime came around, her mother gave her a hug and said, "Get some sleep, if you can."

Peyton knew she was teasing, but it still didn't help. She knew she wasn't going to get any sleep. She had been more worried about the next morning with Noah than she had been going to church. In her mind, she figured this was a good thing because she felt ready to go to church again, but she didn't feel like she was ready to have a boy over at the house again.

As she predicted, Peyton didn't get much sleep at all. All she did was toss and turn, and whenever she did sleep, she had nightmares about the next morning. One of her dreams had her showing up to go running in no pants. Another one was where Noah didn't show up at all, and she was standing on the porch waiting for him to show up. The last dream had Derek show up to run with her instead, and he kept asking her, "Have you forgotten about me already?" or "I thought you loved me?" She woke up crying.

At that point, her mom came in to calm her down and let her know that everything was fine. She held Peyton for a minute to help settle her down, and once she stopped crying, she laid her back down and left the room. This was a common occurrence for Peyton when she would have bad nightmares like this. It happened more when the accident first oc-

curred, and as time went on, the nightmares happened less and less. Regardless of how often she had
them, her mom always came in to calm her down
and let her know that everything was alright. There
were nights when she would wake up and cry all
night and wouldn't sleep much at all. Despite this,
her mom would still stay up with her and hold her
to let her know that everything was okay.

Her mom was her superhero. Not a day went by
that she didn't quietly recognize how much her
mom did for her. She was a hard-working woman,
who always kept herself busy and had other people's best interests at heart before her own. Her
mom was always willing to help at church, she at-
tended all of Peyton's cross country meets, piano
recitals, and her brother's soccer games, and always
made sure to make people meals when they needed
it. Not only that, but she also liked to quilt in her
spare time and give them to mothers who had babies or to elderly women in the winter.

Needless to say, in Peyton's eyes, her mom truly
was a superhero, and thinking about all this helped
put Peyton back to sleep. Thankfully, she slept the
rest of the night until her alarm went off at six
o'clock without any more nightmares. She sat up in
her bed and stared at the wall for a few minutes
and then rolled out of bed. After using the bathroom and brushing her teeth, she walked down-

stairs and saw her dad sitting at the table reading his scriptures as he did every morning.

"Do you want some breakfast, Dad?" Peyton asked.

"Sure, don't you have a date soon though?" her dad mentioned coyly.

"Not a date. We're just going on a run. But I have time to do this, and it will keep me distracted till he comes," Peyton clarified and started pulling out the eggs, milk and bread.

"Are you sure you want to eat, Sis? You don't usually eat before a run. You don't want to throw up in front of the poor guy," her dad teased.

"I'm not going to eat yet. I just thought you might want breakfast. Plus, as I said, I'm trying to kill time," Peyton reminded him and started cracking eggs into a bowl.

"You don't have to make me breakfast. Don't you have to get ready or something?" he asked.

"I'm going on a run. I'm not going to the prom, Dad," Peyton pointed out and began whisking the eggs and milk together.

"Alright, alright. Sorry I said anything," he said and returned to reading his scriptures.

Peyton finished making the French toast and gave it to her dad.

"Thanks, sweetheart, it looks great," he said and started to eat his breakfast.

"Yeah, you're welcome," Peyton said and watched her mom walk into the kitchen.

"Peyton Eva, why are you down here? You should be getting ready!" her mom exclaimed, sounding frantic. "Your dad can take care of himself, so get upstairs and get dressed, put your hair in a cute ponytail, and cover up that nasty zit on your chin, please!"

"Mom," Peyton said calmly in hopes it would calm her mom down, "it's six-thirty, so I have plenty of time."

"Honey, time goes faster than you think. Please, just go start getting ready. He could be here anytime between now and seven, and if you still look like that, well, I don't want him to run away screaming," her mom said sarcastically.

"You're funny, Mom, but if it will really make you happy, then I will go," She gave in to her mom's pestering and started walking up the stairs to get ready.

"Thank you!" Her mom raised her hands in the air as if it were an answer to prayer.

Peyton did exactly what her mom asked. She put on the new outfit her mom had bought her the previous day, put her hair up in a cute ponytail, put a hat on to cover up the frizzy hair, and even covered up the zit on her chin. Secretly, she was grateful her mom had pointed out the zit because she hadn't looked in the mirror all morning.

She knew her mom was excited for her and wanted everything to go as smoothly as possible. Unfortunately, she forgot that her daughter could be a total klutz and was bound to do something stupid.

Peyton walked down the stairs and saw that her mom was waiting by the staircase.

"See!" Her mom held up her phone to Peyton's eye level, "It's six fifty-five, five minutes to spare. Imagine if I hadn't come down the stairs, you might have still had your new friend on your chin, sticking out."

"Heavens, Cheryl, take a breath. Do you need a minute to get ready too? You're all flustered," her dad said in between his snickers.

"Don't mock, not now," she snapped back and walked to the front window to peer through the blinds. She let out an exasperated sigh and spun around to look at Peyton, "He's not here yet, so maybe you should put on some mascara or something, honey."

"Mom," Peyton put her hands on her mom's shoulders and looked her in the eyes, "I'm fine. It's going to be fine, and I look fine. For the love of Pete, I'm going on a run, and I have a hat to hide my face. It's all good!" she explained. Even though she was saying this to her mom, she didn't feel fine. Her stomach was in knots, her heart was beating faster than she knew it should, and she was sweating from pure nerves. However, at this point, she wasn't going to let her mom see any of this because she knew if her mom saw she was nervous, it would make her more nervous.

"Okay, okay. You're right. I'm good. I'm good." She closed her eyes and took a deep breath.

"You'd think she was the one going on the date," Peyton's dad mumbled behind her.

"Walter!" Before she could put her husband in his place, they heard a knock on the door.

"What time is it?" her mom whispered frantically.

Peyton pulled her phone out. "Seven," she whispered back.

"Wow! Right on time! Good man!" She smiled and gave a thumbs up.

"That's great, Mom. Why don't you open the door?"

"Oh!" Her mom spun around and walked quickly toward the door and opened it.

In the doorway stood a tall man wearing knee-length black basketball shorts, a white shirt that accented his muscular physique, and an air of confidence that radiated off him. He didn't seem nervous or worried at all to be at her house. To top it all off, the moment the door opened, he locked eyes with her and smiled at her in a way that made her forget to speak, let alone breathe.

"Hello, Noah! Welcome to our home. Would you

like to come in?" It was moments like these when she couldn't believe how her mom could be a complete basket case in one moment and then compose herself in the next. No one would have ever thought she had been about to unleash on her dad just seconds before. Her voice was even and calm, and her body language reflected it. She was amazing, and Peyton couldn't help but quietly smile to herself.

"Yes, thank you," he said in his deep, even voice. "You have a beautiful home and live on a great piece of property."

"Why, thank you, Noah. That's quite kind. We just completely redid the living room, and Walter works hard on the property every day, and it really shows."

"I don't know about that," Peyton's dad stood up and held his hand out to Noah. "Hi, I'm Walter, Peyton's dad. Cheryl works just as hard. She keeps the house beautiful, and the garden is gorgeous. She truly has quite the green thumb."

"I'll have to check it out. Maybe Peyton will show me after our run or something," Noah was looking directly at Peyton now. Her parents turned their heads in Peyton's direction and awaited her reply to Noah's suggestion.

"Um, yeah. Yeah, I could do that." She looked down at her feet to avoid his gaze and waited for someone to say something to get the attention off her.

"Sounds great! Should we get running?" he asked with almost a hint of excitement in his voice that caused Peyton's head to snap back up.

"Yeah, let's hit the pavement!" She tried to sound enthusiastic, but in her mind, she thought she overplayed it. Nonetheless, Noah chuckled, along with her dad, and her mom gave her a look that she knew meant to tone it down.

"Awesome. I'll see you later," Peyton said as she hugged both her parents.

"Have fun!" her dad said.

"Remember to smile," her mom whispered in her ear.

Peyton followed Noah out the door, and as she was shutting the door, she turned around and gave a sarcastic smile to her mom that caused her mom to roll her eyes and her dad to belly laugh. She quickly shut the door to hopefully avoid Noah asking a question.

"Alright, so how far do you want to go?" she asked, trying to sound as confident as possible.

"Whatever you want to do, I'll just go where you go," Noah said and smiled in a way that made Peyton's heart skip a beat. He wanted to go where she wanted to.

"I was thinking maybe five miles? Is that okay?" she asked hesitantly. The last thing she wanted to do was make him uncomfortable and make him feel pressured to run farther than he was able to. Hopefully she aimed low enough.

"Yeah, that sounds just fine. So, where do you start?" Noah asked.

"I usually run down the driveway and back sometimes when I just want to get out and run without having to think of a route. But, my dad helped me make a trail that goes around the property, and if we run down the driveway and come back, the trail starts by the tree with the swing over there. Then it will follow along the edge of all the trees. Plus, this way, you'll be able to see the entire farm." She looked at Noah, and he was nodding his head, looking around.

"It's very pretty here," he stated. He didn't seem very eager to start running, but then he looked at Peyton and said, "Should we go?"

"Yup." There was a bit of hesitancy as to who would start running first, but then Noah held out his hand and motioned for her to lead the way. She started running, and he followed alongside with her with ease.

"I hope my little legs won't slow you down. Your legs are much longer than mine. I'm sure the stride ratio is your one to my three." She had been looking at his legs. In her mind, she was thinking he was about six feet tall. She also noticed that they were muscular and toned, and she became mesmerized by his muscles flexing with each step he took.

"Oh, so you're checking out my legs now, huh?" he teased. Crap, he had caught her checking him out. Of course, this made her turn about fifty shades of red, and she tried to turn her face away to hide it. Unfortunately, she heard him laugh, and she had reason to believe that he had seen her face turn the shade of a tomato.

"No, not necessarily." She tried to retrace her steps and make it seem as if she wasn't all goo-goo eyes.

He laughed and asked, "So, how long have you lived here?"

Bless his heart, he was letting it go. "My parents have lived here all my life."

"Which would make you…"

"Twenty-four, and you?"

"I'm twenty-six," Noah replied.

"Uh, cool."

They were silent for a couple of minutes to catch their breath from talking and reached the end of the driveway. Once there, they turned around, and Noah picked up the conversation.

"So, do you work?"

"Um, here and there. My dad raises cows, pigs, and chickens for clients and will often butcher them, too, so I help him take care of the billing and the paperwork and run contracts back and forth to the attorney's office. So basically, I do all the be-hind-the-scenes work." She tried to wrap it up quickly because she felt like she had been babbling. However, when she looked up, Noah was staring at her as if he was mesmerized by her.

"Hey, that doesn't sound too bad. At least you get to work from home, right?" Peyton was begin-ning to get the impression that this guy was a half-glass-full kind of person.

"Yeah, it is nice. I can stay at home and bill cus-tomers in my pajamas," she paused as she swerved around a big rock alongside the driveway. "I defi-nitely can't complain."

"I'd say. Granted, I wear scrubs most of the day, and sometimes I feel like I'm wearing pajamas, so I guess I can't either." He smiled his crooked smile, and she smiled back as if now they shared some-thing special in common.

"Speaking of scrubs," she began, "Are you ex-cited to graduate?"

"You have no idea," he laughed and shook his head. "It has been a crazy four years. And I'm ready to have that diploma in hand and begin practicing."

"I can't even imagine. Are you going to open up your own practice?" Peyton asked.

"I'm actually joining another practice in town. His name is Dr. Stocks, and he will be retiring in the next few years and will basically transfer his clients to me, which is especially nice."

"I'll say. I hear building up clients could be the hardest part. That's really nice of him," Peyton said, sounding impressed.

"Yeah, it usually doesn't work out like that. I've been a patient of Dr. Stocks's since I was a kid, and dentistry caught my interest. I always asked him questions about what he was doing and why, what instruments were used for what, and I grew to love it. Eventually, I told Dr. Stocks I wanted to be a dentist, and he was fully on board from day one. He gave me a part-time job to clean the instruments and the rooms when I was in high school, and then I became one of the receptionists while I was doing my under-grad and once in a while if he needed help, I would come sub for his receptionists if someone couldn't make it in. He's kind of been my mentor through all of this. When he found out I got into dental school, he offered me the job once I graduated. During school, he came to me and told me that he was planning on retiring in about five years and that he wanted to give me the practice with all the clients and all the staff. I couldn't believe it, but I think it will work out well because I know most, if not all of the patients, and all of the staff, so I think it will be a smooth transition."

"Wow, that's amazing, Noah. I'm happy for you. I'm sure that's given you some peace of mind. And you know you'll be able to pay off your student loans… someday." She smiled, and Noah chuckled at the comment.

"You have no idea. I've looked at my loan amount only a couple of times and regretted it each time, so I stopped looking. I just decided it's going to be a ridiculously large number for a long time." He laughed, and Peyton joined in. She couldn't imagine being so far into debt. It gave her anxiety just thinking about it.

As they neared the tree swing, she slowed down and turned onto the grassy trail that her dad helped her mow frequently to keep the trail looking good.

"Hey, this is pretty nice," Noah said, sounding impressed.

"Yeah, my daddy is amazing," Peyton admitted and could feel herself becoming teary-eyed thinking of the conversation she had recently had with him.

"This property is beautiful, too," he said as he looked around.

"I agree. I love coming out here to walk around, read a book, or run, of course."

"I can see why. So, if I can't find you, I can assume you're running around out here?" He looked at her, smiling his infamous crooked smile, and it got her heart beating faster than it should've been.

Her face flushed. "Yep," she breathed out. "This is where you can usually find me, somewhere around here." She smiled and tried to regulate her breathing again.

"Do you have a favorite spot?" he asked.

"You know, as a matter of fact, I do."

"Can I see it?" She looked up at him and could swear he had a twinkle in his eye as he smiled down at her. Even though he had sweat dripping down his face, he looked like he had stepped off the pages of a magazine. His shirt was clinging to his chest from the sweat, and she could really make out his muscle definition. His arms were slightly flexed from running, but she could tell he was strong. His hair was even messier, but it still looked like something he had done on purpose. And when he smiled, it just took her breath away every time. His teeth were white and perfectly straight, and laugh lines would wrinkle around his eyes. It was so genuine and playful she couldn't help but react to it every time.

"Sure, sure. Yeah, you can see it. Right now?" She slowed down to a jog and waited for him to answer.

"Sure, if that's okay with you." He had slowed down to a jog as well. "If you want to finish the run though, I understand."

"No, we can go right now," she said and slowed down to a walk. "I think we've done about three miles anyway, and that's good enough for me." Noah walked alongside her but stayed very close to her. Just a few centimeters closer, and they would be touching. It was as if she could feel the energy bouncing back and forth between their two bodies.

"So, I'll show you the garden because it's on our way to the spot, and then we'll head over there. Is that okay with you?"

"Yep! This way I get to see two things."

"Cool, so the garden is just over here…" she trailed off and walked toward the garden. It really was beautiful. Her mom had her build a white picket fence lined with chicken wire all around the garden to help keep critters out. She opened the gate to the garden that had a beautiful arch above it with blush pink roses climbing all over it. With it being spring, all the flowers were beginning to bud and bloom, which made it exciting as everything turned from green to a bounty of colors.

"This is pretty," Noah said, sounding amazed.

"Yeah, it makes it feel like you're entering a completely different world." They walked around the garden as Noah looked around and witnessed all the beautiful colors and greenery around him. Her mom had roses around the entire garden as it was her favorite flower, along with plenty of hydrangeas, sunflowers, daisies, zinnias, pansies, impatiens, and other flowers that Peyton didn't know the names of. In the back of the garden was where most of the vegetables and fruit were grown. She had a few rows of corn along with pumpkins, zucchini, squash, green beans, lettuce, carrots, lots of tomatoes, and just about every herb that she could grow. There were some blueberries and raspberries as well. It was like her mom's own personal Garden of Eden.

"Okay," Noah began, "This is by far the coolest, most beautiful garden I have ever seen. How is she able to keep track and take care of all of this?"

"She spends a few hours a day out here picking the weeds and pruning bushes. My dad set up a sprinkler system that automatically turns on every day so that takes care of the watering. I come out here, too, sometimes when I have all my paperwork done and help pick the vegetables or weed or something. It's a group effort, but she has definitely done most of the work."

"Your mom is a garden wizard," he stated.

Peyton laughed, "I'll be sure to tell her you said that. There are also a couple of fruit trees, too, but they aren't in the garden. There are a couple of apple trees in the horse pasture and some behind the garden over there," Peyton was pointing beyond the garden a little farther. "There is also a pear tree and a plum tree."

"Talk about being self-sufficient. I'm impressed," Noah sounded blown away and kept looking around.

"Yeah, my mom always wanted to be prepared and self-sufficient as you said in case anything ever happened. I guess self-reliance is another way I would call it."

"Well, now I know where I'm going in case anything happens," Noah smiled, and butterflies started flying around in her stomach.

"Anytime." She smiled back and looked into his eyes, and he was staring right back. It seemed like minutes that they stood like this, smiling and staring at each other. In her mind, they probably resembled a scene from a romantic movie where the two love birds were standing in the middle of a beautiful garden about to kiss and live happily ever after. Of course, once she started thinking that, her cheeks started to burn red, and she looked down.

"Well," Noah said, and Peyton looked back up at him, "as much as I have enjoyed seeing the garden, and it definitely exceeded my expectations, I'm ready to see that secret spot of yours."

"Alright, let's go!" She tried to play it cool, but she was pretty sure this secret spot was going to be a major let down after her mom's gorgeous garden. Along the way, she pointed out the barn, the chicken coop, where the cows and horses were, and told the story of the time she was chasing around a calf and slipped in a mud pie. And no, not the chocolate kind.

With a couple of good laughs along the way, they reached the edge of the trees. "So, this is actually part of my little running trail, and it just keeps going and loops around the barn all the way back to the house."

Noah looked around and followed to where she had pointed, "That's cool. So, is this the spot?" he asked coyly.

Peyton shook her head, "No. It's through here." She pointed to another path that cut through the trees.

"Another path? You guys must be outside all the time trying to keep up on everything," he pointed out.

"It's just kind of our way of life out here, I guess. An escape to a simpler place where you're not distracted by the hustle and bustle and the next new thing, ya know?" Peyton shrugged, "I like it. Being this close to nature helps me remember how blessed we are to live on such a beautiful planet."

"I couldn't agree more." Noah smiled his wretched crooked smile again that caused Peyton's stomach to stir again. She smiled back and started walking onto the dirt path through the trees.

"You're not going to murder me out here, are you?" Noah asked playfully. "Because it seems as if you're leading me to the middle of nowhere."

"No, my dad would find you out here eventually, and I would be the first suspect." She smiled up at him, and he laughed.

"Oh, I'm glad that's the only thing preventing it from happening," he teased.

She glanced behind her to look at him and said with a smile, "Not the only thing." Had she just flirted?

Before he could respond, they came into a clearing that revealed a couple of acres of grass and a river flowing slowly not far from them. There was a dock with a bench at the end of it, where her and her dad would often come to fly fish. A few feet away from the river was a fire pit and some picnic benches where they had spent many nights around a campfire staying up late.

They stopped walking just before stepping onto the dock and listened to the water trickling downstream. It was Peyton's favorite sound in the world. Well, now it was. Before her favorite sound was Derek's laugh, and now that it was taken away, all she had to rely on now was this river. Despite it sounding sad, it held a lot of memories. Both good and bad, but she couldn't seem to stay away from it. It brought on a feeling of peace and tranquility to her that it became her favorite spot to pray and talk to her Heavenly Father about her deepest, darkest thoughts and feelings.

"This place is amazing," Noah said.

"Yeah, it really is," Peyton said while scanning around and taking in the scene.

"I can see why this is your favorite spot. How often do you come here?" he asked.

"Almost every day. It's my place to ponder and think, ya know?"

"Yeah. If I had a spot like this, this is where I would go." He stopped talking when he felt a buzz in his pocket and pulled out his phone. "That's my uncle. He needs me to pick him up a bagel before going to the office. I should probably head out."

Peyton thought the last thing Dr. Schoenborn needed was a bagel. "Alright, let's head back." She turned around and headed back to the house with Noah following behind her.

They walked quietly through the trees and past the garden and didn't say anything until they were close to the house, still walking but at a slower pace.

"Well," Noah began, "thank you for the run and for showing me around. Especially your secret spot. It was a lot of fun, and the scenery was beautiful." Noah's eyes seemed to be smoldering. Almost as if he meant a different kind of scenery.

A blushing Peyton answered, "You're welcome. I'm glad you enjoyed it all."

"I definitely did." Noah smiled and looked at his phone again. "I better get going, I have work soon. Will I see you around?" he asked, almost sounding hopeful, but still maintaining a level of mystery to where she wasn't sure if he sounded hopeful or not.

"Oh, I'm sure," she stammered. She wasn't sure if her beating heart could take anymore.

"Awesome. Bye, Peyton, and thanks again!" He waved goodbye and slowly turned around, walking away as if he wasn't sure what he was doing. It made Peyton wonder what he had wanted to do.

"You're welcome!" She waved back and walked up the front steps of the house and through the front door. She jogged over to the window, peered through the blinds, and watched him drive away down the dusty gravel road.

CHAPTER 7

"Well?" her mom screeched from behind her back.

"Whoa!" Peyton felt as if she had just jumped ten feet in the air. She had not anticipated her mom standing right behind her. "Mom, a little warning next time!" Peyton shrieked. She walked away from the window to sit down and pull her shoes and socks off.

"Sorry! I've been waiting around the house this whole time, and I wanted to hear about it as soon as you came in. Is he gone?" Her mom followed behind and sat at the table next to her.

"Yes, he's gone," Peyton confirmed, looking at her hyper mother.

"Well? Are you going to tell me about it?" she asked.

For her sake, Peyton went on to tell her mom about the entire run. She told her about where they ran, how far they ran, and what they talked about, and she answered all of her mother's questions on top of it. She was fine with this and let her mom hear everything she could until her mom asked the last question, "So, did he ask to see you again?" And to Peyton's disappointment, whether she knew it or not, he hadn't asked if they could get together again. Which made her wonder why? Had she done something wrong?

A couple of days passed, and she still hadn't heard from Noah. The last thing she heard from him was a text a few hours after their run saying thank you. She had replied, and then she received nothing else.

She tried not to make anything of it, but it didn't help that her mom kept asking her if she had heard from him yet. She went on her usual runs, got caught up on all her billing and paperwork for her dad, and did extra chores around the house. All these things helped but not completely. She still wondered if she had put him off somehow or said something wrong. Part of her was upset because she didn't want to bother putting herself out there anyway. The last thing she wanted to think was that it was a waste of time, but her thoughts were headed in that direction.

The thing she was genuinely dreading was

going to her therapy appointment. She knew he was working the front desk temporarily, and she didn't know how to act. She couldn't decide whether or not they were platonic, friendly, or extra friendly.

She didn't know. So, when her mom told her it was time to go into town for her appointment, she did what she thought was best. Tried to get out of it.

"You know, Mom. I don't think I'm feeling well," Peyton admitted then coughed.

"You seemed fine this morning when you went on your run," her mom pointed out. Strike one.

"Wasn't there something you had to get done today? If you need to, we can totally reschedule, and I would be fine with that," Peyton said to her mom.

"Nope, I think today is the perfect day for your appointment." Strike two.

Peyton walked over to the back door in one last-ditch effort.

"What's that, Dad?" Peyton yelled and opened the door. "You need my help with the cows? Sure, I'll come right now." Peyton tried to walk out the door, but her mom stopped her.

"Peyton! Get in here," she said sternly. "I know you don't want to go. I know you're disappointed, but the last thing you need to do is make it awkward by canceling and not going to your appointment. You walk in there confident, with a smile on your face, and pretend nothing has happened. You understand me?" Her mom was staring at her, and Peyton knew she was out of hits. Strike three.

"Yes, Mom," she mumbled and sulked out the front door toward the car.

Her mom followed behind her and climbed into the car. "You know I only tell you these things because I love you, right?"

"Yes, Mom, I know," Peyton said and got into the passenger seat. Her mom pulled out of the driveway and began the fifteen-minute drive into town.

Once they arrived at the office, Peyton hesitated before stepping from the car. She knew that she had to regain her composure before going inside the office.

"Are you going to make me hold your hand and walk in there with you?" her mom challenged her.

"No, Mom. No, I'm going, really. I just need a minute to collect my thoughts," she admitted. She leaned her head back against the seat and closed her eyes. She could imagine it going so many different ways, but she knew she couldn't let herself think too much about it. She just had to get in there and be confident as her mom had said.

"Remember what I said, honey—smile. It's all good. And you don't know, maybe it's genuinely nothing, and he's just been super busy. You said he was in dental school, right? And he's graduating this year? Anything could have happened. No worries. Confidence is key." She felt her mom grab and squeeze her hand. She opened her eyes and saw her mom smiling at her. "You can do this," she whispered and smiled.

"Okay, I'm ready." She took a deep breath and opened the car door. "Oh, and hey, Mom," she spun around to look at her, "please don't be late. And turn your phone up." Peyton requested.

"OK, I will. See you later!" She waved.

Peyton shut the door and walked toward the front doors and entered the office. At the front desk sat Noah. He looked up and smiled at her, and for a minute, Peyton forgot she was upset. His hair was tousled around, his crooked smile showed just one dimple on his right cheek, and he was wearing a navy blue shirt that made his eyes pop.

"Hi, Peyton, how are you doing?" Noah asked in his deep voice.

Peyton cleared her throat, "Uh, you know, just fine. You?"

"I'm doing good. Are you here for your eleven o'clock?" he asked.

"Yep. Yep, I am." She looked down at the floor, and he checked her in on the computer.

"Alright, you're all set. I'll let him know you're here, Peyton," He smiled at her, and she felt her heart speed up.

"Thanks," she turned around and sat down in the waiting room.

She tried to pick up a magazine or browse on her phone, but she kept looking up at Noah going back and forth between the computer and a notebook he was writing on. She kept promising herself that she would just look one more time, but somehow she continued looking up. It was getting to the point where she was counting down the minutes in between each glance or trying to stretch herself for as long as she could before looking at him again.

Before she stole another glance at him, Dr. Schoenborn came into the waiting area. "Hello, Peyton, you ready?" He was wearing khaki pants with a purple checkered button-up shirt that appeared to have a jelly stain on it. She was guessing it was from a jelly donut from breakfast.

"Yup, I am!" She tried to sound like she didn't have a care in the world and forced herself not to look at Noah as she followed Dr. Schoenborn.

Peyton followed him into his office and sat down in the same chair she had sat in for months. She looked around the room and nothing had changed. The walls were painted a neutral beige color with a few pictures of mountains that Dr. Schoenborn had no problem telling Peyton he had taken himself. At one end of the room, his desk, scattered with papers, sat in front of a big window.

There were also a few pictures of him and his family on the desk. He had a few file cabinets that Peyton assumed had his patients' files in them with random knick-knacks that sat on top of them. The other end of the room had a big brown couch along with two dark blue accent chairs that Dr. Schoenborn and she preferred to sit in.

"So, Peyton, how was your week?" he asked, pulling out his pen, ready to scribble away on his notepad.

"It was fine. Same thing, nothing new. I ran every day, did some work for my dad, and mostly stayed home," she shrugged, and her shoulders ended her sentence.

"I heard you had some company on one of your runs this week," he smiled and waited for her response.

"Uh, yeah." she looked down, twirling her thumbs. "Noah, your nephew, actually came and ran with me a couple of days ago, and I showed him around the farm. It was fun." She could feel herself blushing and becoming hot. The last thing she wanted to do was talk about his nephew.

"Yeah, he told me about it and said he had a lot of fun." He raised his eyebrows and smiled a frog-like smile that made Peyton squirm in her seat.

"Oh, did he? Well, I'm glad. I did too." she said quietly and continued to look down at her fingers

89

trying to control the sweating she could feel building up in her armpits.

"I'm glad to hear you had a date. It's been a while since you've done something like that, hasn't it?" he inquired, raising an eyebrow.

"Well, I don't know if I would call it a date. We mostly ran anyway. Dr. Schoenborn, this is a little weird to talk about. Not gonna lie," Peyton admitted.

"Peyton, you can talk to me about anything, you know that." Dr. Schoenborn tried to look innocent.

"Yes, but he's your nephew. And I don't want this to turn into you receiving information from him about me like an extra set of eyes. It makes me uncomfortable." Peyton felt bad telling him this, but she didn't want any more questions about it. Especially since she didn't know for herself whether or not it was a date.

"Peyton. I can assure you that all he told me was that he met with you, went running, and that he enjoyed his time with you. The only reason why he told me was that I had asked if he could grab me some breakfast that morning, and he told me he would be a little longer because he was at your house. I am not trying to have someone spy on you or trying to make you feel uncomfortable at all. I apologize if I made you feel that way. However, I wanted to tell you that I was very proud of you for getting out there and going out on this date or whatever it was. You took a huge step last week and made some serious progress. Regardless of it being my nephew. I still want to see how you're doing with this new step and how you're feeling, but I will try to make it sound like I'm not prying, alright?"

Peyton stared at him, and his eyebrows were still raised, but his face was much more serious.

"Okay," she nodded, "I understand."

"Good," he leaned back into his chair as he had leaned forward for his little rant, trying to make a point. "And might I add? The fact that you stood up for yourself just now and told me how you really felt was also very impressive. So, Peyton, good job."

"Thank you," Peyton exhaled and looked at the clock to see that it had only been twenty minutes, and she had forty minutes to go.

"Well, Peyton. I think you made a lot of progress this week. Anything else you would like to talk about?" he asked.

The rest of the appointment consisted of how she was feeling or if she was interested in meeting up with any other friends or having dates. And they talked about her nightmares. He again asked if she wanted something to help her sleep through the night better, but she had no desire to be put on medication. There was a lot of quiet, too, in between each question as Peyton was still feeling a little uncomfortable that Dr. Schoenborn had known about Noah coming to her house. Not to mention, nothing else had actually happened since the run as it had been a very slow week. She thought about bringing up Chris bringing over his new girlfriend, but that would have opened up a whole other can of worms she wasn't up to talking about. She wished that she could leave the appointment early instead of sitting in dead silence with the man, but Dr. Schoenborn told her that she was blocked out for the entire hour, and he was intent on using every minute with her.

"Well, Ms. Peyton, I think we have covered enough today. I have plenty to fill my notes. You are free to go," he informed her, and Peyton secretly did a happy dance. She looked at the clock and saw that it was fifteen 'til, so she was shocked to see that he had ended the session early. He must have been eager to fill his notes.

"Okay, sweet. Well, I'll see you later then." Peyton stood up with Dr. Schoenborn to shake hands and walked out of the office. "Oh wait, Doc, did you want me to schedule another appointment for next week?"

"Yes," he replied, "let's plan on Thursday at the same time again."

Peyton, feeling a little defeated, responded, "Alright, I'll let Noah know." Her heart sank to the bottom of her stomach.

She walked out of the office and forgot that she had to make it past Noah in order to get out of there. She took a deep breath and headed for the front desk.

Noah didn't notice her until she was standing in front of him.

"Oh hey, Peyton! Sorry, I didn't see you. I've been trying to study any chance I can get. Are you done already?" he asked.

"Yeah, we got done early today. Shoot, that reminds me, I need to call my mom," Peyton remembered and pulled out her phone to call her mom. "And Noah, your uncle wants to see me again on Thursday at the same time. Will you make sure I'm on the calendar when you have a chance, please?" she wondered.

"Yeah, I can totally do that," he replied.

"Thank you," Peyton whispered once her phone started ringing.

"Hello?" her mom answered.

"Hey Mom, I got done with my appointment early. Do you mind picking me up, please?" she asked.

"Oh, are you done already? I ran to the store, and I still need to get a few more things. Are you alright waiting?"

"That's fine. I can wait." And then I turned my head away and whispered into the phone, "Are you trying to torture me?"

"Don't be ridiculous!" her mother hissed. "Tell Noah hi for me!" she said cheerily and hung up the phone.

"Crap," Peyton muttered and turned around to look at Noah. "Hey, did that time work out okay for Thursday?"

"Yes, it did," he said. "Hey, is everything okay?"

Peyton looked at her phone and realized what he was talking about. "Oh yeah, my mom is just in the middle of shopping, and since she gave me a ride here, I have to wait for her."

"How long do you think she will be?" he asked.

"I don't know. Depending on how much she needs to get and how many people she sees, it could be a while. But it's okay." She turned around and walked toward the lobby chairs.

"Peyton?" Noah called behind her.

She stopped walking and looked at Noah. "Yes?" Peyton asked and was surprised to see him standing up from behind the desk with his hand wrapped around his neck and his fist stuffed inside his pocket looking a little nervous for whatever he was about to say. Peyton decided it was cute.

"If you would like, I'd be happy to give you a ride home. My uncle doesn't have another patient coming for a few hours, and I could use a break from studying," Noah offered.

Peyton, being caught off guard by his offer, stammered out the next few words, "You don't have to do that. I'm fine with waiting. I have a book downloaded on my phone I could read." She waved her phone and gave him a little smile.

"Are you sure? You would be doing me a favor. I don't think I could read another word. They're starting to swirl and swim off the pages. Plus, it would be a win-win. I give you a ride home, so you don't have to wait, and I get a break from studying. And I guess we would get to spend a little more time with each other too. So, it would be a win-win-win," he chuckled and smiled his half crooked smile. Peyton's face started getting hot, and she looked down at the floor to hide her embarrassment.

"Um, sure if you want to. I don't want to put you out. It's not like I live around the corner." She peered up at him, and he was smiling full on as if he was enjoying the fact she was now beat red.

"The drive sounds nice. Should we go?" He pulled his keys out of his pocket and gathered up his books.

"Yeah, let's go," she said and followed him out the front door and to the parking lot. She looked around outside and noticed that clouds were forming, making it look like it was about to rain.

"Looks like it's going to rain soon," Noah pointed out as if he had just read her mind.

"It does, doesn't it?" She smiled to herself and stopped when Noah stepped in front of a dark green Honda Civic. He walked around to her side, put his books in the backseat, and opened the passenger door for her.

"Why thank you," she said and climbed into the car, buckling her seatbelt.

Noah laughed, "You're welcome, miss." He closed the car door, and Peyton watched him walk around the car to the driver's side. She couldn't help but notice how well he fit into the dark jeans he was wearing. She quickly snapped out of her gaze once she heard the car door open, and she remembered that she should call her mom before she forgot.

"Hey, do you mind if I call my mom real fast and let her know that I got a ride home?" Peyton asked.

"No problem. In fact, I should send my uncle a text letting him know I left..." he trailed off and pulled out his phone to do just that while Peyton pulled out her phone to call her mom. Of course, he was done texting before her mom even answered the phone. He started pulling out of the parking lot when her mom picked up the phone.

"Hello?" her mom answered.

"Hey, Mom. I just wanted to let you know that Noah is going to give me a ride home, so you don't have to rush." Peyton tried to sound as if it was no big deal, but she knew the moment she told her mom this, she would try to play twenty questions with her.

"He's what? Really? That's amazing! Are you in the car with him right now? What car does he drive? Are you on your way home right now? Is he staying at the house for a little bit? Should I plan on another person for dinner?" Her mom tried to ramble on, but Peyton knew she had to interrupt her or else the questions would never end.

"Yeah, Mom, we're in his car and on our way right now. I'll see you when you get home, okay? I love you, Mom," Peyton said as calmly as she possibly could. Luckily, her mom wasn't slow and picked up on the clue.

"Do not leave anything out when I get home. I will be home in an hour." And then she hung up the phone.

"All good?" Noah asked as she was hanging up her phone.

"Yep, it's all good. Thanks again for the ride," she thanked him again.

"It's no problem," he replied. "How have you been?"

"I've been great. Just working at home and helping my dad out. What about you?" She was so grateful she finally had the opportunity to ask what he'd been up to because this man had made her wonder what the heck she had done wrong to make him not talk to her.

"I have been studying like crazy the last few days. I graduate in a couple of weeks, and I have boards coming up. In fact, I hadn't left my apartment all week until today, except to come to work. Even at work, I'm trying to get some studying in." he informed her.

This was sweet music to Peyton's ears. The last few days she had worried that she had said something to offend him or that he just plain didn't like her and that their run date was a huge waste of time. Instead, he had been cooped up in his apartment studying all week. He hadn't had time to text her or do anything else. It was like Peyton could finally breathe again. Boy, her mom was going to be happy to hear this.

"I'm sorry if it seemed like I fell off the face of the earth or something. If it helps, I felt like I've been brought back to it now," Noah smiled, and Peyton could feel the corners of her mouth turn up.

Peyton shook her head, "It's okay. I figured you were busy with school or something."

"Yeah, it's crazy, but I'm almost done, which is such a relief. It's been a long four years," he admitted. He stared out the windshield with his elbow leaning on the window and his hand on his mouth as if he were thinking a serious thought. Peyton figured he probably was, which made her curious.

"You have no idea," she muttered.

"What was that?" His head whipped in her direction.

"Uh," Peyton faltered, "I just agreed with you it has been a long four years."

"Yeah, at least it's almost over. Well, I guess for me. What about you? Do you think things are going to get better with you?" Noah asked, looking back and forth between her and the road.

"I think so," Peyton admitted. And for the first time in a long time, she actually believed it.

CHAPTER 8

*T*he great thing about Noah was that he didn't push Peyton into sharing any details about her personal life. Anyone else she felt would have asked, *"Why have you had a hard year?"* or *"Why are you seeing a therapist?"* For now, things were being kept simple, and she certainly appreciated it. It had almost been a year since Derek had passed, and she wasn't ready to have this conversation with him. Instead, he asked her what music she liked to listen to in the car, what kind of car she drove, and if she had ever been pulled over. Basically, they talked about cars for the remainder of the drive and debated whether or not Rascal Flatts was really a country band or more pop.

Once they finally settled that they were a

country band and he turned down Peyton's old gravel driveway, they got quiet for a minute.

"Is that your car in front?" he asked.

Before she could answer, her brother stepped out of his car with his new friend, Gloria. Chris turned around and paused for a brief moment, obviously trying to figure out whose car was coming down the driveway. Once he realized Peyton was in the passenger seat, he smiled and waved excitedly.

"Nope," she exhaled. "That would be my brother Chris and his new girlfriend, Gloria."

"Ah, got it. They seem nice," he stated while Peyton put her head in her hands. Noah chuckled and put his hand on her shoulder, which gave Peyton a jolt of energy and caused her head to snap up.

She looked at him and he was smiling. "It's all good, I promise."

Unfortunately, Peyton had no idea what he meant by that.

"Alright, well, I better go. My brother is going to be foaming at the mouth ready to ask questions. And Gloria, well, I don't know what she'll do. I don't know her all that well," Peyton admitted and felt a little bad that she hadn't asked Chris more about his new fling.

"Let me open the door for you," he took his hand off her and opened his door.

"No. No, wait…" she stuttered. But before she could stop Noah, he was already out of the car and making his way around to her door. He opened it, and Peyton climbed out. She smiled at him and prayed that her brother wouldn't say anything stupid.

"Hey, Pey Pey, what's up? Who's the guy?" Chris asked. He obviously wasn't very shy.

"This is Noah. He's the guy who ran with me on Monday, and he gave me a ride home from Dr. Schoenborn's office," Peyton explained.

"The one Mom was all worried wouldn't talk to you again?" he said obnoxiously. Peyton's ears started turning red.

"Yup, that's me," Noah said and waved. "Nice to meet you. You must be Chris." He sounded so cool and calm, like what her brother just said didn't even phase him.

"Yeah, I am! I'm Peyton's little bro. And this is Gloria. She's kinda my lady," Chris smiled and shrugged his shoulders.

He put his arm around Gloria, and she waved at Noah, "Hi, nice to meet you."

"Nice to meet you, too," Noah waved back. "Well, I better…"

"Man!" Chris interrupted. "It's been ages since I've seen you get out of a guy's car, Sis."

"Chris," Peyton warned.

"Reminds me of the first time you got out of a guy's car. It was Derek's…" Peyton flinched. Chris either didn't notice or didn't care, because he kept going.

"You came home from school, and Derek had offered you a ride home instead of riding the bus. And then Dad came out the front door and started grilling him! 'Who is this guy? Who are your parents? Peyton, why are you in his car? Why didn't you ride the bus? Are you two dating?' Oh, man! It was hilarious! And the poor sucker still brought you home every day despite Dad staring at him down with his arms crossed on the front porch every time. Kind of ironic after all that driving he died in a car accident…"

"Christopher!" Peyton's dad barked. Chris's talking came to a halt. He turned to look over at his dad, who was standing the exact way he had just described. On the front porch, with his arms crossed, and his eyes narrowed in Chris's direction. Once Chris took in their dad's look, he whipped his head to look at Peyton, and his eyes went wide, realizing what he had just done.

Peyton hadn't realized, but she had tears streaming down her face, and she was trembling. She tried to wipe her face and control her shaking, but the tears kept coming, and she felt like she was in her own personal earthquake.

"Peyton, I…" Chris began, but he was interrupted again by their dad.

"Chris, come in the house, please." His tone was

flat and even, and Peyton knew anyone on the receiving end of that tone was in some serious trouble.

Chris closed his mouth and did as he was told. Gloria, obviously looking a little awkward, followed behind Chris. Clearly, he was her ride, and he wasn't going anywhere yet.

"Peyton, honey, why don't you come in. Thanks for bringing her home, Noah." Her dad's voice had softened up, and he uncrossed his arms.

Peyton shook her head and tried to wipe her face again. "Yeah, thanks, Noah." She took a quick glance at his face, and she noticed three different expressions all tied together—confusion, worry, and concern.

Seeing his face only started to make her cry more. She choked back a sob and walked into the house.

"No problem," she heard him say behind her as she went into the house, her dad following her in.

The first thing Peyton saw when she walked inside was Chris and Gloria looking worried and guilty.

"Peyton, I'm really…" Chris began, but Peyton didn't hear the rest of it. She let herself sob and ran upstairs to her room. She threw herself onto her bed and sobbed. She was angry with her brother for opening his big mouth in the first place. Then he made that insensitive comment about Derek's death and thought it was okay to make a joke about it. For Peyton and anyone with a heart, that was never going to be okay. Lastly, she felt embarrassed. All of this was said in front of Noah, and she could only imagine how confused he must feel. Not to mention, this was not the way she wanted to introduce Derek to him. Her emotions kept ranging from anger to heartache to embarrassment, which all made her cry.

At some point, she fell asleep with her face in her pillow, and when she woke up, she had hair stuck to her face from her tears. Not to mention, she felt like she had been run over by an eighteen-wheeler. She laid down in her bed and looked at her phone to check the time. It read 5:03 p.m. She had been asleep for almost four hours.

"How are you doing, honey?" a voice said out of the blue.

Peyton inhaled sharply and covered her face with her blanket.

She heard someone get up and sit on the side of her bed. She knew that it was her mom, but it still freaked her out that her mom had been creeping around her room.

"Mom," Peyton said underneath the blanket, "I just about peed my pants."

"I'm not surprised," she said from outside the blanket tent. "You've been asleep for a while. I'm guessing you've been holding it for a few too many hours."

Peyton pulled the blanket down, so she was looking at her mom. She still had the same outfit on from this morning, except it was being covered by an apron, and instead of her hair being down and curled, it was clipped up.

"Why are you always right?" Peyton questioned and jumped off her bed to run to the bathroom. After she finished, she felt a whole lot better and returned to her room. Her mom was still sitting in the same spot. She sat by her mom and put her head on her shoulder.

"How are you doing?" she asked.

"I've been better," Peyton tried to wipe her face from her dried up tears and wished she would have washed her face while she was in the bathroom.

"Well, you should know that your dad talked to your brother, and he feels very bad. He wants to apologize when you're ready to hear it, of course," she said.

"Is he still here?" Peyton asked.

"No, he and Gloria left. Gloria needed to go home, but I think he's going to come back for dinner," her mom informed her.

"Mom, I cannot believe he just let all those words come out of his stupid mouth," Peyton breathed and shook her head. "I mean, of all the insensitive, rude things he could have said. It's one thing to talk about Derek like that in front of Noah, but then mock his death?" Peyton started to tear up talking about it.

"He should have never said those things. He was completely out of line. You are right," her mom agreed.

"What did Noah say?" Peyton muttered.

"I don't know. He went home. I don't think your dad talked to him because he was wanting to kill your brother."

"Completely understandable. I wanted to do that. I still do."

"Why don't you come downstairs? Dinner is almost done. We're having hamburgers," her mom told her, and it got Peyton's stomach growling. She realized she hadn't eaten anything since breakfast.

"That sounds really good. Let's go," Peyton got up from her bed. "Mom? Why did he all the sudden say those things about Derek?" She swallowed hard and told herself she was not going to cry. "It was so out of the blue. I think I've made it pretty obvious that I don't want to talk about Derek or anything from the past. It hurts too much." She put her head down and could feel the tears start to flow down her cheeks. "I mean, I know I should be moving past it, but when he started talking about when Derek first dropped me off at home... All those memories just started flowing back. It was so overwhelming. Noah has got to think I'm a complete basket case. I'm sure he's so confused." At this point, Peyton was sobbing and could hardly breathe. Her mother stood up and pulled Peyton into a tight hug.

"Well, your brother has some news, and I think he was so excited that he just lost his head for a minute. And I think when he saw you get out of that car with Noah, he was so happy for you that he became ecstatic and ran his mouth. You know how he is when he gets excited. I'm not making excuses for him, but I'm just trying to help you understand," her mom explained.

Peyton pulled away just enough, so she could look at her mom, "What news?" she asked, but all her mom did was smile and walk away.

"What news?" Peyton demanded, but her mom laughed and walked down the stairs, leaving Peyton to wonder what on earth her brother had gotten himself into now.

CHAPTER 9

*P*eyton walked down the stairs and found her mom stirring something in the kitchen, her dad sitting on the couch flipping through Netflix—typical—and her rotten brother sitting at the dinner table looking at his phone. She stopped on the last stair and leaned up against the wall and crossed her arms. Their dad was the first to look up and put his remote down. He stood up from the couch and crossed his arms, looking at Chris.

When Chris didn't notice either of them for about a minute, their dad cleared his throat, which made Chris jump out of his seat. Apparently, he was still on edge from the talk they had earlier. He looked around and saw his dad first staring him down and then looked over and saw Peyton standing nonchalantly at the bottom of the stairs with a blank look on her face. Although, no matter how blank it was, she knew she couldn't fool anyone. She was sure that her face was all red and puffy, with a few stray tears on her cheeks.

"Hi, Peyton, I'm very sorry about what I said. It was super insensitive of me, and I just got out of my head. Honestly, there was no excuse for it. I shouldn't have ever brought up Derek or mentioned the accident. Really, Sis, I'm sorry," he finished and looked at Peyton with a sad, guilty expression. It reminded her of when he used to get into her bathroom and play with her makeup. She would walk in there and see that he had drawn a mustache on his face with her eyeliner and a heart on his arm in lipstick. Oh, the pirate phase.

"It's okay, Chris," she muttered. She wanted to say more, but she didn't want to make herself upset again, so she just left it at that.

"I hope I didn't scare Noah away! I'm going to feel extremely bad if I did. If he doesn't talk to you again, I'll talk to him myself and apologize," he offered. She could tell he was genuinely sorry for how he acted.

"It's okay. If it scared him away, well, then it just wasn't meant to be," she said. Surprisingly, she truly believed it, no matter how sad it made her feel. Noah didn't even know all her secrets, and if he couldn't handle that, he wouldn't be able to handle the rest of it.

"Well, I don't think it scared him away," her mom called from around the corner.

"Um, what do you mean, Mom?" Peyton asked tentatively.

"I invited him for dinner tomorrow, and he accepted," she said in a matter-of-fact tone and walked around the corner, so she could see everyone.

"You did what?" Peyton shrieked.

"I couldn't very well let him leave on that note. So, I invited him to dinner. Originally the offer was for tonight, but he said something about needing to get back to the office to close up and to make up for some studying. So, I offered tomorrow, and he accepted! Chris, make sure you and Gloria are here." She pointed her finger at him and walked back to the kitchen.

"Is that the news?" Peyton demanded again.

"No!" Her mother called. "Chris, tell her. It's the least you could do!"

"Oh yeah, the reason why I was here with Gloria earlier to begin with was to tell you guys that we're engaged!" he exclaimed and shot his hands into the air.

"Wow! Chris, that's amazing. Congratulations!" She walked over and gave him a hug.

"I really am sorry, Peyton," he whispered in her ear.

"I know. It's okay," she whispered back.

As she was hugging her brother, she started processing that Noah was coming for dinner the next day and realized something.

"Hold on!" She pulled away from her brother and walked into the kitchen to find her mother. "I thought you said that he had left after I walked inside the house with Dad," she gestured toward her father, who was now flipping through channels, standing up, and completely zoned out.

"Well," her mother answered, still mixing the dinner, "I pulled up to the driveway, and he was sitting on the edge of his car talking to your father. Apparently, he was waiting out there to make sure you were alright after seeing you so upset. After your dad talked to your brother, he noticed Noah sitting on the hood of his car and went out there to talk to him. I got out of the car, and after getting a quick rundown of the recent events, I invited him to dinner. Really, Peyton, it was no big deal. After we talked, he left and that was that," she finished and returned to making dinner.

"You lied to me!" Peyton said, completely baffled by what her mother had done.

"Yeah, I did. But I didn't want to tell you while you were still upset. I was going to tell you, so, actually, it was a temporary lie," she tried to explain to her, but it didn't ease Peyton's mind. "Who's ready to eat?" she called out, and everyone gravitated to the kitchen to get ready to eat.

"What am I supposed to do when he comes, Mom?" Peyton asked as she picked up a plate. "Thanks to Chris, no offense, Chris," she looked at Chris, and he held up his hands.

"None taken. I did it," he admitted and grabbed himself a plate.

"He opened up a whole can of worms in front of Noah, and I don't even know where to begin to explain." Peyton finished her thought and began assembling her hamburger with all her favorite toppings.

"You know what you need to do, honey?" her dad said, scooping up his own plate of food, "Pray about it. Tell Him everything, and you'll know what to say tomorrow."

"Okay, Dad," Peyton said sarcastically and made her way to the kitchen table.

Her mom, dad, and Chris followed Peyton, and this time her mom spoke, "Your dad is right, Peyton. Pray about it. He'll help you say just what you need to tomorrow."

Peyton nodded her head and started eating her dinner. Ever since Derek died, she hadn't prayed very often because part of her was angry with

Heavenly Father for taking Derek away even though deep down she knew everything happened for a reason. She knew, though, what her parents said was true, and that she needed to pray every moment she could get.

"What did you tell him, Dad?" Peyton asked after she had finished all the food on her plate. She really was hungry.

"I just told him that you and your husband were in a car crash about a year ago. You were fortunate enough to walk away from it, but Derek was not." He shrugged his shoulders. "If I hadn't, the poor guy really would have been confused. Sorry, hun," he explained.

"It's fine. He was bound to find out eventually. Not how I wanted him to find out," she said pointedly to Chris, "but yet, here we are." She leaned back in her chair and folded her hands in her lap.

"Again, sorry!" Chris said sounding more exasperated than apologetic. He stood up to clear his plate and kissed his mother on the cheek. "Thanks, Mom, for dinner. I gotta go. Gloria and I are facetiming her parents to tell them the news."

"Hey, congrats again, little brother. I want to hear more details tomorrow," she stood up to give him a hug and clear her plate as well.

"Will do. See you guys later. Bye, Dad," he waved and walked out the front door.

"Well, that was fun. Not exactly how I envisioned this day going," her mother cleared the table.

"You can say that again," Peyton muttered and helped her mom clean the dishes.

"What are you going to tell Noah, Sis?" her mom asked.

"I don't know. I honestly don't want to talk about it at all. I was planning on just telling him little bits slowly. Now, I feel like that plan is out the window."

"Just be honest with him. You don't necessarily need to share everything, but be honest. If you are truly interested in this guy, he deserves to know everything upfront. Wouldn't you want the same treatment?"

"Yeah. But Mom, it's not like we're dating or anything. It's just been a meet and greet at the mall, a run last week, and he drove me home once. This is all being blown out of proportion!" She threw her hands up into the air. "I feel like now I'm having to do things or say things that I feel like I shouldn't even have to do because nothing has actually happened! What if he's just trying to be friendly? You know, make a new friend. It's not like we've been on an actual date, and that there are any feelings there," Peyton protested. She realized she had raised her voice and felt bad, but her parents didn't seem phased.

"I understand why you're frustrated. I understand where you're coming from, but I think now more than ever he deserves a couple of answers. Maybe not all the answers, just enough to give him a little clarity."

"Fine," she conceded and started drying dishes.

"You are absolutely insane if you think there aren't any feelings there," her mother stated.

"What?" she questioned.

"Each time you've been with that boy, he's put himself out there, wanting to see you. Not to mention, after the thing with Chris, he stayed behind to see how you were doing. What baffles me is that you still don't think he has any feelings for you," her mom persisted.

"How could he?" Peyton barked, now feeling more frustrated. "I'm tainted! I'm an old widow. Why would he want something that's already been used once?"

"Peyton, you are not an old widow, and you're definitely not tainted. He obviously just likes you for you, sweetheart, and that's all that matters. Isn't that what you want?" her mom countered.

"Well, yeah," Peyton conceded.

"Then please, just be nice and let things run their course," she pleaded and finished drying the dishes.

Peyton wanted to keep arguing. She thought her mom was being absolutely ridiculous and trying to push this thing between her and Noah. She also didn't believe her mom about Noah even liking her. Sure, he'd been nice and friendly to her, but she didn't have any other reason to believe he might actually like her. Even though deep down, she hoped he did.

CHAPTER 10

That night, before Peyton went to sleep, she grabbed her phone to set her alarm and realized she hadn't looked at her phone since calling her mom earlier that day. She unlocked her phone and noticed she had a text that had been unopened.

It said that it was from Noah.

It read, *"Hey, I just wanted to make sure you were alright."*

Peyton thought it was so nice that he had made the effort to text her and check on her.

She responded back to his text, *"Yeah, I'm okay. Thanks for asking."*

She set her alarm and put her phone on her nightstand. When she started to get comfortable, her phone buzzed. It was another message from Noah.

"Good. Your mom invited me for dinner tomorrow, and I told her I would come. I hope that's okay."

She appreciated him checking with her and thought it was very considerate and texted back, *"My mom told me she invited you. It's all good with me!"* Peyton felt a little bad because, at first, she really wasn't okay with it. However, now she was really looking forward to seeing him tomorrow.

She stared at the blank screen on her phone wondering whether or not to put her phone back on the nightstand, but then her phone lit back up, *"Awesome. Well, I'll see you tomorrow!"*

Peyton smiled and replied, *"See you tomorrow!"* She put her phone back on her nightstand, got into her comfortable sleeping position, and went to sleep with a smile on her face.

Peyton ended up having a couple of nightmares during the night. One of them consisted of her walking downstairs for dinner to meet Noah when she realized she was only in her underwear. The other dream was Peyton walking down to the dining room and seeing not only Noah but Derek as well. When she sat down at the dinner table, Derek would constantly ask her, *"Why?"* or *"Did you forget about me already?"*

She woke up crying, and her mother came into her room and hugged her while she cried. "Well, you woke up a lot later than usual," her mom pointed out.

"What time is it?" Peyton whimpered.

It's seven. You made it through the whole night. Well, kinda. But still, I'm impressed," she said scratching Peyton's back.

"Thanks, Mom, but I gotta tell ya," Peyton sniffed and continued, "I'm so tired of these nightmares."

"I know, sweetheart. I have a feeling though that they're going to start getting better."

"You think so?"

"Yes," her mom smiled, "I do." Her mom kissed her forehead and left her room.

Peyton couldn't justify going back to sleep, so she got up and went running. She figured if anything could make her feel better, it would be that instead of risking another nightmare. She ended up running seven miles instead of her usual five. Her legs didn't feel as tired, probably because of her long nap yesterday, so she pushed out a couple more miles.

During her run, she thought of her nightmares. She worried about her dinner with Noah and how that was going to go. Especially with her brother and his new fiancé coming tonight as well. She knew that Chris was sorry and felt really bad for running his mouth, but she couldn't help feeling a little worried about it. Hopefully, everyone would just focus on Chris and Gloria's recent engagement. Her last nightmare bothered her the most. Part of her felt like she had no place talking to another man. She felt lucky enough to have met her sweetheart in high school and get married to the love of her life. Was it truly possible to fall in love again? Was she being fair to Noah? There she went again jumping to conclusions. She'd only seen this guy a handful of times, and love wasn't even on the radar. Was he handsome? Most definitely. Was he as sweet as honey? Oh, yeah. Thoughtful and considerate? Check and check. Did she think she could fall in love again? Peyton didn't know the answer to that question. She was going to take her mom's advice though and just be nice. Not try and force anything or read more into anything. She was reminded of the first time she had met Derek during her junior year of high school...

Derek was new in school, and she had noticed him from a distance in the hallways but didn't make an effort to talk to him. She was super shy, and so was he, but he was also adorable, which made it hard for her to approach him. She still remembered what he was wearing that day. He wore light-colored jeans that had oil stains splattered all over them with a dark blue zip-up jacket. His hair was messy like he had just woken up, and his eyes looked tired.

She was sitting at the lunch table reading her book. Her nose was always in a book. She was in the middle of a sentence when someone sat across from her out of nowhere, and she jumped at the sound of the lunch tray being set down on the table. She looked up from her book and saw it was the new boy, Derek, opening up his milk.

"You're Peyton, right?" he asked confidently.

"Yeah," she squeaked and cleared her throat, "I mean, yes. I'm Peyton, and you're Derek?"

"Yup, that's me," he replied, staring at her. It almost made Peyton uncomfortable except that he was nice to look at.

"Awesome," she stated simply and picked up where she left off in her book.

"Are you always reading?" he questioned with a tone of sarcasm. At this point, he finished opening his milk and started drinking it.

"Pretty much," Peyton informed the milk drinker and started reading again.

"How do you read and walk at the same time?" he asked and took a bite of his pizza. "I mean, I swear I almost saw you collide with this poor little freshman, and at the last possible second, you swerved out of the way. Seriously, is it like some superpower?" he asked, clearly trying to keep her away from her book, which Peyton thought was annoying but kind of cute. He took another bite of his pizza with a sort of smirk on his face that hinted he was totally teasing her. Peyton decided to play along.

"I don't know," she replied. "Maybe I'm not so much of a superhero, but rather the villain. And I zap people away, so I can read my book." She smirked and picked up her book, so it was blocking Derek's face.

"Now it makes sense." Peyton peered over the top of her book and saw he was looking straight at her. "I thought you were more the villain type," he said, trying to look serious, but Peyton could see he was trying not to smile.

Peyton gave up, marked the page, and slammed the book down. "Really?" she exaggerated.

"Yup," he began. "You act like an innocent school girl who pours herself into her books when, really"—he stopped to put his finger on his chin—"the human race drives you crazy, so you're pretending to read and are plotting to take over the world."

"Wow, you are so smart," she put her hands up in the air as if she were being arrested, "because you caught me. Is there something I can help you with?" she snapped.

"Yeah. I was just wondering if by chance you would put your book down long enough and go on a date with me?" he asked, and Peyton realized he wasn't as shy as she thought.

"You are very bold," she observed out loud to him.

He shrugged his shoulders, "Only when I want to be, I guess. So, what do you say? Will you risk waiting to read about Prince Charming for one night and spend it with me?"

"If I said yes, what would we do?" she asked curiously.

"Well, I can for sure say it will not include a library," he laughed and finished the rest of his pizza.

"Bummer, that's a deal-breaker for me," she teased and went for her book.

"If it involves dinner, would that sway you?"

"Now, you're speaking more my language," she admitted.

"Great! If you give me your number, I'll let you know details," he reached his hand out. Peyton was tempted to high-five him and say forget it, but she conceded and handed over her phone.

"There," he said while looking at her phone. "You just sent me a text." He pulled out his phone and read the text. "Oh, look, you just asked me if I would walk you to your next class! The answer is yes, I will." He stood up to put his lunch tray away and stood by the table. "You ready?" He handed her phone back to her and waited for her answer.

"Yeah, I think I am," she said. Later that day, her phone had buzzed, and when she looked to see who the text was from, the name read *Your Hot Date…*

She walked inside the house after her run and went for a glass of water.

"You were gone for a while today," her dad, who was sitting at the dining room table reading his scriptures, pointed out.

"Yeah, after that nap yesterday, I just had a little more energy, so I pushed a couple more miles out," she explained and began chugging water.

"Peyton, you are dripping sweat all over my floor. You either get a rag or go shower before I make you mop," her mom threatened and sat down next to her dad.

Peyton grabbed a rag from a drawer and started wiping her face. "You know, Mom. I'm sweating so much that maybe I should mop the floor with it," she teased and heard her dad start to laugh.

"Ha ha, very funny. That's disgusting," her mom scolded and opened up her own scriptures.

"Hey, Peyton," her dad called, "will you help me check on Betsy later? I think she's going to have her calf soon."

"Yeah, Dad, just let me know when you need

me. I'm going to go shower before Mom has an aneurism," Peyton joked.

"Again, you're hilarious," she said.

Peyton went upstairs to shower and got ready for the day as she did every morning. After she got dressed, she went downstairs and started working on her dad's business. She organized her dad's notes, invoices, and receipts, and then she called clients and updated them on the animals. This usually took a few hours because the man had a thing about sticky notes.

She ran out to the barn to ask him a question about a note and heard him talking to a cow that was lying down in her stall.

"Peyton, good thing you're here. Will you get some fresh hay for Betsy and fill her bucket up with water, please? I think she's about ready to go into labor, and she's hardly eaten," he informed her.

"Sure thing, I'll do that right now. While I'm getting it, do you mind telling me what this says? It looks like there's cow poop on it," Peyton said. She handed him the hot pink sticky note with cow pie on it, and he started laughing.

"Sorry, Sis!" he bellowed. "This must have happened when I was wrestling Lucy out there." He turned away from her to check on the poor mama cow.

Peyton loved being out in the barn. There was something about the smell of the hay and warm sunshine shining into the barn that brought back good memories…

"I wouldn't do that if I were you, Derek," Peyton warned.

"What are you talking about?" he questioned, laughing in an arrogant tone.

A baby calf had jumped into the goat pasture and needed to get back to his mama to feed. The heifer had been mooing loudly for an hour, and when Peyton had finally decided to check on the darn animal, she saw that her calf had gotten away. Derek was sitting on the edge of the fence about to jump in with the goats and the lone calf. Little did he realize that the goats loved a good chase.

"You're going to get your butt kicked," she said flatly.

"By you or the goats?" he challenged and looked at her as if he were asking for it.

"Oh, I won't need to do that. Billie and Millie, along with their offspring, will do that for me," she laughed and pointed out the goats that were staring down Derek.

"Not a chance!" he retorted.

Peyton put her hands up and chuckled, "You go right ahead then if you're so sure!"

"I will!" he exclaimed and jumped into the pen. Right as he did that, it was as if all the animals went quiet, except for the mama cow in the background desperately needing her calf to nurse. The calf was walking around eating grass, minding his own business, but the goats were watching him like a hawk. Or goat.

Derek took a few steps toward the calf, and the goats remained still, with one of the baby goats bleating every once in a while. Peyton knew he was in trouble. He took a few more steps, and the goats started moving together into the corner of the pen. Once Derek was within reaching distance, he made a quick grab for the calf, turning his back on the goats. Peyton knew immediately that was a mistake because when he turned his back, the mama goat started running toward Derek.

"Derek, get out of there!" Peyton squealed and ran toward the gate, ready to open it.

Derek turned around and realized he had made a big mistake. He picked up the calf and started running, but before he could get to the gate, the mama goat caught up to him and butted him right in the buttocks.

"Ow!" Derek yelled yet somehow managed to hang onto the calf, which was mooing loudly in his ear. Derek ran faster, only to have the papa goat come up and take his turn at butting him.

"Ow!" Derek yelled again, still holding firmly onto the calf. "Peyton, open the gate!" He was only a few feet from the gate with a herd of goats behind him bleating and wanting to get their turn.

At the last minute, Peyton swung the gate open, and Derek rushed out with the calf in his arms, slightly limping now with sweat dripping down his face. Peyton quickly slammed the gate and locked it before any goats could escape.

She rushed over to Derek, trying not to laugh, and roped the calf, so Derek could put the calf down. Once the rope was around the calf's neck, he put the cow down and wiped his face. Peyton knelt and scratched the calf behind the ears, trying to hide her face because her laughing was almost impossible to hide now.

"See?" he said, panting. "I told you it would be no big deal!" He was standing up straight and rubbing his backside, trying not to look like he was in pain.

Peyton couldn't contain herself any longer. She laughed so loud that the goats freaked out and started bleating loudly, running around their pen and into each other. She was laughing so hard her stomach started to hurt and tears were welling up in her eyes.

"That was the best moment of my life!" she declared and wiped the tears from her eyes.

"That's not good," Derek said, limping toward her.

"Why?" she asked, her laughter calming down

to a chuckle. Now she was worried she had upset him.

"Because now, I'm going to have to spend every day of the rest of my life trying to top that," he said quietly, walking closer to her.

"That sounds like a lot of work for you," Peyton pointed out, whispering now.

"It's worth it," he whispered back and pulled her in for their very first kiss…

After she filled up the bucket of water, she brought some hay over to her dad, who was still checking over Betsy.

"How's she doing, Dad?" she asked.

"I think she's going to be going into labor soon. We'll have to keep an eye on her. You're okay to help me today, right? You don't have anything planned?" her dad verified.

"Besides having a boy come to dinner who was invited by Mom, nothing," she grumbled.

"Honey, your mom didn't mean anything by it. And if she did, which she probably did, you know her heart is in the right place," he explained.

"Yeah, yeah. I know, Dad. I'm going to go inside and grab some lunch. Do you want anything?" Peyton offered.

"I'd take a sandwich or leftovers from last night.

Thanks, honey. Oh, and that note says to charge Mrs. Donald for that cow I butchered last week."

"You know, Dad, it's a good thing I go through these notes. Otherwise, you would be working for free."

He laughed, "You're amazing, Sis!"

"All in a day's work, Dad," she chuckled and jogged back to the house.

Peyton walked into the house and made herself and her dad the lunch she promised. After running it back to her dad, she sat down at the table and started working through all the notes again courtesy of him.

She didn't mind working for her dad. When she was married to Derek, she worked as a bank teller, which was a fine job and paid the bills. However, it didn't ever make her happy, and she didn't mind saying goodbye to it. Her dad offered her a job helping him with the paperwork and finances because when her mom tried to do it, she would become flustered. It was also so she could have something to do and earn a little money. Not that she needed to though because she had received a lot of settlement money from the insurance company from Derek's accident. Her parent's attorney made sure that piece of work who was stupid enough to drive drunk and then kill her husband would pay out the nose. Regardless, working with her dad ensured that she could work whenever she wanted and stay at home.

After she was done going through all her father's notes and billing clients, she decided to do a little cleaning before Noah showed up. She cleaned the bathrooms, swept and mopped the floor, and vacuumed the living room. She thought about working her way upstairs when her mom stopped her.

"Peyton, do you want to help me make dinner?" she asked. Peyton turned around and saw that she had her gardening hat and gloves on.

"Yeah, I can do that. Let me put the vacuum away," Peyton replied and wound up the cord and put the vacuum in the coat closet.

"Thanks, honey. How do tacos sound? I figure that's easy enough for everyone to personalize in case he's allergic to something," she explained.

"Yeah," Peyton agreed. "I think it's a great idea. You can't go wrong with tacos."

"Great, I'll put you on chopping duty."

"Alright, just as long as I don't have to shred cheese," Peyton countered.

Her mom reached into the fridge and pulled out a bag of pre-shredded cheese.

"Wow, Christmas came early," she said sarcastically and amazed all at the same time. Her mom never bought shredded cheese. She would tell us only lazy, rich people bought it, and we could easily save money buying a block of it and shredding it ourselves.

While her mom was in the fridge, she pulled out an onion, tomatoes, cilantro, avocados, and limes and handed it all to Peyton. She sighed and started chopping away on all the vegetables.

"What time did you invite Noah over, Mom?" Peyton asked.

"I told him to come at 5:30."

"You realize that's in like twenty minutes, right?" she informed her mother, who appeared as cool as a cucumber. "And you're wanting to make guacamole?"

"The two of us can get it done. No problem!" she encouraged, and as if on cue, Chris and Gloria came through the door. "Oh, look! More help. Chris!" she called, "Get in here and grab a knife."

"Let me guess. She told Noah an unrealistic time and is scrambling to get everything done now," he said nonchalantly.

"Right on the button, bro!" Peyton pointed her knife in the air and then continued chopping her onion. "Gloria, how are you at making guacamole?" Peyton asked.

"Oh, man, Pey Pey, she makes a mean guac! Definitely have her make it!" Chris insisted.

"Are you okay with that, Gloria?" Peyton didn't want to make her feel uncomfortable, but she also wanted to include her. She knew how weird it was to adapt to a new family. The first time Peyton had dinner with Derek's parents, they asked her what she wanted to do for a living. Being Peyton, she wanted to be honest and told them that all she truly ever wanted to be was a mom. She couldn't find a career that she wanted to do. The looks on their faces told her that they were super nervous, and after she left, Derek's parents gave him the sex talk again and told him that she and Derek could never be alone together.

"Yeah, I would love to!" Gloria said enthusiastically. Peyton handed her all the makings for the guacamole, and before she knew it, they all were like a bunch of sous chefs, working together to get dinner out.

"How much time do we have now?" Peyton asked after she and Chris finished chopping all the vegetables.

Chris looked at his watch, "Ten minutes."

"Okay, let's quickly set the table!" She grabbed a handful of plates while Chris grabbed the silverware, and they scrambled to set the table.

"Don't make it look like a bunch of toddlers set it, you two," her mom chided.

"Now I want to do it just for spite," Peyton muttered.

"Don't tempt me," Chris teased. "Hey, Gloria, can I try that guacamole?"

"No way!" her mother called. "Once you start

eating that stuff, you can't stop! We're having dinner any minute, so you can wait."

"Not even one chip?" he begged.

"You can wait," she repeated.

Before Chris could try and take a chip, there was a knock on the front door.

CHAPTER 11

"Peyton! Go open the door!" her mom whispered and pointed toward the door.

"No!" she protested, "You're the one who invited him, you do it!"

"Are you kidding me?" She put her hands up in the air to exaggerate that she was irritated even though Peyton already knew she was.

"No, I'm not! Now, are you going to answer it before he knocks again?" Peyton said, knowing it would bother her mother.

Her mom set her spoon down and scowled at her daughter, "You're ridiculous!"

Peyton shrugged her shoulders, "This isn't news, Mom."

Right before she answered the door, she turned around, "Start putting the food on the table! And

Chris, keep your fingers out of that guac!" she threatened.

"Mom, just open it!" Peyton said exasperated.

Her mom opened the door and put a big smile on her face. You would have never guessed she was just arguing with her kids.

"Hi, Noah! Come on in!" She waved into the house, and Noah entered.

"Thank you," Peyton heard him say in his deep voice. She turned the corner and saw that his hair and his rain jacket were covered in water droplets. She hadn't even noticed it was raining.

He took off his shoes and his rain jacket. Before he could wonder where to put it, her mom spoke again, "I can take that, honey. I'll put it in the coat closet."

"Thank you, Cheryl," Noah said and smiled when he saw Peyton, revealing the laugh lines around his eyes. It looked like he had stepped off the pages of a magazine. He was wearing dark wash jeans with a shirt that clung to his chest and outlined his muscular upper body. He brushed his hand through his hair to get rid of some of the water droplets, and Peyton had to remember to breathe.

"Hi, Peyton," he said affectionately.

"Hi, Noah," she breathed, taking in his gaze. It was brief, but he looked at her as if no one else were in the room. She was stuck in what felt like a trance, but she didn't mind. Peyton would never admit it to her mom, but she was so happy he was here. Even though her heart was racing, and she forgot to breathe every once in a while, he brought a sort of peace to her mind. A feeling of comfort and safety she hadn't felt in a long time.

"Thank you for inviting me to dinner," he said while still looking at Peyton. He turned his head to look at her mom, "It smells very good."

"You're welcome. Should we eat? Walter, put the remote down." she called over to her husband, who had been sitting in his chair flipping through channels again.

"Yes, dear," he said. Her mom whipped back her head and gave him a look that Peyton knew meant he would get in trouble for that later. She hated being called "dear."

Chris and Gloria were already sitting, and Peyton looked at her mom, questioning where she wanted them to sit.

Her mom caught her eye and understood what she was asking. "Why don't you and Noah sit on the opposite side of Chris and Gloria," she suggested.

Peyton did as she was told. She knew that was the safest bet. She and Noah sat down next to each other, and they briefly touched hands, which sent an electrical shock through her body. She shook it off and folded her arms.

They blessed the food and started building their tacos. Chris finally was able to get a big spoonful of guacamole without his mom smacking his hand.

"Honey!" Chris said around a mouthful of chips and guacamole, "I think this is the best guac you have ever made!"

"Thanks, Chris," she said and focused on her tacos. She seemed a little embarrassed, which Peyton didn't blame her for. Her brother was pretty clueless sometimes.

"So, Noah, Peyton told us you were in dental school. How's that going?" Peyton's dad asked.

"It's going good. I only have a few weeks left, so I've been studying a lot preparing for my board exams," Noah explained.

"I bet you're excited to graduate," her dad said in between taco bites.

"Yeah, I am. It's been a long four years, and I'm ready to start practicing," he admitted.

"Well, good for you!" her dad raised his taco in the air and then took a huge bite of it.

"Thank you, sir," Noah nodded and started eating his own taco.

They sat for a few minutes in silence finishing up their food, and then Chris decided to pipe up again.

"So, Noah, where did you and my sister meet?" he asked boldly. At this point, Peyton began choking on her chip, and she felt a hand pat her back. She looked over and saw that it was Noah, and he smiled at her. "You okay?"

Peyton put her hand on her chest and nodded, "Thanks." Noah dropped his hand, which made her heart drop along with it.

"I met her after her appointment at my uncle's office. And then I saw her again at the mall, and we went running together last week," Noah told her annoying brother.

"Wait, you guys haven't been on a date yet?" Chris questioned, raising an eyebrow. Peyton was now ready to reach across the table and pummel him.

"Nope, not yet. I was actually going to ask her out for this weekend." Noah turned to face Peyton. "Would you like to go out with me this Saturday?" Peyton could feel her face burning up and knew all eyes were on her.

"Yeah," she nodded. "That would be great." She smiled at him, and he smiled even bigger at her.

"You're welcome, Sis," Chris said arrogantly, and Peyton whipped her head around to scowl at him. She took the opportunity to kick him in the shin. "Ow!" he cried and leaned down to rub his leg.

"You deserved that," her mom mumbled and took a sip of her water. Her mom cleared her throat, "That sounds fun, you guys! Noah, how do you like dinner?"

"It's very good. Thank you again for inviting me," Noah repeated.

"You are welcome anytime. Do you like peach cobbler?" she asked him.

"I love it," he informed her.

"Perfect, that's what I made for dessert. I should have asked you what you liked when I asked you for dinner! Speaking of, Gloria," she turned to face Gloria, "what are we going to have at the wedding reception? Are we going to have some Mexican cuisine there?"

Peyton turned to Noah to explain, "Chris and Gloria are engaged."

"Wow! Congratulations!" he told the engaged couple.

"Thanks, man," Chis said, wrapping his arm around his lady.

"Thank you, Noah. We're extremely excited," Gloria giggled. "We're thinking about June!"

"June!" her mom blurted. "That's in two months! That's really soon, and I don't think we will be able to get everything done in time!" It was as if Peyton saw her mom start to go into a downward spiral. Her mind was running a million miles a minute, and Peyton didn't want to be around when she went ballistic on Chris because the look she was giving him was not a good one.

"Yeah, Mom, isn't that the month to get married? It's barely summer, and there will be good weather for pictures, and there will be lots of flowers available for picking. Also, that's when a lot of Gloria's family will be available to come for the wedding," Chris explained quickly, but her mom's look didn't improve. She stood up and started clearing the table.

"Walter, will you help me clear the table?" she called, walking toward the kitchen.

"Sure thing, honey," he responded and looked at Peyton, "Save me!" he mouthed and picked up a couple of plates and followed his wife into the kitchen.

"Do you think she's mad?" Chris asked sarcastically.

Peyton snorted, "I think you need to go talk to her."

"I don't want to stress her out! It's just when my family is going to be able to visit. I feel so bad!" Gloria covered her mouth and looked back toward the kitchen.

"Look," Peyton began, "You just need to communicate with her. Be open about what you guys want and be honest. Especially with a two-month timeline. I struggled with my mother-in-law and not being completely honest with her about what I wanted, and it made the wedding planning especially hard until I finally got the courage to tell her what I wanted. She wanted to have carnations for the center tables and wanted the guys to wear bowties! I almost let her have her way until she informed me that she had ordered the bowties and carnations, and that's when I told her I didn't want that. Luckily, there was enough time to cancel the orders, but all I'm saying is don't let it get to that point. Be upfront. Everyone deserves that, and things go smoother."

"Wow, Peyton, that's the most you've talked in months. Thanks, Sis," Chris said, genuinely looking surprised and appreciative.

"Yeah, thanks, Peyton. You're right, we do need to make sure to communicate," Gloria admitted and looked at Chris, who started pigging out on the last of the guacamole. "Let's go talk to your parents."

"Are you sure you want to do that right now?" Chris asked. "We could wait for her to cool off a bit and…"

"No," Gloria cut him off, "now."

Chris sighed and put the chips and guacamole down. "Wish us luck," he said sarcastically. Peyton was happy to see who truly wore the pants in the relationship.

They stood up, cleared their plates and headed toward the kitchen to face their doom. Peyton looked sheepishly at Noah, who didn't seem to be fazed at all. She hadn't thought about what he would think about her talking about a previous relationship.

She tried to break the ice with her next statement. "So, I'd love to tell you that dinners usually aren't this dramatic, but I would be lying."

Noah laughed and turned his body so that he was facing her, "It's all good. It didn't bother me at all. I thought it was a completely normal dinner with its usual highs and lows."

"You've got that right," Peyton agreed and leaned her head against the back of the chair. She was very worried about what he thought about her big ol' speech to her brother. Especially about the part where she had already put on her big white dress and married the love of her life.

"That was really nice of you to share that with your brother. Ya know, to help him. It was very sisterly of you, and I think you explained it perfectly. I even liked the story about the bowties," he chuckled.

"Well," Peyton put her hands in her lap, "it was all true. She was so set on having bowties, and I just didn't like them at all, and for some reason, the woman loved carnations, which I don't get. I always thought they were a funeral flower, and I didn't want that to be a bad omen on my wedding day." *Of course, she didn't need the carnations as a bad omen because Derek ended up passing away anyway*, she thought to herself.

Her mom walked into the dining room to gather more dishes, and Noah tried to stand up and grab his plate until her mom stopped him. "No, Noah," she said while shaking her head and grabbed his plate, "you're a guest. You don't have to worry about it. You and Peyton just sit, relax, and talk."

"Thank you," he smiled and sat back down as he was instructed.

"Yeah, thanks, Mom," Peyton offered.

"No problem. I'm pretty sure your brother will be on dish duty every time he comes home," she re-marked and pursed her lips.

Peyton laughed as her mom walked away and shook her head. Once her mom was out of eyesight, she looked at Noah, "My mom can get a little worked up. Sorry."

Noah shrugged his shoulders, "It's all good. She's just a mom."

"Thanks for understanding."

"Of course," he assured her and put his hand on her knee. "Is your mom wanting to do dessert right now? Because I was hoping we could go for a walk."

Peyton, feeling flabbergasted, blushed and stuttered, "Uh, let me ask her! Hang on." She pushed herself away from the table and walked into the kitchen where Gloria and Chris were doing dishes, and her parents were putting food away. "Hey, Mom?"

Her mom spun around, looking surprised to see her, "Peyton! What are you doing here? Get back out there! Did he leave already?" Her dad put his hand on her back the way he usually did to signal for her to relax. She took a deep breath, realized she was getting worked up, and waited for Peyton to speak.

"I was just going to ask when you wanted to have dessert because Noah was wanting to go on a walk with me," Peyton explained, her voice becoming quieter with every word.

"Oh, honey, that's fine! When you guys come back, we can have dessert. No worries. I'd like to talk to Gloria and Chris anyway." She rubbed Peyton's arm and smiled, "Go for it."

"Thanks, Mom. Good luck, you two," Peyton implied to the love birds.

"Thanks a lot, Sis," Chris called.

"Anytime, bro." She walked back out to Noah, who was sitting at the table like a male model. "She said it's all good. Let me grab my shoes and a sweatshirt."

"Great," he stood up from the table to put his own shoes on and get his jacket.

Peyton rushed upstairs to her room and found her Converse to wear and her old sweatshirt she had gotten during high school. She checked herself in the mirror and pulled her hair into a ponytail. She quickly touched up her makeup and lastly checked her teeth to make sure there wasn't any food stuck between them. After she went through her personal checklist and decided she was suitable, she ran downstairs to meet Noah by the door.

"Ready?" he asked.

"Yup! Let's do it!" she said enthusiastically and opened the front door. She motioned him to walk forward, and he laughed walking through the door. She chuckled and followed him out the door and closed it behind them. "Well, I'll follow you. I'll go where you go."

"Can we go check out the barn?" he asked.

"Yeah, I should probably check on one of the cows anyways. She's about to go into labor," she told him.

"Cool, then instead I'll follow you because I didn't realize how dark it was out here, and don't really know which way the barn is," he admitted.

Peyton laughed and pointed, "It's this way."

Noah followed alongside her through the wet grass and looked up at the sky, "Wow, there are so many stars out."

"Yeah, the stars are beautiful out here. I would prefer country living any day compared to city living. There's a kind of innocent beauty you can't beat with the stars, the sound of the river in the background, and the crickets chirping. It's my favorite," she explained.

"You know, I think you're beautiful," Noah admitted and stopped walking.

"Really?" she asked and stopped.

"Yeah, I do. There's an innocence to your own beauty that is so attractive. Like, the way you stutter when you get nervous. Or when you look down and tuck your hair behind your ear to hide your face when you blush. It's so cute, and it makes my heart race." He grabbed her hand and gently pulled her into his chest, so she could hear his heart beating. It sounded a lot like how hers felt. They stood in the grass, halfway from the barn, for a while embraced in each other's arms underneath the stars, and Peyton couldn't imagine a more perfect moment.

"I like you, Peyton," Noah spoke. Peyton pulled away a little, so she could look at his face while his arms were still wrapped around her. "I like you a lot. I know we haven't known each other for very long, but every time I'm with you, I feel like I can be myself, and I'm comfortable. And now, whenever I'm not around you, I miss you like crazy. And I gotta apologize. I know after that run you didn't hear from me for a while, and that wasn't fair, but it was nothing against you. I could tell you were acting a little funny when you came in for your session. I honestly was just studying for a test I had later that week, and now, I'm trying to study for boards, so I promise if it seems like I'm ignoring you, I'm really not. I'm just trying to finish out these last few weeks. Because, honestly, I would much rather be with you than study."

Peyton couldn't believe what she was hearing. The deep-down part of her knew that she sincerely liked Noah and loved being around him. But still, there was something that held her back, and she knew it was the thought of Derek in the back of her mind. Then her mother's words entered her mind, *"Peyton, he would have wanted you to be happy. He would have wanted you to move on."* Her mom was always going to be in the back of her mind telling her things, and she knew that if she were here right now, she would be telling her to open her mouth and say something.

"I like you, too, Noah. I really do. My life is a bit complicated though. I wouldn't want to make your life more complicated, especially with you about to graduate and whatnot. You have enough going on," Peyton looked down in shame. She genuinely did like Noah and having his arms wrapped around her made her feel safe and secure. A feeling she hadn't felt in a very long time. Sure, she had been hugged by her mom and dad plenty of times, but this was different.

"Peyton," Noah whispered and put his hand underneath her chin and lifted her head, so he could look into her eyes. "Please don't think of yourself as being complicated. That is the furthest from the truth. I know some things have happened in your life, and when you're ready to talk about them, I'll be here to listen, okay?"

Peyton took a deep breath and smiled, "Okay." She put her head down and pulled away from Noah, "Do you want to go to the barn?"

Noah smiled and nodded, "Sure, let's go to the barn." Noah unwrapped his arms but grabbed her hand and let her guide him to the barn. Peyton's stomach did a flip. She loved the feeling of his warm hand in hers.

She felt guilty for not saying anything else, but if she was being honest, she had no idea what to say. She was shocked and caught off guard and didn't know how to portray her feelings to him. Her feelings were so mixed up with thoughts of her late husband and wondering if she was crazy for entertaining the thought of another man. Then again, she couldn't help thinking about Noah every now and again, wondering what he was doing, when would be the next time they saw each other, and if he was thinking about her like she was thinking about him.

"What are you thinking?" he asked as they walked toward the barn. They were only about a hundred yards away by now.

"I don't know. I'm trying to process everything. I'm not trying to be rude, I promise," she offered. "I guess I never thought of myself ever being liked by another guy again. Do you believe that a person can only fall in love once? Like truly fall in love, or do you think it can happen more than once?"

Noah looked straight ahead, clearly thinking

about the question and deciding how to answer. Granted, Peyton knew it was a loaded question, especially with him knowing now that she had already been married.

"I think that people are put in our lives when they're supposed to be, and that everything happens for a reason. And I think you can fall in love with anyone if you let yourself. So no, I don't think there's only one specific person for everyone. I mean, I sure hope not. I was determined in the seventh grade that I was going to marry Holly Stewart, and, thank heavens, I didn't. After high school, she went a little crazy and has already been through two divorces." Noah laughed and Peyton joined in. Thank heaven he had a sense of humor.

"Alright, you make a good point," Peyton admitted. They walked into the barn, and Peyton turned on the lights.

"Wow, this is bigger than I thought it would be," Noah said.

"Well, my dad does house a lot of cows for people, so he needs the space. We have a couple of horses, too, and a chicken coop in the back. In the last stall, though, is a cow named Betsy, and we're waiting for her to go into labor. Wanna see her?" Peyton asked, curious at Noah's expression. Of course, he had a calm demeanor and didn't seem phased in the least.

"Yeah, let's check on Betsy."

He and Peyton walked to the back of the barn, and she let go of Noah's hand to open the stall. She noticed that Betsy hadn't eaten any hay, but that her water bucket was a little low, so she grabbed it to fill it up with fresh water.

"Hey, mama," Peyton said to the heifer and scratched her head. She was standing up now, which made it a little easier for Peyton to examine her.

"That is a big cow," Noah stated.

Peyton laughed, "You know she can hear you, right?"

"I'm just saying that it's obvious she's carrying a calf in there," Noah chuckled and watched Peyton as she checked out Betsy.

"Oh boy, it looks like she's freshening," Peyton noticed. "And she's discharging cervical mucus. You're about to be a mama, Betsy!"

Noah cleared his throat, "I'm sorry, but what does freshening mean?"

Peyton snorted, "I'm sorry. It just means that her milk supply is coming in, and she's lactating. She's probably very uncomfortable."

"It's moments like these when I'm glad to be a guy," he admitted.

"That's not the first time I've heard that. I am quite grateful that I am not a guy," Peyton informed him and picked up the bucket of water and headed to the hose.

Noah followed behind her, "So am I." He smiled his crooked smile, and Peyton blushed.

She emptied the old water and refilled it with fresh water for the mama cow. She took the bucket back to Betsy's stall and locked it back up. "Is there anything else you want to see?" she asked Noah, who was quiet while she helped out Betsy.

"No, I think I've seen it all," he said sarcastically, and Peyton busted up in laughter.

"Yeah, you definitely got the behind-the-scenes tour," she giggled, and Noah joined in. He grabbed her hand again, and they walked back toward the house.

Peyton finally decided to be brave and tell Noah about Derek. He earned it after seeing mucus draining from the backside of a cow.

"Derek was my high school sweetheart, you could say. He moved to my high school our junior year, and we were together every day from day one. After high school, we dated for another year, and shortly after that, he proposed, and we got married. We were married for four years. Last year we were driving back from my doctor's appointment. I was six months pregnant at the time," Peyton stopped, trying to choke back tears, and Noah squeezed her hand in comfort.

"It was raining very hard," she continued, "and

Derek had a green light through an intersection. But a guy in a truck wasn't paying attention and T-boned our car on the driver's side, where Derek was." Peyton had tears running down her face and was trying to keep it together as best as she could, but she could feel herself start to lose it.

She had stopped walking, and Noah was staring at her with a concerned look on his face, but she kept going, "The driver was drunk, and Derek was killed instantly. I woke up in a hospital bed only to find out that my husband was dead, and I had lost the baby." Peyton let loose and cried. Noah pulled her in again and held her tightly.

She had never recounted the events of Derek's death before, and it felt as if she was reliving it all over again. Also, she had never told anyone outside of family about her losing a baby in the accident. She felt heartbroken all over again, but at the same time, she had this huge weight lifted off her shoulders. She assumed she was feeling some type of closure. She felt so embarrassed for crying the way she was in front of Noah. She was not one for showing her emotions to others, and she could only imagine what he was feeling. She figured he wanted to run the other way and say *"forget this broad."* Instead, he embraced her affectionately and let her cry all over his jacket.

"Peyton," he whispered, "I am so sorry. I can't even imagine the heartbreak you must be feeling."

Peyton took a few deep breaths and willed herself to get her emotions under control. Noah must have noticed she was trying to calm herself down because he started to stroke the back of her head. Then she felt him press his mouth against her head. Did he just kiss the top of her head?

That seemed to snap Peyton out of it, and she wiped her face. "Ugh, I'm sorry, Noah. I promise I don't usually do that. I've just never ever told anyone that before. And it felt like I was just reliving it all over again, and now I feel like I'm remembering all these little details like our conversation before the crash and brief memories of being in the ambulance and the nurse's names in the hospital." She put her head in her hands and held herself there for a minute to try and shake it off. "I promise I'm usually much more composed than this."

"Don't even worry about it. It's natural for you to feel this way. You lost so much," he said. "I'm sure you miss him."

Peyton shrugged her shoulders. "I think I'll always miss him. But I think I've finally come to a point where I need to start living life again. My mom told me that there's a time to mourn, and then there's a time to start forgiving and move on. Within the last couple of weeks, I've really felt that it's time for me to start moving forward and start living life again. Every time I pray, I get the feeling that I need to forgive and realize that Derek would want me happy and not spend my days on this earth so unhappy. But to take advantage of being alive. It was a miracle I even survived that accident."

"I'm sure he would be proud of you. For what it's worth, I think you're doing an amazing job. Is that why you go see my uncle?" Peyton knew this question was going to come up.

"Yep," she nodded her head, "I was prescribed therapy to try and work out how I was feeling and help me move past all this. I especially struggled in the beginning. My mom always drops me off because before I really put up a fight to go. Now, it's just become a habit for her to take me to my appointments."

"Ah, that all makes sense now," Noah replied.

"I thought you would have already known that by looking at my chart when I would check-in," Peyton questioned.

"I try not to look at them. Plus, once you caught my eye, I didn't want to look at your chart. I wanted you to be the one to tell me why you were in therapy, rather than read the opinions of others on your chart. Plus, that stuff is private. I don't read it unless I need to," Noah explained, and Peyton shook her head.

"You truly are amazing," she whispered.

Noah chuckled, "I could say the same about

you. Should we go back to the house? I bet your mom is ready to serve dessert."

"Yeah, we should," Peyton agreed.

"Hey," Noah said and took her hands in his, "thank you for sharing with me tonight. I really appreciate it. I know it wasn't easy for you, but it helps me understand more what you've been through and where you're at."

"You're welcome," she said and they walked hand in hand back to the house.

CHAPTER 12

They walked into the house, and everyone was waiting for them to have dessert. While they were gone, it seemed as though everything had calmed down between Chris and her mom. Chris was back to his usual sarcastic self, Gloria didn't look as worried, and her mom had her company smile back on her face. They all sat in the living room to enjoy their cobbler, and everyone had their own side conversations. Peyton's dad was talking to Noah about some tooth pain he was having while Chris, Gloria, and her mom were talking about wedding plans. Peyton sat back, listened, and enjoyed her cobbler, lost in her thoughts.

She couldn't believe that she had opened up to Noah the way she had. She also couldn't believe how he had opened to her about his feelings. She didn't know what to do with herself, or how to act. The only person she had ever dated was Derek, and everything was so easy with him. With Noah, as she had gone through so much, she was trying to figure out how to open herself back up and believe that she deserved a second chance at love.

After Noah left, she helped her mom clean the kitchen, informed her dad about Betsy, and then walked upstairs to her room. Shortly after she put her pajamas on, there was a knock on her door.

"Come in!" Peyton called.

The door opened, and her mom walked through. "Hey, sweetheart. How are you doing?" she asked.

"Oh, you know, as good as ever," Peyton replied sarcastically.

"What happened on your walk? Your face looked all blotchy. Had you been crying?" her mom didn't miss a beat.

"Yeah. I told Noah about Derek and the accident. And about me being pregnant and losing the baby," she explained.

"Wow!" Her mom looked shocked yet eager at the same time. "How did he take it? What did he say?"

Peyton shrugged her shoulders, "What could he say? He said he was sorry, and he let me cry all over his jacket. It was completely embarrassing, but he didn't seem phased at all. He took it very well, I think. I just didn't explain it very well between my blubbering."

"Well, it seemed like he understood, and he stuck around for a while and let your dad talk his ear off. He must like you, Peyton." She smirked and looked as if she were jumping up and down on the inside.

"Yeah, I know. He told me," Peyton admitted.

"He did!" her mom shrieked. "Oh my goodness, this is so exciting! What did you say? How did he say it?"

"He said that he would much rather be with me than study all the time, and I told him that I liked him too."

Her mom started clapping her hands and laughed. "Peyton! I'm so excited for you! Are you happy? He is such a nice guy and patient and, he even stuck around when your brother decided to drop the ball of a June wedding."

"By the way," Peyton wondered, "how did that go? Did you forgive them?"

Her mom rolled her eyes. "Hardly. The boy is forever going to cause me trouble," she huffed. "They explained to me that it was the best time for Gloria's family to come, and that their family was willing to help with whatever we needed. Quite frankly, all I need is for them to send a check, and then I can take it from there. I don't think they have any idea how long it takes to plan a wedding. All the things we have to order like flowers, dresses, picking a cake, booking a venue… Speaking of, do you remember when Derek's mom ordered those ugly pink carnations? And the bowties? When I found out she actually ordered them, I had a heart attack. It's not like anyone was dying that day. Carnations only belong in funerals!"

Peyton chuckled, thinking that she had just explained this to Chris and Gloria earlier. "Yeah, thank heaven we were able to cancel the order in time. She looked so caught off guard when I told her I hated carnations, and that we were going to go with neckties instead. Anyways, I'm glad they finally explained to you the situation and brought you in the loop."

Her mom smiled, "You know, Chris told me you opened up to them. And told them to open up to us and said that communication was the best thing they could do to make this wedding planning go as smoothly as it can."

Peyton waved her hand, "I may have said something. It was no big deal. I just wanted to make sure you're treated fairly, and that this experience is as much fun and great for you as it is for them."

Her mom hugged her. "Thank you so much," she whispered in Peyton's ear and kissed her on the cheek. She stood up from the bed and smiled at her. "You know, you had a pretty amazing wedding yourself."

"Yeah, it was the perfect day," Peyton nodded. "Thanks to you."

"I do have good taste," her mom confirmed and laughed. "I already have ideas for your next wedding," she winked and walked out of Peyton's room.

Peyton's jaw dropped. "You've got to be kidding me!" she sputtered.

She heard her mom laugh down the hall and go into her own room. Peyton chuckled to herself and shook her head in disbelief.

She laid down in her bed thinking about what her next wedding would be like and what she would do differently and who she thought might be at the end of the aisle. She fell asleep smiling, imagining Noah in a suit and her walking toward him in a big fluffy white dress.

The next day, Peyton was sitting on the couch reading a book when her mom came down the stairs. "Hey, Peyton, do you want to go to the grocery store with me? I need to get a couple of things for several dinners, and I don't want to end up having to go on Monday. Plus, I need to make sure I have everything we need for tomorrow. Just brace yourself, though, because you know going to the store on a Saturday guarantees it's going to be busy and the cashier lines will be ridiculously long."

"Mom, what if we run into one of your friends?

Then we're going to end up being there even longer," Peyton queried.

"I promise if we run into someone, I'll make it short and try to hide you as best as I can, so they don't bombard you with questions. And then we will run away as fast as we can!" she teased.

"You're hilarious," Peyton quipped. "Fine. I'll go with you."

"Thank you, I appreciate it. I know it's such a huge inconvenience," she said sarcastically, and Peyton rolled her eyes. "I can't seem to get your dad to come with me anymore. Do you have any ideas for dinner tonight and tomorrow?"

"Well, Mom, I don't really blame him. And I don't know. Meatballs sound good. I'm going on that date tonight with Noah though, remember?" Peyton reminded her.

"That's right! I'm so excited for you, Peyton. You're going to have a blast," she squealed and grabbed her purse.

"Yeah, it will be fun, I think. Plus, you know how much I love free food," Peyton teased and got up from the couch and stretched her arms. "Do you think I should bring my book just in case you see one of your girlfriends?"

Her mom narrowed her eyes at Peyton, "I'll throw that book away," she threatened. Peyton just laughed and tossed the book onto the couch then followed her mom out the door and to the car.

During the drive, all her mom wanted to talk about was Chris and Gloria's wedding. She was still ranting about how they hadn't told her about the date, and evidently, Chris had asked if some of Gloria's family could stay at their house. There were a couple of extra bedrooms in the house, and Gloria had aunts and uncles who wanted to come to the wedding too. Her mom never liked being put on the spot when asked questions like that in front of people. It never ended well. There were many times while she and Chris were growing up that they tried to ask their mom to have friends over while they were on the phone with the friend. She would make them hang up the phone and then ask her the question because she felt uncomfortable and up-set. Then Gloria had told her mom that she wanted the colors red and green, but her mom thought that was ridiculous because those were Christmas colors. The whole drive she ranted about it, and all Peyton had to do was nod her head and say "mm-hmm."

When her mom parked the car in front of the grocery store, she handed Peyton the list.

"Don't let me forget anything! I'm telling you if I have to come back here on Monday, I'm dragging you back here with me!" she reiterated and opened the car door. Peyton followed behind her and read the list.

"Um, Mom, did you write the list?" Peyton asked.

"Yes, I did. Why?"

"So, you want Oreos, ice cream, bbq chips, and root beer?" Peyton read.

Her mom took the list back and read it. "Your father! If he thinks I'm going to get him all that junk, he's crazy. He doesn't need it. I swear that man is going to end up with diabetes!" She thrust the list back at Peyton, and Peyton laughed.

"I don't know, all those things sound good to me," she snickered. "I think he has good taste."

"You are your father's daughter," her mom verified as she walked into the store and pointed to the shopping carts. "You get to drive," she informed her and started walking toward the aisles.

Peyton rolled her eyes. "Figures," she muttered.

"I heard that!" her mom called and turned around to smirk at her.

"There's no way!" Peyton challenged, but if she was being honest, her mom probably did in fact hear her. She had insanely good hearing.

Peyton followed her mom up and down every aisle, slowly checking each item off the list. There were multiple times where they forgot an item and had to go back down an aisle they had already been to. Just as Peyton suspected, her mom grabbed the items her dad had written on her list.

As Peyton and her mom were waiting in line for

the cashier, Peyton looked around the store, and out of the corner of her eye saw a familiar face coming down the cereal aisle. It was Noah. With another girl. A blonde one, in fact, with beautiful bouncing curls and make-up perfectly done. They were both laughing at something, who knows what, and she kept affectionately touching his arm.

Peyton felt her heart hit the floor, and she inhaled sharply. She turned around quickly and lifted her hood to hide her face.

"What on earth are you doing?" her mom inquired.

"Mom, I beg of you. Give me the keys, so I can go to the car," Peyton pleaded.

"What? No. We are almost done," her mom said and started putting groceries on the belt.

Peyton turned her head around slowly and saw that Noah and the blonde were heading in their direction.

"Mom, I promise if you forget something today, I will come to the store myself and get it, so you don't have to come. But please, let me go to the car. Please!" Peyton urged.

"Not until you tell me why!" she demanded and folded her arms.

Peyton grabbed her arm and turned her so that her back was facing the happy couple.

"Don't look now. But Noah is behind us and has a

bubbly blonde hanging on his arm. They look very cozy and friendly, and I don't want him to see me. That would be so awkward and embarrassing, so please, let me run while I still can. And if he sees you, don't tell him I was here!" Peyton whispered. Her mom slowly turned around to look and spun back around quickly.

"Oh, my word! I can't believe it!" She put her hands in her purse and handed Peyton the keys.

Without hesitation, Peyton took the keys. "Thank you!" she hissed and strode off to the car without looking back.

About ten minutes later, she saw her mom walking toward the car with her cart full of groceries. Her brow was furrowed and her eyes looked distant, and Peyton could tell she was deep in thought. Peyton jumped out of the car and met her mom at the back to quickly load the bags of groceries and put the cart away. By the time she got back, her mom was already in the driver's seat ready to drive. As soon as she was in the car and buckled up, her mom drove away with the best timing because not a minute later. Noah and the bubbly blonde walked into the parking lot. She had her arm wrapped around his arm while he was pushing the cart to his car.

"What a trollop," her mom stated.

"Which one?" Peyton asked.

"I don't know. That's the sad thing." She bit her

lip, which was what she usually did when she was worried or stressed.

"Did he see you?" Peyton wondered.

Her mom shook her head. "No, they walked right past me toward the produce department. Thank heaven. I don't know what I would have said if I saw him. I mean, I guess I do. I would play it cool and not bring you up, of course. But I'm glad I didn't have to. I wanted to throw one of my apples at his head," she surmised.

"I would have cheered you on." Peyton put her head in her hands and fought back tears. She felt so ashamed and embarrassed. She couldn't believe that she had let herself permit a guy to waltz back into her life, let alone allow herself to have feelings for one. It was at this moment that she realized that she had been falling in love with him. She could see him with her every day—laughing, cooking, traveling, having a family, growing old together, and being together forever. Little did she know that it was all a lie. He had played her, and she fell for it.

"Sweetheart, it's okay," she felt her mom put her hand on her back. "Maybe it's not what we think it is."

Peyton lifted her head and scowled at her mom, "Okay then, Mom. What else could it be? It was nothing but a tease, and I freaking fell for it. I feel so stupid. I should have never let you push me into this. I wasn't ready!"

"Yes, you were! And you are! Honey, I know it's scary to put your heart back out there, but you deserve to be loved. You know as well as I do that nothing compares to the happiness you feel when you have someone by your side who truly, truly loves you and who stands by you no matter what. Someone that you can constantly rely on and go to and trust! You deserve that! You should have that!" she protested and put her hand back on the steering wheel.

"Mom, I already had all that. I crave it every day. For him to be by my side again. He's the one I've desperately wanted to talk to these last few months, up until Noah maneuvered his way into my life. Then I started feeling all those mushy-gushy feelings again like being excited when I saw him or got a stupid text from him, and now, as soon I realize I really like the guy, I found out it's all a lie! He's a two-timing, two-faced jerk, and I never want to hear from him again. There's no way on this earth I'm going out with him tonight." Peyton was fuming. She folded her arms and looked out the window, letting tears trickle down her cheeks.

"Peyton, you don't know that! You don't know…" her mom stopped once she heard her cell phone ring. She picked it up to look and see who it was and decided to answer it.

"Hello?" she answered. Peyton listened closely

to the muffled voice coming from the cell phone and recognized it to be her dad's.

"Oh, really?" her mother queried. She was listening to her dad's voice rattling on, and it sounded as if he was worked up.

"We're about ten minutes away," she informed him. "I'll call the vet right now." She stopped talking to listen to her husband's voice and Peyton made out the words *"Thank you"* and *"Love you."*

"Love you too. Bye." Her mom hung up the phone and immediately started dialing what Peyton assumed to be Dr. Stapleton. She was our vet and lived a couple of miles down the road. She was usually available to come whenever her dad needed her.

"Mom, what's going on?" Peyton asked and wiped the tears off her face. Her feelings had now switched from anger to worry.

However, her mom ignored her and waited for the doctor to answer the phone. "Hello, Nicki? Hi, it's Cheryl. Are you at home?" she asked.

Peyton was straining her ears at this point to try and make out the words but couldn't do it.

"Good, it's an emergency. Can you head over to our house? There's a calf being born, and my husband says he thinks it's a breech birth," she informed her.

Peyton covered her mouth and started to panic.

She had just checked on Betsy last night, and everything had looked fine.

"Thank you so much, Nicki. See you soon." Her mom hung up the phone and set it back in her purse.

Peyton stared at her mom, who was staring at the road intently with her hands wrapped around the wheel so tight that her knuckles were turning white. Peyton reached over and put her hand on her mom's shoulder.

"It's going to be alright," she consoled.

Her mom looked over at her and smiled. "I hope so. Nicki is heading there right now. Hopefully, the cord isn't wrapped around the poor thing's neck. Your dad was really banking on this calf."

"Well, at least she will be there," Peyton sniffled.

CHAPTER 13

*P*eyton and her mom were home not more than five minutes later. Peyton had looked over at the speedometer and noticed that her mom was going fifteen miles per hour over the speed limit. Luckily, they saw Dr. Stapleton's car in the driveway, which caused Peyton to breathe a sigh of relief. She was happy to know that her dad had support now. Once the car was in park, they both jumped out and sprinted toward the barn.

When they reached the stall, they looked over to see Dr. Stapleton checking the calf's vitals. Her dad was stroking Betsy's back and watching intently over Dr. Stapleton and the calf. They waited silently for what seemed like forever until finally the doctor looked up and shook her head. Peyton choked back a sob and opened the stall door. Her mom walked over to her dad to hug him, and Peyton knelt next to the calf. Despite it being slimy, she touched the top of the calf's head and looked at it.

"What happened?" she asked glumly.

"Well, multiple things, I think. The calf is huge, and I think it was too big to turn around. And on its way out, it got tangled in the cord and choked. The poor thing didn't have a chance. There was nothing we could have done," Dr. Stapleton lamented.

Peyton nodded her head and wept over the cow. Her mom knelt down next to her and hugged her tightly. "Thank you for coming on such short notice, Nicki." her mom sniffled.

"Anytime. I'll check everything on Betsy and make sure she's not bleeding too much before I go."

"Thanks, Nicki," her father said. "Peyton, Cheryl, I'll walk you back to the house. Do you need my help with anything?" he asked the doctor.

Dr. Stapleton shook her head, "No. I'll take care of everything here. You guys just go ahead and head back to the house. I'm so sorry."

"Thank you," he said, and they walked out of the stall and headed to the house.

As soon as Peyton walked into the house, she started bawling. Seeing the poor dead baby cow laying helpless in the hay broke her heart into pieces. She blamed the death of the calf on herself. She had sworn that from last night's check, the head had felt like it was turned the right way. She felt absolutely guilty and helpless.

Not to mention she was still upset with Noah. Seeing him so happy and laughing with that other girl made her feel worthless. She had nothing on that other girl. The blonde was beautiful, vivacious, and bubbly, and Peyton felt like she was damaged goods. It was a no brainer for Noah. Why would he want to have leftovers when he could have a brand new meal?

"Peyton, it's going to be alright," her dad informed her and sat by her on the stairs, wrapping his arm around her. "I checked on the other cows this morning and discovered that two of our other cows were pregnant. I don't know how far along, but Nicki is going to check them out after she looks over Betsy. Our neighbor's bull that escaped into our fence a couple of months ago must have done the dirty work before we got him out. It's going to be okay."

"Oh, really?" she blubbered. "Well, that's good. At least we have that. That poor little calf. Just lying there, helpless. I could hardly stand it."

"I know," her dad rubbed her shoulder. "He fought so hard."

"And it was all for nothing. He worked so hard and fought for his life only to make his strangulation worse and end his poor innocent life! It would have been better for him to not have even existed.

The poor calf didn't deserve that. He didn't do anything wrong. He just wanted a chance at life—to be happy and live happily ever after. The poor little calf!" Peyton wailed and cried into her dad's shoulder.

"Um, honey. I have a feeling we're not talking about the calf anymore," he pointed out.

"That's because she's not," her mom stated.

"Mom," Peyton moaned and leaned away from her dad and tried to stop crying.

"She already told me, Sis," he informed her.

Peyton rolled her eyes and put her head in her hands, "Great."

"Maybe it's not what we think it is. That bubbly blonde, as you two put it, could be anybody. He said that he really liked you last night, right? And that he would rather be with you than study?" her dad coaxed.

Peyton's eyes narrowed at her mother. "You told him?"

"Peyton, I tell him everything. You have got to know that by now," she deflected.

"Peyton," her dad said, trying to get her attention back. "Did he say those things to you?"

"More or less, yes. But, I mean, wouldn't people want to do anything else besides study?" Peyton countered. "Dad, it looked like they were together. She was hanging all over him, and he was laughing and smiling and looked really happy. And you know what, honestly, if he's happy, I don't want to mess with that. I don't want to get in the way. I just wish that he had never messed with my feelings."

"I do too. Plus, he seemed like such a nice guy, and it didn't seem like he was the kind of guy to mess with a girl like that. I guess only time will tell," her dad said.

"Yep. Time. I've got lots of that now," she mumbled.

"Hey, it's all going to be okay."

"Thanks, Dad," Peyton smiled. "I sure hope so."

"I'm going to go see if Nicki is still here. I want to know how the other cows are doing." He stood up, walked over and kissed his wife on the cheek then walked out the front door.

Peyton continued to sit on the stairs and stare at her mom unloading all the groceries. She couldn't believe the day she had had. Last night, she had been told by an incredibly sweet, handsome, kind guy that he really liked her and wanted to be with her. She had woken up with the realization that she was beginning to fall in love with him. By noon, he became a two-timing scumbag, and she was fooled. Only moments later, she saw a poor, helpless baby animal die, and then not long after that, she was comparing herself to the dang calf. Her life had become so complicated in just twenty-four hours that she missed her life of a couple of weeks ago when Noah wasn't in the picture at all. She didn't think she could miss being miserable.

Her phone buzzed in her pocket. She pulled it out and saw that she had received a text from Noah.

"Oh, no," Peyton mumbled and opened the text. *Hey, Peyton, how are you doing today? I was wondering where you wanted to go out to eat tonight.*

Peyton snorted and texted back, *Sorry, I had something come up. I won't be able to go out tonight.*

"What are you doing over there?" her mom asked.

"Noah just asked where I wanted to go out to eat tonight, and I told him that I wouldn't be able to make it," she informed her.

"And you're okay with that?" she questioned.

"Yeah, Mom, I am. I have no desire to go out with him. I don't deserve that. I can't compete with gorgeous blonde locks accompanied with perfect makeup and long legs. And I shouldn't have to." Her phone buzzed again in her hand, and she opened the text. *Okay, does another day work better for you?*

Peyton responded, *Yeah, I'm busy all week, sorry. Have a good weekend!* She decided to turn her phone off for the night. She didn't want to be tempted to call him and give him a what-for or to wait around for a text that might never come. She needed some time to herself.

She helped her mom prepare dinner, which was a simple spaghetti with salad and garlic bread. Then she helped clean up the kitchen, sweep and mop the floor, and start the dishwasher. Once she was done in the kitchen, she picked up her book that she had previously thrown on the couch, sat down, and lost herself in her book. She figured the best way she could get through this weekend without spending too much time thinking about Noah was busting out a book. She was reading *Pride and Prejudice* again. She had read it so many times that she lost count, but she didn't care. She loved to read, especially Jane Austen.

When it got to the point where her eyes were getting fuzzy and she couldn't make out the words on the pages, she decided it was time to go to sleep. So, she trudged up the stairs to her room, completed her nightly routine, sprawled out on her bed, and passed out.

Her dreams consisted of Elizabeth and Mr. Darcy hashing it out and arguing, and then it would turn into Peyton and Noah fighting. This was what she dreamed of back and forth all night until the last dream she had, which was about Derek, of course. He was sitting on the fence that housed the goats, and he was shaking his head. He kept saying, *"You can't fall in love twice"* and *"Why have you forgotten me so quickly?"* Once she heard him ask that a couple of times, she woke straight up with sweat beading down her face, panting as if she had just gotten done running. She never wanted to feel like she was replacing Derek. In Peyton's mind, he could never be replaced. But, she also knew that she deserved to be loved and cared for, which was something Peyton was lacking. Of course, her parents loved her and took care of her every day, but being married to somebody who was as dedicated to the relationship as you were was just the best kind of love. It was nice with Derek because he was very open about his feelings, whether it was verbal or by his actions. She never doubted that he loved her. It scared her to think that she had already been fooled once and didn't want it to ever happen again. Oh, the joys of dating!

The next couple of days passed, and Peyton did her best to not mope around the house. When she wasn't reading *Pride and Prejudice*, she was helping her mom in the kitchen or helping her dad with the cows and checking on them. To really help pass time, she hopped on the riding lawn mower and mowed the grass. Luckily for her, this took a couple of hours, and to avoid letting her thoughts get away from her, she plugged in her headphones and blasted music in her ears, singing along. At one point, her mom walked by her on her way to the garden, and she looked at her and started laughing. Peyton smiled but didn't care. For those couple of hours, she felt like she was on another planet far away from her troubles.

Occasionally, she would receive texts from Noah asking how she was doing and what she was up to. Peyton would give him brief answers, saying she was fine or say that she was working a lot with her dad. Thankfully, Noah wasn't one to press for answers and seemed satisfied by her simplified replies. Peyton did wonder why he still bothered texting her. She thought she was giving off pretty good hints about not wanting to go out with him or text him. But still, every once in a while, he texted to check on her, and even if it could be considered sweet, it was beginning to annoy her.

Before she knew it, it was Thursday morning, and Peyton was getting ready to head into her appointment with Dr. Schoenborn. Of course, she was dreading it. The last few days had gone by so fast that she didn't even realize it. It felt like she hadn't even done anything, and still, the days flew by.

"Mom, if there were ever a time to let me stay home, today would be the day," Peyton insisted, leaning over her breakfast.

"Honey, you have to go. You can't miss any of your appointments unless you're throwing up or dying. It's going to be fine. Maybe that other lady is back, and he won't even be there," she encouraged.

"She's not going to be back for a while. He's definitely going to be there," Peyton started rubbing her temples. "Do headaches count as excuses to not go?"

"No, they don't," her mom said and sat down next to her at the table. She held Peyton's hand and squeezed it in encouragement. "It's going to be fine. Just put a smile on your face and don't let him see you upset."

Peyton did her cheesiest smile possible and her mom laughed, "That's my girl. Now let's go. Why are you eating so late anyway? Usually, you're done by now."

"I couldn't sleep last night, so I let myself sleep in and run a little later than usual," Peyton explained.

"I can tell. Your hair is still kind of wet. What kind of impression are you trying to give off? At least you did your make-up a little bit. Although it's not your best job," she pointed out.

"Hey, Mom, you're not helping," Peyton admitted.

In a short fifteen minutes, they were parked in front of the office and Peyton was hesitant to get out of the car. She slowly unbuckled her seat belt and reached her hand up to open the car door but couldn't bring herself to open it. She dropped her hand and put her hands over her eyes.

"Get out and get it over with already," her mom groaned.

"Mother. Will you just, okay?" Peyton stammered.

"Honey, I'm meeting with a couple of ladies at some new restaurant they want to take me to, and at this rate, I'm going to be late. So, can you please just be a big girl and do this already?" she pleaded.

"Fine!" Peyton exclaimed and burst out of the car.

"Call me when you're done!" her mother called, and Peyton slammed the door.

She turned around and marched up to the doors only to hesitate again once she looked through the windows and saw Noah at the front desk. She drew in a deep breath and opened the door slowly. She walked into the office, and Noah looked up right away. When he realized it was her, he smiled and stood up from his chair.

"Hey, I was waiting for you to come," he grinned. He was wearing a lighter wash pair of jeans but paired them with a blue and green flannel shirt that was opened up, revealing his white shirt underneath. The sleeves were rolled up three-quarters of the way, and he had a pencil behind his ear, which led Peyton to believe that he must have been studying for his board exams again.

"Oh, really? Well, I'm here now. Will you let your uncle know?" The question stumbled out of her mouth quickly, and she hoped he had understood what she had asked him.

"Yeah, I'll let him know." He bent over the computer and started typing, which Peyton assumed meant he was messaging him. While he was typing she walked over to the lobby area and sat down in her favorite chair. She wanted to appear busy to try and ward him off, so she pulled out her phone and started playing Mario Kart.

Out of the corner of her eye, she could see Noah stand back up from typing on the computer and noticed that he looked confused when he saw that she wasn't in front of him anymore. He did a quick scan of the room and found her sitting on the chair.

"How was your weekend?" he asked with curiosity.

"It was good. My dad needed my help with the cows. It got pretty hectic for a little bit." This guy just didn't see the *"don't talk to me"* sign on her forehead.

"Did that cow end up having her calf?" Noah wondered and slowly walked around the desk so that he was standing in front of her. He leaned up against the desk and crossed his arms, waiting for her to respond to his question. Peyton herself wondered why he had to look like a supermodel all the time. It wasn't fair. She couldn't keep her eyes off of him no matter how irritated she was.

Peyton nodded, "Yeah. Yeah, she did. It didn't make it though."

"Oh, man, I'm so sorry, Peyton. That had to

have been hard. What do you think happened?" Noah asked.

"It was breech. And as it was trying to come out, the cord wrapped around his neck and strangled him," Peyton sighed, feeling the sadness wash over her again thinking about the poor helpless calf.

"I'm sorry. Is there anything I can do to help?" he offered, but Peyton shook her head.

"Nope, we're all good now. We found out that two of our other cows were pregnant, so we should be just fine. Hopefully, the same thing won't happen to their calves," Peyton lamented.

"I sure hope so. Maybe since it sounds like you guys have everything figured out, we could try again for our date this week?" Noah asked. Peyton was taken aback at how persistent he still was about taking her on this date. Didn't he have a boisterous blonde to go back to?

Before Peyton could answer his question, Dr. Schoenborn opened his door and walked out. "Hello, Miss Peyton, are you ready?"

"Ready as I'll ever be," she said sarcastically.

"I'll see you when you come out," Noah said and walked back over to the computer.

"Great," Peyton muttered and followed Dr. Schoenborn back to his office.

CHAPTER 14

"How've you been, Miss Peyton?" Dr. Schoenborn asked cheerfully. Peyton quickly looked over at him and noticed that he was wearing a light blue pinstripe shirt, which was not the most flattering shirt on him, with a pair of khaki pants. The weird brown stain down his shirt especially didn't help his full ensemble. It just encouraged the stereotype.

"I'm just dandy. How are you, doc?" Peyton questioned and sat back waiting for his response.

"I've been good. Thank you for asking. I have some family visiting, I got to go fishing, and I tried out the new restaurant in town. Have you been yet?" he asked and got his notepad and pen ready to go.

"No, not yet, but my mom is going today, so

we'll see how she likes it," Peyton told him and twirled her thumbs in her lap.

"I heard you were supposed to go on a date this weekend, but it didn't end up happening. Can you tell me what happened with that?" Dr. Schoenborn inquired. Peyton really didn't like the fact that not only did she have to spill her guts out to him once a week, but that he was getting a behind-the-scenes earful outside of their sessions.

"Um, well, my dad had some problems with the cows this weekend and needed me to stay home," Peyton informed him.

"Oh! What happened?" He pushed his glasses up the bridge of his nose and adjusted the earpieces while waiting for her to answer.

"We had a calf die," she stated.

"I'm so sorry to hear that. That could not have been easy for you. How did you feel about that?"

"Well," Peyton put her head down. "I was really upset. It's hard seeing something so innocent and helpless die like that when there's nothing you can do about it. It was completely out of my control. We had called the vet and gave her a heads up when my dad noticed that the calf was breech, but there was nothing she could do. It had strangled to death while struggling to come out."

"Did that remind you of anything in particular?" Peyton could tell he was hinting at something, so she went ahead and took the bait.

"Yeah, it reminded me of losing the baby after the car accident," Peyton said in a monotone voice.

"Yeah, I can see why you would feel that way. Your poor baby died of circumstances that were unknown and out of your control!" he sympathized. "What helped you recover after having these feelings dug back up?"

"Pride and Prejudice."

"Excuse me?" Dr. Schoenborn questioned.

"Pride and Prejudice," Peyton verified. "The book? I read all weekend, and it helped me move past it. I simply read, so I didn't have to think about it."

"Peyton, if you're struggling with something, I would strongly encourage you to be open about it and talk to someone. Don't bottle up your feelings, otherwise, you're going to blow up," he theorized.

"Blow up?"

Dr. Schoenborn nodded, "Like a volcano." He went on, "When you bottle up your feelings, it's inevitable that something is going to set you off, and you're going to end up spewing out all your thoughts and feelings."

"That's quite a visual," muttered Peyton.

"What?" He turned his head in an attempt to listen harder.

"Nothing," she waved off. "Besides, isn't that why I'm here? To tell you these things and get them off my chest so that I feel better?" She did air quotes and continued, "I don't like talking about my feelings, Dr. Schoenborn. I never have. Especially when it comes to sadness or, in this particular case, death, which I've had a lot of in my short twenty-four years of life. You know as well as I do that I have no desire to be here. None. It's not like I look forward to coming here every Thursday and think, 'Gee, I wonder what I'm going to talk to Dr. Schoenborn about today?' No! I would rather be at home by myself reading or helping my parents around the house or be working. But I'm trying to do the right thing here and come to my appointments, so I can get them over with and finish up. So forgive me if I always don't go around day by day telling people how I feel or what I'm thinking. I feel like my life has already been out in the open much more than I ever wanted it to be, and there are some parts like my brain that I would like to be kept private." Peyton took a deep breath and covered her mouth after her little speech. She couldn't believe that she had just ranted to the doctor like that. What had gotten into her? First, she gave a big speech to Chris and Gloria about wedding plans then she completely opened up to Noah about the accident and now to Dr. Schoenborn.

Dr. Schoenborn leaned back in his seat and stared at her, processing everything she had just said. He hadn't even written anything down during her rant.

"Dr. Schoenborn, I'm so sorry. I…" she stopped when she saw a smile spread across his face, and he started clapping.

"Miss Peyton, I cannot believe it! That's the most you have ever said in a session! You were so expressive and raw and open about your feelings. I think you're feeling and cracking out of your beautiful shell!" He started scribbling away on his notepad, and Peyton sat in her chair staring at the overly excited man. He had completely caught her off guard, and she had no idea what to say. In her opinion, this man was by far the oddest person she had ever met. She felt like he got excited and happy at all the wrong times, and it left her just wanting to give him the slip and run out of his office.

"I think," he began, "that you only have a couple more sessions left with me. That is unless you want to keep going past the suggested time frame your family doctor and I have prescribed. But from what you've told me, it doesn't sound like you'll want to do that."

"Really?" Peyton breathed. "I only have a couple left?"

"Yes," he confirmed. "The last couple weeks you have been showing improvement. You've been happier, alert, and willing to make little changes in your life. Like reaching out to Derek's parents, making friends with Noah, and going on a date with him. And you've been opening up to people more than you have in months."

Peyton smiled and nodded her head, "Well, that's great news. Thank you so much for everything you've done for me. I know I haven't been the easiest person to work with, but I really do appreciate you and how patient you've been."

"Thank you, Miss Peyton. I think we're done for today, and I'll send a message to your regular doctor letting him know your diagnosis. As always, thanks for coming in." They stood up and shook hands.

"You're welcome, and see you next Thursday," she called as she walked out the door.

Peyton didn't realize she still had a smile on her face, but Noah had noticed and chuckled. "Well, you look happy," he pointed out.

Peyton was caught off guard and stammered out the next sentence, "Uh, yeah, I guess I am."

"I'm glad to hear it. Did you need me to set up another appointment for you?" he questioned.

"Yeah," she said, slowly walking away from the desk. "Next Thursday, same time, please."

Noah hadn't noticed that she was backing away from him because he was so focused on the computer and scheduling her appointment. By the time he straightened up and wasn't staring at the computer, Peyton was already by the door.

"Alright, you're all set," he looked up and slightly frowned. "Are you okay?"

"Yes. I just need to get back home to get some work done," Peyton said, trying to come up with the best excuse possible so that he didn't see past her.

"Oh, okay. I thought you might want to reschedule our date," admitted Noah. The sad thing was that he honestly looked disappointed, which made her heart leap a little bit. She didn't like to see him sad.

"Well, I... Whoa!" Peyton almost fell straight back when the door all of the sudden opened.

"Excuse me!" said a lady behind her, and Peyton did her best to maneuver out of the way without falling on her behind. She somehow grabbed the door frame and held herself up. The lady walked around her, and Peyton recognized the bouncing blonde curls and realized it was the same girl from the grocery store.

"Hey, sweetie," the blonde chirped. She was wearing a dark green rain jacket with the tightest skinny jeans Peyton had ever seen and knee-high, high-heeled boots. She looked like she had just walked off the runway, and Peyton then realized he was the Ken to her Barbie. "I was wondering if you wanted to come and grab a bite to eat with me." She leaned over the desk and twirled one of her curls around her finger. "There's a new restaurant in town that all my friends seem to be raving about, and I thought we should both check it out. I know you've got to be hungry since it's lunchtime after all!" Peyton thought she was going to break out her pom-poms and start cheering.

Poor Noah looked completely caught off guard. He was staring at the blonde, who was trying to capture his full attention, but then he would look at Peyton in bewilderment. He seemed to not know how to handle the situation because he kept looking back and forth between the two women.

When Miss Cheerleader realized he was distracted, she turned to find the culprit who was distracting him and locked eyes with Peyton. Was it possible for someone to become even more beautiful in such a short period of time? Her make-up looked even more perfect than before. Her light blue eyes with perfectly done eyeliner and mascara were now staring at Peyton as if to say, *"Who's this loser."* Her eyebrows had a great arch and looked as if they had just been filled in. Her cheeks were rosy, her nose had the perfect slope, and her lips were ruby red. When she lost interest in glancing at boring old Peyton, she turned back to Noah and smiled to show her pearly white teeth.

"So, what do you think, you want to go?" She flirted and reached across the desk in an attempt to touch his hand.

At this point, Peyton had seen enough and

walked out the door. Thankfully, her mom was waiting for her out front, and Peyton bolted for the car.

"Mom, go!" Peyton yelled.

"Are you serious? Again?" her mom screeched.

"Yes! Just drive, Mom. Go, go, go!" Peyton pleaded and buckled her seatbelt.

"I can't believe we're doing this again. I feel like we're trying to get away from some type of bad guy. We have the treasure, and we're running from pirates."

"Well, if that helps you to drive then, by all means, Mom. Blackbeard is right behind us, and he will do anything to get the treasure, so you need to drive like you've never driven before! I'm not walking the plank today!" Peyton beseeched, and her mother did as she was told. Her mom weaved in and out of traffic and went as fast as she could for Peyton's benefit. Whenever her mom drove like this, Peyton automatically knew she was on cop duty and scanned the streets for any black and whites waiting around to ticket someone.

Once they were out of the city limits, her mom slowed her speed and calmed down her driving.

"Okay, I want an explanation," she ordered, and Peyton did as she was told.

"Remember the stupid blonde? Well, she showed up right as I was about to walk out the door. She practically ran me over, and I almost fell," complained Peyton.

"Is that what I saw?" her mom interjected.

"If you mean me almost eating the pavement? Yes. She basically cat-walked right up to the front desk where Noah was sitting, and being her flirtatious, flamboyant self, she asked Noah out to lunch. You should have seen Noah. He was so caught off guard when he saw her walk in. And then when he noticed me still standing there by the door, his face just fell. He looked so embarrassed to know that I had figured out he was two-timing me and dating Miss Runway. And then, when she noticed Noah looking away from her, she turned around and saw me, made this face like I was the scum of the earth, and asked him out again. At that point, I left. I had heard and seen enough, and well, you know the rest of the story," grunted Peyton and she stared out the window. The trees were all blooming with beautiful pink and white blossoms. It reminded Peyton of popcorn.

"You didn't say anything? You just ran out like a chicken?" her mom called out.

"I am not a chicken!" Peyton argued.

"Well, it sure sounds like you were. You didn't even give him a chance or wait to see what he was going to tell Blondie."

"Honestly, Mom, I didn't want to hear it. I've had enough. If he wants to be with someone like that, then I certainly don't want to get in the way. I am definitely not Project Runway," admitted Peyton. She looked down at herself and frowned when she noticed grass stains on the jeans she was wearing. She really didn't look great. She was wearing an old high school sweatshirt, and her hair was wrapped up into a bun. When she had woken up earlier that morning, she had some deep purple bags underneath her eyes and had applied a lot of concealer to try and hide them. She pulled down the car roof mirror to check her makeup and was disappointed to see that most of it was gone. She put her hand to her forehead and remembered she had forgotten to spray primer on her face to help the makeup stick and stay. If she didn't do this, her makeup always had a hard time being applied and staying on. Today was not the day for her to forget an important step like that, but she had felt completely sleep-deprived when she was putting on her makeup, so she wasn't surprised she'd forgotten the primer.

"I don't blame you, sweetheart. And that's very big of you to say even though I personally want to run him over with your dad's truck. I won't, but I will admit the thought has crossed my mind a couple of times. He was just so nice and easy-going, and he seemed to like you. I just feel like we missed something, but from what you just told me, it sounds like he was just taking advantage of you.

I'm so sorry, Peyton. I feel like I pushed you into this, and now your heart is being broken all over again," her mom sniffed. "I just wanted to see you happy again."

"It's okay, Mom. I'll be happy like that again. Someday. It's just obviously not the time quite yet. It will come though," Peyton assured her mother, who looked just as confused as ever.

"Wait, now you're consoling me? Peyton, are you okay?" she asked with concern in her voice.

"You know, Mom, I'm not doing that bad."

They drove down the driveway, and Peyton noticed Chris's car in the driveway.

Peyton groaned. "Okay, I don't know if I can handle those two right now."

"I don't think I can handle those two either. Maybe we should just let your dad take care of them," her mom suggested. She parked the car next to Chris's and stepped out. "They probably have wedding stuff to go over though." She sighed and walked up the steps of the porch. She turned around and noticed Peyton still standing by the car.

"Are you coming?"

"You know, I think I'm going to go for a walk. I need to get some things sorted in my brain before I face the happiest couple on the planet," Peyton decided and started walking towards the trail.

"Alright. Well, be careful. Are you going to the river?" she asked.

"Yeah, I haven't been there for a while, and I need some privacy. Please don't tell Chris where I am. I don't need him to come looking for me and hounding me with questions about Noah. I'm not even sure how I completely feel about the situation."

"Okay, see you later," waved her mom as she entered the house.

Peyton walked onto the trail and followed it back to her most favorite spot in the whole entire world.

CHAPTER 15

She sat on the edge of the pier and closed her eyes, taking in all the sounds around her. She heard the sound of the water trickling below her feet and moving downstream. She heard a frog nearby croaking and then hopping farther away from Peyton. She heard crickets, the wind rustling through the trees, and the birds chirping all around her, warning the others that there was a human around. They were all sounds that Peyton welcomed and loved to listen to. This was a special place to Peyton that brought peace to her mind, helped clear her thoughts, and where she often went to pray.

She laid down and looked up at the sky, watching the clouds roll by. Off in the distance, she could see that a weather system was coming in, and it looked like there was going to be some rain. She wasn't worried though because it wasn't going to come for a while, so she had time to relax and enjoy the sun.

She started thinking about Noah and wondered what he had told the blonde who had strutted into the office. He had looked completely taken aback and, obviously, didn't know how to handle the situation. She imagined they were out to lunch, sitting across from each other and talking and laughing just as they had at the grocery store. She imagined the blonde trying to reach across the table and grab his hand, but Peyton didn't know whether or not he would take it. He probably would, just to be nice or maybe he would because he liked her.

Peyton covered her eyes with her hands in frustration because she had no idea how he was feeling right now. Last week, he had told her that he had wanted to be with her, hugged her, and held hands with her. He was very affectionate and sweet and, what seemed like to Peyton, very honest and transparent. But now, a week later, seeing him interact with this other girl, Peyton didn't know what he was thinking or if he had changed his mind. The idea of that made Peyton's heart sink and her stomach queasy.

She didn't like seeing him with the other girl at the grocery store laughing like they didn't have a care in the world and having a good time. She hated watching that girl walk up to him and very flirtatiously ask him to lunch and try to reach over and grab his hand. Peyton thought that it was her hand that she got to hold, and the blonde was overstepping boundaries. Evidently, those boundaries were not set by both her and Noah, but just Peyton. She didn't realize how much she had truly liked Noah, but seeing him with this other girl was slowly making her go crazy.

She then started thinking about all the things she liked about him. She liked the way his hair laid and how it was sort of messy but in a good sort of messy like he had done it on purpose. She liked how polite he was and always wanted to make her comfortable. She liked how patient he was with her family and noticed how well-mannered he was. She was attracted to him on a physical level and could stare at him all day long. His physique was very muscular as if drilling teeth made muscles, but who knew? His eyes always looked like they were lively and alert, like they had enjoyed a good few laughs in his lifetime. And then there was his smile. His crooked smile, which took her breath away every time. It was as if nothing in the world was more perfect than his smile. When he smiled, his eyes would almost twinkle, and the world seemed to glow brighter. Nevertheless, no matter how perfect Noah seemed, he had disappointed her, and she really wished that he hadn't.

She stood back up and walked off the pier. She went to the water's edge and picked up some rocks to throw into the water. She tried to find some rocks with smooth surfaces to skip into the water, but she had no luck. They would just drop to the bottom of the river. She would try over and over again but failed to get a single rock to skip. With frustration, she threw the last rock she had overhand and walked away from the river.

"You've got quite an arm on you," said a male voice from a few feet away.

Peyton jumped and looked up and saw Noah walking toward her from the forest trail.

"Holy crap, Noah! I just about jumped out of my skin!" Peyton cried and put her hand on her heart as if she were trying to slow it down. "What are you doing here?"

"I came to your house looking for you, but your mom answered the door and told me where you were," Noah said to her.

"That doesn't answer my question. What are you doing here?" Peyton repeated.

"I wanted to talk to you. I've missed you, and I feel like you haven't wanted to talk to me. Did I do something wrong?" Noah asked.

"Noah, truthfully, I don't want to talk about this right now," she admitted. "I…" she trailed off when Noah came within a couple of feet of her and stopped.

"Please talk to me."

"I can't believe you're even asking me. I'm so sick of these mind games!" Peyton shook her head and closed her eyes.

"What mind games? What are you talking about? Please tell me!" Noah begged.

"The blonde, Noah!" she cried. "The blonde who was all over you today at the office asking you to go out to lunch with her. And then at the grocery store where she was all over you, and you were giggling and flirting and walking arm in arm."

"Wait, what?" Noah asked with a look of confusion.

"Oh, please, you know who I'm talking about!" She waved him off.

Then she saw his eyes widen and his cheeks flush. It was as if a light bulb had gone off in his brain. But instead of looking embarrassed, he started smiling and shaking his head.

"Uh, Peyton," he whispered and took a step toward her.

Peyton's face started to burn up. She was getting more upset as the seconds ticked by, and she stood with her arms crossed, fighting back tears and waiting for him to explain himself.

"Peyton, that wasn't what you thought," he stated.

"I beg to differ," she gritted through her teeth, determined not to let any tears escape her eyes.

"That blonde, as you referred to her as, was someone I used to date in high school. It didn't last very long because I'm sure you can tell she's a bit out there, and I am not," he replied.

She shrugged her shoulders, "How was I supposed to know you weren't interested in very flirtatious supermodels?"

Noah chuckled and took another step forward so that they were only inches apart now.

"My cousin Sarah is best friends with that very flirtatious supermodel, whose name is Brittany, by the way," informed Noah.

"Brittany, the bubbly blonde. It just keeps getting better," Peyton muttered.

Noah laughed louder this time and wiped his hand over his face. "Brittany came home during her school break and has been hanging around my cousin a lot, which seems to translate to tracking me down and wanting to be with me. When you saw us at the grocery store I'm assuming, she had just ambushed me and started hanging on me as if I were monkey bars or something. I was laughing out of pure terror."

This time Peyton laughed and put her head down, tucking a piece of hair behind her ear.

"And then, well, you saw what mostly happened at the office today. What you missed was me saying no and that I wasn't interested in going to lunch with her. When she asked why not, I told her that it was because I was hoping to go with someone else. But, by the time I finally got her to leave, you had already left. So, I told my uncle I was leaving for my lunch break, and now, here I am," he explained and smiled his crooked smile, and Peyton could feel her spirits lifting.

"So, you're not interested in Brittany the bubbly blonde after all?" Peyton clarified and uncrossed her arms to put them behind her back.

"No," Noah shook his head and chuckled, "I most certainly am not. I like brunettes." Noah moved in and wrapped his arms around Peyton, and she looked up at him. His eyes were staring intently into hers, and they were locked into each other's gazes. Before she knew it, Noah was bending his head down to her face, placed his hand on her cheek, and gently touched his lips to hers. They were kissing. She hadn't been kissed in a long time, and she felt like there was electricity running through her veins. It was the perfect setting—the sound of the river in the background, the birds singing, and the sun shining on them. She felt like she was in a fairytale, and she wanted to stay in it forever.

He pulled away after a few seconds and leaned his forehead against hers. Peyton's breath was taken away, and she tried to steady her breathing. She couldn't believe what had just happened. She hadn't been kissed in over a year and wondered if this was all a dream. She knew it wasn't because her dreams were never this good.

"Do you believe me now?" he whispered.

Peyton chuckled and nodded her head, "Yeah. Yeah, I do."

He stood up straight but still kept his arms wound tightly around her. "Did you cancel our date because you thought I was going out with Brittany behind your back?" he smirked and waited for her to answer his question.

"Yes," she answered sheepishly and looked down at the ground.

"Oh, Peyton," he pulled her in for a hug. "I would never do that to you. I think you've been through enough. All I want to do is make you happy. Not cause you any more pain. And believe me when I say that I really like you and would like to take you out. Tonight, if you'll let me."

"Okay," she smiled and looked at him, so he could see that she was happy, "Let's do it."

"Great! Where do you want to go?" Noah asked.

"Not the new restaurant," Peyton quipped and he tipped his head back and laughed out loud.

"Deal. I think I know a place you might like," he decided.

"I trust you. Plus, I'm not very picky. I just love food," Peyton admitted.

"Me too." Noah looked at her so intently that it felt like he was staring straight into her soul. As if he were memorizing her face so that he would never forget it. He gave a little smile, barely turning up the corners of his mouth, but it wasn't a forced one. It felt tender and sweet. He reached his hand up to brush her hair out of her face, and Peyton shyly smiled back.

"I think I should head back. I've been out here a while, and my mom is probably wondering where I am. Especially now that she knows you're out here," Peyton said thinking about it. She imagined that her mom was wandering around the house doing meaningless chores like straightening up the bookshelf or wiping down the counter for the third time and repeatedly looking out the back window to see if they were coming back or not. Then she would turn around in a huff, muttering under her breath and asking herself if they were ever going to come back.

Peyton smiled to herself, realizing that's probably exactly what she was doing, and unwrapped her arms from around Noah's waist. Even if Noah looked a little bummed, he didn't let her go completely because then he took her hand and kissed it before they walked back to the house together.

Once they reached the front of the house, Noah hesitated at the front porch steps.

"I would love to come in, but I need to get back to the office." He pulled out his phone to look at the time, "Yeah, I really need to get going. I'm sorry. I wish I had more time."

"Don't worry about it. It's all good," Peyton hummed. He grabbed her other hand, so they were standing straight across from each other.

"Are we still on for tonight? I'm not going to get a text saying you're busy again?" he chortled and eyed her in a flirtatious manner.

"Nope. I'd say so far so good," she teased. "I'll let you know though."

Noah laughed and shook his head, "You think you're so funny."

"I don't think," she paused for effect, "I know." They both laughed, and he pulled her in for another kiss. This time he wasn't as gentle but was more persistent in an affectionate sort of way. He held her tightly and placed his hand on the back of her head. Peyton couldn't believe that this was happening to her. Her heart felt as if it was beating out of her chest, and she could almost feel herself becoming lightheaded.

"Now I really don't want to go," he whispered.

Peyton giggled. "You'll see me tonight," she encouraged.

"At least there's that," he admitted. "Is six okay? I get off at five, so that should give me enough time to run to my apartment, shower, and then come pick you up."

"Yeah, six works great," she confirmed.

"Great. Well, I will see you later tonight then," he restated. He kissed her on the cheek and walked to his car. He waved before climbing in and driving away.

Peyton waved as he drove down the driveway and didn't start walking inside until she saw the car disappear.

CHAPTER 16

*P*eyton was welcomed into the house with screaming from her mother.

"Peyton!" she squealed as she ran over and hugged her tightly. "Peyton! I can't believe what I just saw! I can't believe he just kissed you! Like actually kissed you. Oh, I never thought I could be so happy, honey. Are you happy? What happened? What did he say? What about the blonde? You have to tell me everything!"

"Mom! You were spying on us?" Peyton said, feeling completely embarrassed.

"It wasn't just me! Your dad was too," she informed her.

"What?" Peyton screeched. "Dad?" She spun around and saw her dad sitting in his chair, flipping through channels again and trying to act non-chalant.

"Honey, we were both curious to see whether or not he would come back to his car hand in hand with you or with an imprint of your hand on his face," her dad admitted. "Thank heaven it wasn't the latter. But I did see him on your face. I don't know if I liked that much better."

"Daddy!" she exclaimed.

"Peyton," her mom said to turn her daughter's attention back to her. "What happened? What did he say?"

Peyton sat on the stairs and recounted everything that had happened to her mom. She explained to her about Brittany the bubbly blonde, about the office, and about how he had kissed her, twice.

When Peyton told her mom about the first kiss, she swooned and put her hand on her heart. Then when she realized she had seen the second kiss, she clapped excitedly and smiled so big that it looked like her cheeks were going to start hurting.

"Are you happy?" she asked again.

"Yeah," beamed Peyton. "Yeah, I am. He's picking me up at six, and we're going out to dinner."

"Please, let me help you get ready. I can help pick out an outfit. You're going to shower, right? You smell like the river," her mom looked over her and scrunched up her nose in disapproval.

"Yes, Mom, don't worry. I plan on it," Peyton rolled her eyes and tried to smell herself without her parents noticing what she was doing.

"Uh, actually before you do that, Sis, do you mind mucking out the stalls for me? They absolutely need to be done, but I'm not going to have enough time today. And then after you're done, will you make sure to put more hay down and check the cows' water?" her dad asked. "I would really appreciate it. The stupid cows messed with the fence on the back of the property, and I need to go all the way out there and fix it."

"Yeah, Dad, sure thing. I need something to do anyhow to help the time go by," decided Peyton.

"Make sure you give yourself enough time to get ready though. I want you to look beautiful tonight," her mom pestered.

Peyton sighed, "Yes, Mom." She quickly walked out the back door before her mom could say anything else.

She felt grateful for her dad because working out in the barn did help the time go by. She spent the entire time thinking about Noah. She hadn't expected him to show up today and kiss her no less. She felt she had gotten herself all worked up over nothing and was truly embarrassed. She had wasted time and energy worrying and being upset over something that she had completely misunderstood. Despite being embarrassed, Noah made her feel like it was okay and that she was human. He made her feel comfortable and safe with him, and she didn't like when he was away. It was like she noticed this safety net being taken away from her the moment they parted ways. She hadn't felt so head over heels in a long time. She wondered whether or not she was moving too fast and if it was a good idea. It had been barely a year since Derek had passed, and she didn't want to rush into anything. However, whenever she was with Noah, she couldn't help herself. It was easy to be around him and be herself when she wasn't in her own head.

By the time she was done cleaning out the stalls, she looked at her phone and noticed she had been out there for three hours. She ran back to the house and hurried up the stairs, hoping her mom didn't notice that she hadn't showered yet.

"Peyton!" called her noisy mother, "Is that you? Have you still not showered yet? I can smell you all the way from in here!"

"I'm going now, Mom!" Peyton replied and shut her door quickly and jumped in the shower.

When she walked out of the bathroom to grab some clothes, her mom was sitting on her bed waiting for her.

Peyton jumped and grabbed her towel to make sure she was covered up. "Oh geez! Were you sitting there the whole time?" she screeched.

"Most of the time. It's been a while since I've heard you sing in the shower," her mom pointed out. "You sound good."

"Gee, thanks," she stalked over to her dresser and found some old sweats and a baggy shirt to throw on quickly while her mom played dress up. She walked into the bathroom, quickly put on the clothes, and walked back out.

"Alright," Peyton jumped onto her bed and spread her arms out, "the closet is yours."

Her mom sprang from the bed and started whirling around Peyton's room throwing clothes everywhere, encouraging her to try everything on from jeans and a blouse to a skirt and cardigan and then Peyton's least favorite dress with heels. Her mom made her walk around the room in the heels to practice, but she kept stumbling and tripping over her own feet. She realized she hadn't worn heels since Derek's funeral. She sat on the edge of her bed and felt a tear fall from her cheek.

Her mother had another dress in her hand when she spun around, and her face fell when she noticed that Peyton was crying.

"Honey, what's wrong?" She sat down next to Peyton and put a hand on her knee. "You don't have to wear a dress if you really don't want to."

"Am I doing the right thing?" Peyton whispered.

"What do you mean?" her mom questioned.

"I mean," Peyton's voice became louder, "should I be going out with someone so soon? Won't people think that I'm rushing? What if someone sees me?"

She shrugged her shoulders, "Who cares? You need to worry about yourself and what's best for you. You deserve happiness just as much as everyone else. Enjoy your time with Noah and be in the moment. Don't spend the whole time worrying about what other people think. It's impossible to please everyone. Plus, who are you worried about seeing?"

"No one in particular. Just in general, people have their personal ideas of what grief is, and I'm just worried I might set someone off if they see me with another boy," Peyton explained.

"Or they would be happy to see you get out of the house for a change," she offered.

"Yea, maybe," she thought out loud and stared at the heels that were crushing her toes together.

"So, what do you want to wear?" her mom prompted.

Peyton decided to go with dark skinny jeans and a yellow flutter sleeve blouse, but to make her mom a little happier about that option, she told her she would wear her booties. That way, she was wearing some type of heel to look dressy but not so tall of a heel that she couldn't walk. Her mother had especially wanted her to wear a dress and strappy heels.

Her mom followed her like a little puppy dog around her room and into her bathroom, constantly asking questions and offering suggestions. Once Peyton started working on her hair and makeup, she let her mom take over and do it because she didn't want to risk messing up and causing her mom to have a heart attack. With a lot of guidance from Peyton, her mom curled her hair into loose waves and pulled some of it up so that she didn't have to worry about hair falling in her face. Then her mom started on her makeup, and even though it was a little darker than what Peyton preferred, she kept her mouth shut because it was going to be dark out, so she could get away with a little darker makeup.

When she was all done getting dressed, she looked at herself in the mirror and gasped. She hadn't seen herself done up and all put together in a long time. Lately, she figured she cried so much that it was pointless to put on any makeup besides the occasional concealer for breakouts.

Her mom walked up behind her and hugged her shoulders. "You look so beautiful," she breathed.

"You don't think it's too much?" she hesitantly asked about her new look.

"Not at all. You are going to blow him away.

What time is it?" She patted her shoulder implying for her to find the time.

"It's fifteen till," she answered, looking at her phone. "Oh, look, he texted me a while ago. My bad," she muttered.

"What did he say?" her mom asked, being her usual nosy self.

"He just wanted to make sure I was still planning on coming and wasn't going to bail on him again," she explained. "How was I supposed to know that blonde wasn't his special someone?"

"I don't know. Because he told you he wanted to be your special someone?" her mom retorted.

"Okay, okay, you were right. I get it," Peyton waved her off and walked out of her room and downstairs.

"I just love hearing those words," gloated her mom as she followed Peyton down the stairs.

"What are you guys going to do tonight?" asked Peyton.

"I think Chris and Gloria are going to come over, and we're going to plan some things for the wedding. Don't worry, they aren't coming until after you're gone. I don't need your brother saying something that's going to embarrass all of us."

"You talking about Chris?" her dad called out from his chair.

"Yep. Mom was just telling me that Chris was coming over, but he isn't coming over until after

I'm gone," Peyton walked over and sat down on the couch closest to her dad. Her dad looked over at her and his eyes widened.

"Holy smokes, Peyton, is that you?" he marveled and looked her up and down.

"Very funny, Dad," she mumbled and slumped into the couch.

"Honey, you look beautiful! I didn't mean anything by it!" he complimented.

"Yes, so sit up straight. You're going to wrinkle your shirt and flatten your hair," her mother pointed out.

Peyton did as her mother said and straightened out her shirt and fluffed her hair back out. "Better?" she sassed.

"Yes, thank you! Sarcastic punk," her mom deflected.

"I heard that," Peyton sang, and she and her dad snickered.

"Are you excited?" he asked.

"Yes and no," Peyton admitted. "This whole last week I thought he was playing me and that turned out to be wrong, so I think I'm still trying to digest that. And I'm worried about the timing of everything and wondering if we're moving too fast. More specifically, me."

"Well, after what you've been through, I don't think there's a specific timeline of when to start moving on. If you're happy and he's happy, that's all that matters," he smiled and grabbed her hand. "You look absolutely beautiful. And I gotta say, I haven't seen you smile this much in a long time. I've missed your smile." Peyton noticed tears welling up in the corners of his eyes, and it caused Peyton to start tearing up as well.

"Oh, Daddy!" Peyton lunged forward and hugged her dad, trying to not let any tears fall from her eyes. She didn't want to mess up her makeup and, more importantly, give her mom another reason to put a makeup brush near her face.

There was a knock at the door, and her mom rushed over to answer it. Before she opened it, she noticed her husband and Peyton hugging and getting emotional.

"You guys!" she whispered frantically and waved her hand around like a crazy person, "Stop it! Shake it off. Peyton, go quickly check your makeup in the bathroom. Walter, pull yourself together." Peyton rounded the corner and checked her makeup quickly. Once she was done, she walked back into the living room and straightened out her clothes again.

The man did as he was told and grunted, "Yes, dear."

Her mom rolled her eyes, "You two will be the death of me." Then she swung the door open and greeted Noah. "Why hello, Noah! Nice to see you again! Come on in."

"Thank you, Cheryl. How are you doing?" Noah asked. He was wearing khaki pants and a nice navy blue pullover sweater. He searched around the room for Peyton, and when he finally found her, he caught her eye and winked.

She blushed and looked over at her dad to see if he had noticed the affectionate gesture. By the look of it, he had noticed and teased her by making a funny face and winking at her. Peyton attempted to stifle a laugh but didn't do a good job because then her mom gave her a look, and she tried to make a straight face. Her mom narrowed her eyes and turned back around to look at Noah to answer his question. Peyton spared another glance at her dad, and they both smiled at each other mischievously. Noah caught her eye when her mom wasn't looking and shared a silent chuckle, shaking his head. She had been caught.

When they were done exchanging pleasantries, Peyton walked over to Noah to get ready to walk out the door.

"Alright, what time will you be home?" her father asked.

"Daddy," Peyton warned.

"We'll be home no later than nine. I have to get up early and study in the morning," Noah explained.

"Good man, nice and early. Have fun, Sis." Her

dad kissed her on the forehead and sat back in his chair and grabbed the remote.

"And Dad's assumed his position, which means we can go. Mom, I'll see you later," Peyton kissed her on the cheek and opened the front door.

"Have a good night, Cheryl," Noah said and walked out the door, and Peyton followed behind.

Like a true gentleman, Noah opened the car door and waited for her to climb into the car.

"Well, aren't you nice," Peyton teased and walked over to the passenger side.

"I'd like to think I am. By the way, you look beautiful," he crooned and shut the car door, walked over to his side, and got into the car.

"Thank you," Peyton said bashfully. She was grateful it was getting dark to hide her red cheeks. Noah grabbed her hand and squeezed it as if he knew she was embarrassed.

"Hey," Noah began, "I'm glad you're here."

"Yeah, I am too. So, where are we going?" she asked.

"Well, there's a good restaurant here in town called Maxwell's and it has an assortment of food. Burgers, pasta, seafood—all sorts of stuff. I wanted to go somewhere where we had a lot of options be-cause I didn't know what you would be in the mood for," explained Noah.

"I think it sounds great. And very smart on your part," she added.

It didn't take long for them to drive to the restaurant. They parked the car, and Noah walked around to open the door for her again.

"Are you ready?" he teased as she hesitated to get out of the car. Her nerves were starting to get to her. She hadn't been in public like this in a while, and she didn't want to see anyone. He held out his hand and smiled, waiting patiently.

"Yeah," she swallowed hard and took his hand. She couldn't resist a smile like that, and somehow it gave her courage to step out.

"You okay?" He eyed her suspiciously.

"Yes," she nodded, "let's go!" She tried to sound enthusiastic, but she didn't fool him because then he started laughing.

"Alright then, I'll just let you tell me later. I'm hungry since I didn't eat lunch," he added. He looked at her with a twinkle in his eye, and it took Peyton a second to realize that he had skipped his lunch to come to see her.

"Noah, I would have made you something to take with you! I feel bad you came to see me and didn't eat," Peyton said as Noah kept hold of her hand and led her to the entrance of the restaurant.

"It's all good," he reassured and stopped at the front doors. "It was worth it," he smiled his crooked smile, and she couldn't help but smile back. He leaned in and gave her a quick kiss.

"Definitely," she breathed and looked at him, realizing she was head over heels for this man.

"I'm glad you think so," he concluded then opened the doors and led her to the front desk to request a table. The hostess took them straight back to a booth, and they sat across from each other.

The restaurant was big and open. It felt like a big lodge but had lanterns and candles all over the restaurant to help it feel romantic. The hostess let them know that their waitress would be with them soon and left them alone.

"This place is great. It feels romantic yet comfortable," Peyton described.

"Yeah, it's a nice little place," Noah agreed and looked over the menu.

Peyton decided to do the same but was having trouble deciding between pasta or a burger.

"Are you guys ready?" said a familiar female voice above her.

Peyton looked up at the waitress and felt a chill run down her spine.

"Peyton?" said the female waitress in a shocked voice.

"Hi, Lucy," Peyton stammered and could feel her cheeks start to flush because the look on Lucy's face showed that she was not happy.

"How do you two know each other?" Noah asked, noticing that Peyton was very uncomfortable.

"This is Derek's little sister, Lucy," Peyton mumbled.

"Derek? Who's..." Noah paused and his eyes widened ever so slightly, realizing he knew the answer to his question. "Oh, that Derek." He sat back in his chair and said nothing else.

"Yep," Peyton nodded her head.

"Yes, I'm Derek's little sister," huffed Lucy and put her hand on her hip. "I'm the sister-in-law Peyton hasn't talked to in about a year and has ignored our family ever since the accident. You know, we're still your family and could have needed you throughout this past year. The only thing we get from you is one phone call. One phone call! That's it! We used to talk and hang out all the time, but the moment Derek was gone, you were too. I needed you, Peyton! I tried to call you and text you for the first few months. Did you get those? Apparently you're getting some messages because you're out tonight with this guy!" She pointed to Noah, and he smiled sheepishly. "But I guess you're doing just fine because you've moved on and forgotten all about us! Glad you've been able to move on so quickly and completely abandon us! The worst part was that it didn't just feel like Derek died, but you did too! And it didn't need to be like that. But I'm over it. Enjoy your new guy." She turned around and stalked off.

Peyton could feel that her face was on fire. She

looked around the restaurant and everyone was staring at her. As calmly as she could while biting back tears, she stood up from the table and walked toward the front doors. Noah must have picked up on what she was doing because she heard him stand up from the booth and follow her.

She refused to turn around and look back until she was out of the restaurant and by his car.

"Peyton," Noah called behind her. She stopped walking once she reached the car, but she wouldn't turn around. "Peyton, are you okay?"

"Um," Peyton sniffled, "I don't know." Her tears were starting to escape out of the corners of her eyes. She was really hoping her makeup wasn't going to mess up too much.

Noah touched her shoulders and turned her around so that he revealed her tear-stained face and pouty lips. "Peyton, are you okay?" he repeated.

Peyton proceeded to collapse in his arms and cry all over his sweater. She didn't know how long they stood there, but it must have been a while. She was so embarrassed. It was their first date, and she was already so nervous about seeing someone she knew, but then it had been Derek's little sister. The sad part was that Peyton felt like everything she said was true. Lucy and she had been very close. They used to shop together, stay up late to watch movies, and talk about the boys Lucy was into. However, after the accident, Peyton couldn't bring herself to talk to her in-laws. They were a constant reminder of Derek, and it hurt her too much. She had only called her in-laws once because Dr. Schoenborn had told her to, and she wanted to be done with that place.

"Peyton, do you want to get out of here?" he asked.

Peyton nodded her head, and Noah guided her toward the passenger seat.

CHAPTER 17

*N*oah drove away from the restaurant and kept sneaking glances at Peyton, who was staring out the window.

"Would you like to go somewhere else?" he offered to her.

Peyton shrugged her shoulders, "Not really. Especially after what just happened. But I know you're hungry, so we can do whatever you want to do. It doesn't matter to me."

"I'm okay, Peyton. I'm more concerned about you right now. Would you like me to take you home?" he asked quietly.

Peyton looked at Noah and nodded her head, "I'm really sorry. I'm just not hungry anymore. I just want to go home."

Noah took her hand and gently squeezed it,

"That's okay, we can try and do this again another night."

Peyton smiled in response because she didn't want to tell him what she actually thought. At this point, she didn't want to go out in public ever again.

Noah stopped the car in front of the fully lit house and turned off the engine. Peyton stepped out of the car, and Noah did the same.

"Do you want me to go in with you?" he asked, opening his arms in question.

"No, I think I'm just going to go in. I'm sorry about everything," Peyton was looking down at the ground, trying not to make eye contact. All she wanted was for him to leave, so she could continue crying in her room.

"Can I do anything for you? I feel bad leaving you like this," he explained to her. Peyton looked up at him and noticed that when he was worried, his eyebrows furrowed. She felt herself smirk a little bit and shook her head.

"Don't. You couldn't have predicted this happening. I just need time to process this. I don't mean to leave you hanging like this. I'm sure you have a lot of questions, but I just need to figure things out," said Peyton.

"Okay, I hope you feel better. I'll text you tomorrow," Noah informed her. He took a step forward, kissed her on the forehead, and walked to his car.

Peyton felt bad. She could tell he was confused and wanted to help her, but she just wanted to be alone. She walked into the house and saw four sets of eyes turn to look at her.

"Peyton, what are you doing here?" her mother demanded and stood up from her chair.

"You've only been gone about an hour," her dad stated and stood up behind his wife.

"Have you been crying?" her mother asked, walking toward her with a look of concern.

"Do I need to go teach this guy a lesson?" Chris stood up from his chair and pounded his fist into his hand.

Gloria rolled her eyes and tugged on Chris's shirt, "*Sientete, mi amor.*"

Peyton looked between the four people and started feeling anxiety swell up in her. Her eyes became fuzzy, and she started seeing stars. Before she knew it, her dad was rushing toward her and everything went black.

Peyton woke up staring at the ceiling. She looked around and realized she was in her room, and her mom was sitting by her bed, asleep. She sat up slowly and looked around to see if she could locate her phone but didn't see it lying around. She assumed it was probably still in her purse, wherever that was.

She sat up straighter and accidentally knocked down a book that had been sitting at the edge of her bed. The noise woke up her mom, who looked dazed and confused for a moment until she saw Peyton awake.

"Peyton, you're awake! How do you feel?" she asked, rubbing her face.

"I'm okay. How long have I been out?" Peyton wondered.

"Well," her mom paused to pull out her phone, "you've been out all night. After you passed out, your dad carried you upstairs. You woke up for a minute, but you were very groggy and fell back asleep. You were completely out of it."

Peyton leaned her head against the wall and shook her head in disbelief. "Wow, I didn't think I was out that long. What time is it?"

"It's twelve," her mom informed her. "You've been asleep for about seventeen hours."

"Holy crap," Peyton put her hand on her forehead. "Half the day is gone already."

"Well, you obviously needed the sleep, sweetheart. Can I ask what happened?" her mom asked carefully and leaned forward in her chair, waiting for Peyton to respond.

Peyton sighed and decided it was better to get it over with and tell her mom now rather than wait. "I saw Lucy last night."

"Who?" her mom questioned, and then Peyton

watched the realization hit as her mom's eyes widened. "Wait, Derek's sister, Lucy?"

Peyton nodded, "Yeah, she was our waitress last night at Maxwell's."

"What did she say?"

Peyton began recounting what Lucy had said to her in front of the entire restaurant last night, including Noah. Her mom looked at her intently while she was telling her what had happened the night before. Peyton noticed she became more still as she went further into the story and relaxed when she got to the part when Noah hugged her and asked if she was okay.

"So, why did you come home then?" she asked.

"Mom. There was no way I was going to go to another restaurant after that. I was so embarrassed by what had happened, and I can't imagine how Noah felt. He looked so confused and uncomfortable. I just needed to get away," Peyton sighed and closed her eyes, wondering what Noah had been thinking during that whole incident.

"Did he say anything else?" her mother prodded.

"No. He just kept asking me if I was okay and if he could do anything to help me. I kinda pushed him away," admitted Peyton.

"Honey, you should have let him help you!" her mom's voice became louder by a couple of notches.

"Mom, I told you right before I left that I was

worried about going out in public, remember? I told you that I was worried I would run into someone I knew and that something might happen. And what happened not twenty minutes into our date? I ran into Lucy, Derek's little sister, who yelled at me and humiliated me in front of the whole restaurant!" Peyton exclaimed. "And you know the worst part of it all? She was right. Lucy and I used to talk all the time. She was usually our third wheel when Derek and I would go on dates. She would ask me for dating advice, ask me to do her hair, and watch chick flicks with me. She would stop by our apartment a couple of times a week just to hang out. I completely left them high and dry after Derek passed. I'm a terrible person! I can only imagine what she thought when I was sitting there with Noah. I never should have gone out last night. I had a feeling, and I completely ignored it. Why didn't I just trust my gut?" Peyton finished rambling and felt a tear trickle down her face. Her mom stood up from the chair to sit next to Peyton and hug her.

"It's okay, sweetheart. How were you supposed to know Lucy was going to be at the restaurant last night? Besides that, she never should have yelled at you like that in front of everyone. That was not kind. Everyone has their own way of mourning. She can't fault you for that," her mom encouraged.

"I just didn't realize that I was hurting her. I've

been so wrapped up in my selfish feelings that I haven't been thinking about anyone else's. Have I become self-absorbed? I mean, it was her brother that died. Marie and Andrew's son. I mean, they are or were my in-laws, and I haven't been concerned or thought about them at all. It's been about me, me, and me. Again, I'm a terrible person!" Peyton screeched.

"No, you're not! That's enough of that. You have been through a very hard time! Not a lot of young adults go through losing a spouse. You aren't giving yourself enough credit. You have done amazing, and if it meant secluding yourself and giving yourself time to work through this then that's okay! Don't let anyone, even your in-laws, make you feel guilty over this. That's not fair of them to treat you like that. Above all else, you are absolutely not selfish." she paused and pulled away from Peyton to look her in the eyes. "You hear me, Peyton? You are not selfish. Remember what I told you, there's a time to mourn, which you have done. And now is a time to move on and start living your life again. Which is what I thought you were doing with Noah, no matter if serious or not, it's a step. A step in the right direction."

"You sure, Mom? I haven't turned into some self-absorbed beast?" Peyton asked.

"No, honey, you haven't. Just don't push Noah

away. He's been so patient and sweet with you. Not all men are like that," she said.

"Nope. No, they aren't," Peyton reiterated.

"Are you going to be okay?" her mom yawned and stood up from the bed.

"Yes, I am. Do you by chance know where my phone is? I don't see it anywhere," Peyton wondered and started looking around the room again.

"I don't know," her mom responded. "I bet it's still in your purse from last night. Your dad carried you upstairs right after you passed out, and then I sat in here waiting for you to wake up." she recounted.

"Well, thanks for staying in here and taking care of me, Mom. I really appreciate it. I should probably get up too. I can't believe how late it is," Peyton admitted and stood up next to her mom and gave her a hug. "I can't believe you still put up with me," Peyton muffled into her shoulder.

"It's only because I love you. Otherwise, I would have kicked you out by now," her mom laughed and walked out of the room.

"How rude!" Peyton yelped and followed behind her down the stairs where she found her dad sitting at his desk.

"Peyton!" her dad called, "how are you feeling? Does your head hurt at all from falling? You fell straight back onto your back."

"I feel fine, surprisingly. Do you know where my purse is?" she asked.

"Yes, it's on the kitchen counter," he pointed over into the kitchen. "I heard some buzzing earlier this morning but didn't know where it was coming from."

"Oh boy," mumbled Peyton and she walked over to grab her phone out of her purse.

She had a few texts from Noah asking if she was alright and if she felt any better plus a missed call from Chris.

"That's weird," Peyton muttered.

"What?" her mom asked.

"Chris called me this morning. How long was he here after I passed out?" Peyton wondered. Chris usually never called. If he ever wanted to get a hold of someone, he would just text. Calling usually meant it was important and could not wait, whatever it was.

"He was only here for a few minutes, and then he left pretty quickly with Gloria. It surprised me because before you showed up we were trying to figure out a venue for the reception. With the reception only a few weeks away, we really needed to figure that out. Oh, that reminds me..." she trailed off and started writing down her thoughts on a notepad going into wedding mode.

"I guess I better call him back then," Peyton decided and started calling her brother.

"Peyton?" Chris answered.

"Yeah, it's me. What's up?" She noticed a hint of worry in his voice, which made her nervous about what he was about to tell her.

"I may have done something bad," he told her.

"Oh no, Chris. What did you do?" When she asked him that, both her parents looked up, listening intently to the phone conversation.

"Well," Chris began, "when you came home last night upset about your date and passed out, I assumed something bad happened with… Noah."

"Oh no, Chris," Peyton repeated.

"What is going on?" quizzed her mom, but Peyton waved her off, so she could hear her brother better.

"Something just came over me. I snapped. After all that you had been through with Derek and watching you go up and down with this Noah guy… Well, it's been hard for me to watch. I hate seeing you so sad and upset, especially when you used to be so happy and bubbly and a lot of fun to be around. And then after last night, you came home early without Noah and so upset, I assumed the worst," Chris continued.

"Get to the point, Christopher," Peyton pleaded. She knew using his full name would get his attention and let him know she wasn't messing around.

"You mentioned that he worked at the therapist's office you go to. So, this morning, I went to your therapist's office to confront Noah and do the brotherly thing, you know?" Chris said sheepishly. "Well, I was walking in to give him a piece of my mind, but then I saw his car parked outside, and something just came over me. I felt this uncontrollable anger boil up inside of me, and I went over to his car and started kicking it." He stopped talking to wait for a response from Peyton, but she didn't know where to begin.

"You kicked his car?" Peyton said in disbelief.

Her mother gasped, "Chris kicked someone's car? Whose?"

"Mom!" scowled Peyton and narrowed her eyes at her mom. "Go on, Chris."

"Yes," he continued, "I kicked his car. I'm pretty sure I got a couple of good dents in it. After about five minutes kicking his car, the alarm started going off, and then Noah stepped out of the office to switch it off and saw me standing by his car."

"Uh oh," Peyton said quietly, trying not to get her mom worked up again.

"Yeah, he came out, and I started yelling at him," Chris admitted. "I told him that he needed to stay away from you and that he completely broke your heart. I told him that you had been through so much, and you didn't deserve to be taken out by some jerk who has blonde bimbos hanging all over him and who messes with people's emotions. Especially my big sister's. He tried to defend himself, but then I punched him in the face. Unfortunately for me, there was a cop nearby, and he arrested me."

"You got arrested?" Peyton shrilled.

"Peyton, you have to tell me what is going on!" her mother shouted.

"Are you okay? Are you calling from jail? Do I need to come bail you out?" Peyton asked quickly.

"No, you're fine. Gloria came and got me, and we worked everything out. She gave me a tongue lashing, and the officer gave me a ticket, but it's fine. I did it to myself. I let my anger get the best of me. Anyway, if you don't hear from Noah for some reason, it's probably because of me," Chris reckoned.

"I cannot believe you kicked his car, Chris. What were you thinking? And then you punched him?" quizzed Peyton.

"I know, Peyton, I know. Trust me. A couple of hours locked up definitely gave me some reflection time."

"I cannot believe you were arrested. I can't believe this. Poor Noah. I wonder if he has texted me since that happened. What time were you there?" Peyton asked.

"It was about nine this morning," said Chris.

"Okay, well. Thanks for sticking up for me, I guess. But I gotta tell you, it was all in vain."

"What do you mean?" he asked.

Peyton began to explain to Chris about the misunderstanding with the bubbly blonde Barbie, and she told him about Lucy yelling at her from the previous night.

"Wow! I was seriously wrong," Chris groaned.

"Yeah, you really were. Did you break his nose?"

"I don't know! I didn't stick around to ask him. Right after I punched him, a police officer ran up to me and grabbed my arms and leaned me up against Noah's dented car," Chris said with a tone of irritation.

"Listen, I'm not the one who punched him, so don't get annoyed with me. Well, thanks for calling me and letting me know that Noah is probably never going to talk to me again," she teased.

"Yeah, you're welcome. Sorry, Sis," sighed Chris.

"It's okay. You were just trying to be a nice little brother. Is Gloria still going to marry you, by the way?"

"So far she still is. We're going to try and avoid telling her parents that I ended up in jail a few weeks before the wedding."

"Probably a good idea. Tell them the day after and let me know how it goes," she joked

"Very funny. Alright, I'll talk to you later. I need to go and apologize to Gloria again for being a total idiot," he informed her.

"Good luck with that. Talk to you later," Peyton ended the call and looked up to see her mom glowering at her.

"What? I couldn't hear him with you yelling at me," she stated.

"What in the world happened?" her mom snapped. Peyton sighed and recounted the entire conversation. Her dad walked over and put his arm around his wife and looked intently at Peyton as she told them what Chris had done earlier that morning.

"That stupid boy!" her mother seethed.

Her dad crossed his arms, clearly upset, and asked, "Is Noah okay?"

"I don't know. It looks like the last time he texted me was this morning at about eight. Chris probably freaked him out so much that he's never going to want to talk to me again. He probably thinks I'm way too much drama or something. I mean, I can't really blame him, I kinda am but not this much. Chris took it to a whole other level," Peyton rambled.

"I'm calling your son!" her mother snarled and stormed off to her room.

"My son? Weren't you the one who said you wanted a boy?" her dad retorted and followed her mom up the stairs.

Peyton tried texting Noah, asking if he was alright, but he didn't respond to any of her messages.

She even tried calling him a couple of times to apologize for Chris's behavior and say that it was all a misunderstanding, but he never called her back. Days went by, and she heard nothing from him, and it drove her crazy. She would trace her steps from the barn to the driveway where they had walked and embraced each other. She ran up and down the driveway reflecting on their first date. She walked along the trail all the way to the river and would remember him showing up and assuring her of his feelings. She expected him to be at the front desk greeting her for her therapy appointment but instead was welcomed by a younger gal. He had disappeared from the face of the earth, and she once again felt completely and utterly alone.

CHAPTER 18

*T*he wedding was in two weeks. Her mother was running around the house like a chicken with her head cut off, and her father had done a lot of work to make it look in tip-top shape for guests. Chris and Gloria decided that it would be better to have the wedding and reception at the house, where it was more homey, familiar, and cost-effective. Peyton would have thought it was a great idea had it not been for her mother. Her mom had turned into a wedding lunatic, making tons of lists, including a honey-do list for her dad, to make sure the house was freshly painted, the lawn was well maintained, and no broken fences where any animals could get loose. She was working in the garden tirelessly day in and day out because that's where Gloria wanted to walk down the aisle, so the garden had to be beautiful and kept up. She enlisted Peyton in doing the yard work. She was supposed to mow the lawn every few days, pull every weed in sight, and keep the trail trimmed up. Not to mention, she helped keep up on cleaning the house for her mom, which she would usually do anyway, but at this point, it kept her busy. She knew that she probably didn't need to mop, vacuum, and clean the bathrooms every day, especially with only three people living in the house, but she needed to stay occupied.

Noah hadn't talked to her in weeks. The first week, Peyton tried getting ahold of him, sending him the occasional text message asking how he was and how his studying was going, but she didn't hear anything. No response. Nothing. She figured he was getting ready to graduate, but she didn't know any details. When she went into her last couple of therapy appointments, he wasn't there, and Dr. Schoenborn didn't bring him up at all. On the last appointment, he gave her a pudgy handshake with his cheeky smile, and then she was free to go. She never had to go to therapy again. She wanted to celebrate this gigantic feat but realized the only person she wanted to celebrate with was Noah.

He was constantly on her mind, in her every thought, and she couldn't get him to leave. She hoped that he would show up to the house randomly and pretend that everything was okay, but she knew that wouldn't happen. Deep down, she had blown it. Or her brother had. Either way, he wasn't going to come back. He had probably moved on by now, and somehow Peyton had to do that too.

Unbeknownst to her mother, all she did was cry. She hid it well, too, because she knew that if she cried in the house, her mother would hear her and then drill her with questions. So, no one would hear her, she would cry while on the riding lawn mower, while she was edging the trail, anywhere far away from the house, when she knew her mom was gone, and sometimes she would become a rebel and cry while weeding. Her heart had been crushed. She had let herself open back up again and could see a future with him. But now that was gone, along with Noah.

Little did she know, while she was weeding the flower beds in the backyard, that her brother would catch her crying.

"Peyton, are you okay?" Chris asked and crouched down next to her in the dirt.

"Oh, yeah. I'm fine. It's just my allergies," she lied.

"Like I believe that," said Chris sarcastically.

Peyton tried to smile but was so upset that her emotions took over, and she started crying even harder than before. Chris put his arm around her, and she leaned her head onto his shoulder.

"I'm guessing he still hasn't talked to you?" Chris assumed. She shook her head, unable to form words, and he sighed, "I'm going to fix this."

"No," cried Peyton, "if he wanted to talk to me and hear my side of the story, he would have gotten ahold of me by now." At this point, she was blubbering and highly doubted Chris understood what she was saying.

"I don't care. He deserves to hear the whole story and how I made a complete idiot of myself. He should know that you had nothing to do with it, and it was my own doing. He liked you, Peyton, maybe even more than that from what I could tell. Those kinds of feelings don't go away. He's probably just really confused. You and I both know that your situation is not an easy one, and it sounds like you guys had some obstacles, and I probably pushed him over the edge," Chris explained.

"No, I'm sure I did. I was probably too much for him," Peyton decided. She moved off of him and kept pulling weeds, thinking that it would help her not to cry, but she still had some tears escape.

"You probably were," Chris agreed and Peyton spun her head around to glare at him.

"Excuse me?" she fumed.

"Peyton, listen to me. You kinda have baggage.

A lot more baggage than most women in their twenties have, right?" Chris said.

"He knew all that, Chris! I told him everything, and he was fine with it! Or at least he said he was!" Peyton snapped.

"I know, and maybe he was. But then you got mad at him for Brittany, thinking she was his mistress, and then you had Lucy yell at you like that in front of him. The guy is probably freaked out. I mean, you were in therapy because your husband was killed, and that's a lot for a guy to handle!"

"So, you're saying I'm too much drama? That I'm destined to be alone till the day I die? That's great, Chris, thanks!" She stood up and stomped away from him, but Chris followed behind her.

"No! That's not what I'm saying. He's about to graduate dental school, right?" Chris asked her.

"Yeah, I think so. I don't know since he won't talk to me, remember?" she howled and was about to open the back door when Chris jumped in front of her to block the door.

"Okay. Well, imagine how he feels. He's put in four years' worth of time and money to graduate. Don't you think he's feeling a little overwhelmed already? And then throw you and me into the mix…" Chris trailed off.

"It's not like I sought him out. He sought me out," Peyton said tartly.

"Well, can you blame him? You're a catch!

You're beautiful, funny, considerate, and strong. Any guy would be attracted to you. Why wouldn't he approach you? I'm telling you, I bet he's just taking a step back to focus on school and to think. Guys do that. I do that. I'm not saying it's the right thing to leave a girl hanging or ignore her like this, but I promise it's a guy thing," Chris insisted and put his hand on her shoulder. "He likes you. I would bet he loves you. I mean, he knew you were going to therapy and still wanted to get to know you. Therapy is usually the biggest red flag ever, but he thought you were special regardless."

"Are you trying to make me feel better?" Peyton insinuated, "Because I've got to say, you keep offending me then complimenting me, and it feels a little like whiplash."

"I'm trying to give you the perspective of a guy. Sometimes we're idiots."

"Sometimes?" Peyton interrupted.

"Hey!" Chris said, pretending to be offended. "Anyway, what I'm trying to say is sometimes we don't handle situations in the best way. So, maybe consider cutting him a little slack?"

"It's been almost three weeks, Chris," Peyton retorted.

"I said consider it. You don't have to. It's your prerogative. But I have a feeling you might because, if I were a betting man, I would say you love him too. And deep, deep, deep down, I think you know that," he pointed out.

"So, what? It doesn't matter. He won't talk to me. He's obviously avoiding me," Peyton faltered.

"I told you that I was going to take care of it," Chris reminded her and touched her nose.

"What are you going to do?" Peyton asked.

"I don't know, but I'll let you know," he shrugged and walked away from her back to his car.

"I don't even know where he lives!" she called after him.

"I've got this! I'll see you later. Tell Mom that I'm coming for dinner and bringing Gloria, will ya?"

"Yeah, sure," Peyton agreed and headed into the house. She shook her head in disbelief. "There goes one of the biggest idiots of them all," she muttered to herself and walked upstairs to wash off all the dirt… and tears.

"So, Chris is coming for dinner? I don't even think I pulled out enough meat for two more people!" her mother said perplexed when Peyton returned from upstairs. "That boy kills me. Gloria is going to have her hands full with him."

"Well, the great part about that, Mom, is that

she's going to have to put up with him, not you," Peyton chuckled.

"Yeah, right. He always shows up when he wants something. That boy is never really going to leave me!"

"Oh, brother," Peyton rolled her eyes, "you love it. He keeps you on your toes."

Her mom snorted, "You got that right. Well, what are we going to do with only a pound of hamburger?"

"Tacos, again?" Peyton suggested.

"That's such a cop-out," her mother said.

"How about enchiladas? You can fill it with other things like beans and cheese, and then you won't have to worry about pulling out more meat and trying to get it thawed in time," she offered.

"OK, that's a good idea. Will you pull out some enchilada sauce and tortillas then, please? Dinner is in an hour. I should probably tell your brother."

"Is it five already?" Peyton asked, sounding surprised.

"Yep, we gotta get moving if were going to finish before they show up," she said.

"Wow, this day has flown," Peyton said quietly.

Peyton did what her mother asked and started setting the table. "Where has dad been at?" she asked.

"He's working on that stupid fence again," her mom replied. "The last couple of days he's been saying that he's ready to shoot all the cows and be done."

"I'm surprised he didn't ask me to come and help him. I haven't seen him all day, and it must have given him a hard time."

"Well, he noticed you were having a hard time, and then after your conversation with Chris, he didn't want to bug you," her mom explained.

"Oh, okay," muttered Peyton.

"By the way, have you heard from him since that talk?"

"No, I haven't. I don't know what Chris could possibly do to fix what he's done. I feel that if Noah wanted to see me or clear the air, he would have done that by now. But Chris has it in his mind that boys think differently, and that it's innocent and whatever," Peyton prattled.

"Well, I'm curious to see what he does," her mom said as she started cooking the meat and preparing the enchilada mixture.

"Me too," mumbled Peyton. "I'm going to call Dad and see if he needs my help," she decided and walked over to the dining room to call him. As the phone began ringing, there was a knock at the door.

"Peyton, will you get that? My hands are covered, and it's most likely your bratty brother," she called.

"Yeah, I can," she said and lumbered over to the

door. She opened the door to find Chris, Gloria, and… Noah.

"What the…" Peyton trailed off, but Chris cut her off.

"Peyton, don't be mad. I know I shouldn't have surprised you. Especially considering what you're wearing," he pointed out. Peyton happened to be wearing a pair of her old high school sweats, one of her dad's t-shirts, and her hair up in a high, messy bun with hair shooting out every which way.

"Thanks for pointing that out, Sherlock," Peyton scowled. She hung up her phone, once she heard it go to voicemail and crossed her arms.

"But it turns out he was getting ready to come to see you anyway, so I just helped move the process along. See? I told you I would fix it!" he said cheerily. However, the smile on Chris's face made her want to punch him right in the mouth.

"Okay, thanks, Chris," Peyton spat out. She looked at Noah and noticed he was smiling. She wondered why on earth he would be smiling right now and if maybe she missed a joke somewhere. He looked as handsome as ever. Especially with a smile spread across his face, he was irresistible, and Peyton couldn't seem to look away once they locked eyes. It was as if the last few weeks never happened, and they were walking hand in hand by the river again, falling in love.

"Chris, I think I can take it from here now,"

Noah said in his deep voice, and Chris spun around to see him staring at his older sister.

"Alrighty, dinner smells good. Although we probably freaked out Mom by coming early," Chris laughed and walked past Peyton, who was still standing in the doorway as if she had been petrified.

"You did!" her mom called from the kitchen.

"Good luck," Chris whispered in her ear, and, in response, Peyton swatted his back.

Chris shut the door behind her and forced her to step out onto the front porch. She looked down at herself, regretting her choice of clothes, but decided to own it and squared her shoulders.

CHAPTER 19

"Hi," Peyton said curtly.

"Hi, Peyton, do you mind if we talk for a minute?" Noah asked.

"Sure," she responded and sat on the porch bench.

Noah sat next to her and noticed the cold manner she had, so he thought it was better to not try and hold her hand.

"How have you been?" he wondered.

"Well…" Peyton fussed with her hair and straightened out her shirt, "I've been good. Just getting ready for the wedding."

"The wedding?" Noah questioned and then he remembered, "Oh, Chris and Gloria's, that's right. How's that going?"

"It's going good. My mom has been keeping my

dad and me busy. They decided to do the whole thing here outside since there's so much room, so we've been trying to clean up around here and keep up on it. What have you been up to?" Peyton asked, genuinely curious how he was going to answer this question.

"The last couple of weeks I've been studying like crazy for finals and boards," Noah answered.

"How did that go?"

"It went great. I finished up a couple of days ago," he added.

"Wow! That's awesome. How do you feel? I bet you can finally breathe again like a huge weight has been lifted off your shoulders," she said as she imitated lifting something.

He chuckled and revealed Peyton's favorite crooked smile. "Yeah, I have to admit it feels pretty amazing. I officially graduate this weekend," he informed her.

"That's great," she nodded. "I bet you're very excited."

"Yeah, I am. I was actually going to ask you if you would come," Noah wondered.

"Wait, what?" she said perplexed.

"I want you to come to my graduation ceremony," he stated again.

"Are you serious?" She could feel her eyebrows furrowing and her head tilting, but she didn't bother relaxing.

"Yeah," he smirked, "I am." He sounded so relaxed and calm. His tone was so even, it was like he experienced a completely different last couple of weeks than what she had.

"Noah, I haven't heard from you in weeks," she stated.

"I know," he replied.

"I tried to get a hold of you. You got my texts and phone calls, didn't you?" she quizzed him, becoming more and more irritated by the minute.

"Yes, I got them," he admitted.

"So, you ignored me," Peyton challenged and felt her face becoming hotter, which meant she was starting to turn red.

"I know and I'm sorry. There was a misunderstanding, but your brother cleared it up," Noah explained. "I should have messaged you back and heard your side of the story. I was a little freaked out from our dinner date, and then the very next morning, I found your brother kicking my car, and then he punched me!"

Peyton put her head in her hands, shaking her head. She still couldn't believe her brother had done that and was still embarrassed about it. Especially hearing Noah recount his part of the story.

He continued, "I guess you could say I got lost in my studies and didn't realize it had been so long since I had talked to you. I never thought sitting in the same room studying for days on end would make time fly by so much. When I wasn't studying, you were constantly on my mind. I missed you every day and wanted to make excuses to come out here to see you. I also wanted to text you and see how you were doing, but I was too afraid you would be upset with me and ignore my messages as I had done to you. Not that I wouldn't have deserved it, but I was a chicken. It was your brother who finally gave me the boost of confidence."

"Oh boy," Peyton rolled her eyes.

Noah laughed. "It wasn't that bad. He did have to do a little bit of hunting. First, he went to my uncle's office to track me down and ask how he could find me. Luckily, my cousin, who's been working the front desk for me while I've been studying…" He trailed off and smiled at her as if he read her mind, and she smiled sheepishly in response. "And no, it wasn't because I was trying to avoid you. Well, she told him I was studying on campus, which is where I have practically lived the last few weeks, and he tracked me down. I guess he kept asking people on campus if they knew who I was and where he could find me. He eventually found me and told me the whole story. He assured me that he had acted completely on his own and misunderstood the situation. And of course, he explained this in a very 'Chris' way."

"I felt terrible about what had happened that night. I know I shouldn't have blown you off the

255

way I did, but at the time I just didn't know how to handle the situation. So, I'm sorry about that," Peyton apologized.

"It's okay. I don't blame you. I wouldn't have known what to say either. Your brother mentioned you passed out after you had gotten home. Are you okay?" Noah asked.

"I think I was just overwhelmed. Just as I walked through the door, I was hounded with questions. When I agreed to go out with you, my biggest fear was that something like that would happen. That someone would see me going out with another guy and confront me the way Lucy did. And it happened. Not twenty minutes into our date, I get yelled at in front of the entire restaurant," Peyton shrugged her shoulders, unable to find her thoughts.

"Peyton," Noah whispered. "I know you're still trying to get over the death of your husband. And that's okay. I know you're always going to love him, and why wouldn't you? He sounded like a great guy. I just hope you'll still give me a chance because when I'm with you, I feel complete. I know what I want to do, where I want to be, and what I want in life. I really did miss you like crazy the last couple of weeks. I missed the touch of your hand," he took her hand gently when he said this. "I missed your infectious smile," naturally, she smiled, "and I missed pulling you in close and holding you." Peyton could feel that her face was beet red by now, and she tried to look down at their intertwined hands in an attempt to hide it, but Peyton knew she couldn't fool him. "Man, I missed that blush too," he chuckled, which didn't help Peyton's case at all. "I know I wasn't the smartest person in the world the last couple of weeks, but I'm here now, and there's no other place that I would rather be. Do you believe me?"

Peyton looked up at him and nodded. "Yes, I do."

"Good," he smiled crookedly at her, and she smiled back.

"That smile kills me every time," she admitted. "You could get away with murder with that smile."

"Does that mean I'm off the hook?" he teased. He scooted closer to Peyton and wrapped his arms around her so that their faces were only inches apart.

"Maybe," Peyton asked, "Are you ever going to drop off the face of the earth again?" she asked, trying not to sound so serious. However, she genuinely wanted to know the answer.

"I promise I won't ever drop off the planet again. That wasn't fair to you, and I'm sorry," he said.

"Thank you. I promise not to blow you off and to open up more to you," Peyton vowed.

"Thank you. You know you're pretty amazing, Peyton," Noah beamed at her.

"Really? You don't think I'm too much drama?" she questioned. This is what she had feared the most from him.

"No, Peyton. I think you've been through way too much for someone your age, but despite your trials, you've handled it extremely well. You're stronger than you give yourself credit for." Noah bent over and gave her a sweet kiss on the forehead that sent an electric shock through Peyton's entire body.

"You're just trying to butter me up now," she flirted and smirked up at him, waiting for his retort. He was so handsome that just looking at him made Peyton's heart skip a beat.

Noah slowly started inching toward her lips, which made Peyton feel jittery. "Is it working?" he whispered, only mere centimeters away from locking lips.

"Maybe…" she stammered out.

"You sure like that word. Do you love me?" he asked.

"Maybe…" she giggled, and Noah laughed in response.

"Oh, Peyton, what am I gonna do with you?" he teased.

"Kiss me."

Noah urgently and passionately pressed his lips

onto hers, and she melted into his arms. Peyton could feel her heart racing a million beats a minute, her face flushing, and tingles running down her spine. She was falling in love with this man more and more by the minute.

He gently pulled away but kept his arms wrapped around her in a tight embrace. Peyton never wanted to leave this moment. She wanted to stay forever if that meant always being able to be with Noah.

"I like the sweats, by the way," he chuckled, and Peyton tried to escape his arms, but he squeezed a little tighter so that she couldn't wiggle out so easily.

"You think you're so funny. I didn't expect you to be showing up today! I've been doing yard work all day and didn't see a reason to get ready," she complained and hid her face in her chest.

"Are you glad I came?"

She turned her head to the side, so he could hear her clearly, "Yes, I am." He couldn't see, but below his chin, she had a big smile spread across her face.

Peyton and Noah walked back into the house hand in hand, and her mother started jumping up and down ecstatically at the sight of them.

"It just makes me so happy to see the two of you together again!" she gushed and ran over to hug them both, "Noah, are you staying for dinner?"

"I'm sorry, but I have to get going. I'm picking

up my parents at the airport in a couple of hours, and I need to make sure I have everything together before they come. But thank you," he said graciously.

"You know you're always welcome, Noah! How exciting that your parents are coming into town! What's the occasion?" she inquired.

"I'm officially graduating this weekend, and we're having a party at my uncle's. I would love to have all of you come. I would invite all of you to the ceremony, but I don't have enough tickets," Noah explained and continued, "Here, let me write down the address. The party is on Saturday at five in the evening. There will be food, so don't worry about eating before."

"That sounds great! We will be there," her mom assured. "We have nothing going on Saturday right, honey?" she looked over at her husband.

"Nope, just Noah's party now," he affirmed.

"Yeah, we will stop by too," Chris pointed to himself and Gloria. "Thanks for the invite, especially after everything," he said with a concerned look.

"Hey, it's all good, man. You were just looking out for your sister, and I respect that. Forgive and forget. My car though, it doesn't forgive and forget as well as I do," he laughed.

Chris laughed sheepishly in response, "I'm sorry about that, man."

"You'll never do that again, will ya?" Gloria said sternly.

"No, *mamacita*. No, I will not."

After a moment of awkward silence, Noah finally piped up and said, "Well, I better get going. I have errands to run, and I don't want to be late to the airport."

"I'll walk you out," Peyton offered. After saying goodbye, they followed each other out to the car, and Noah spun around to look at her before getting into his car.

"So, will you come to my graduation?" he smirked at her and leaned up against his car.

"Of course. If you want me to be there, I would be happy to be there," she smiled.

Noah beamed, "I do want you there." He took her hand and pulled her gently into his arms. "It means a lot to me that you would come. Peyton, I don't want to go another day without seeing you. Quite frankly, I don't even want to go pick up my parents because I just want to stay here and be with you."

"I want you to stay too. But it wouldn't be fair to leave your parents at the airport. I bet they're so excited to see you," she encouraged. She didn't want him to leave. She felt like she just got him back, and now he had to leave so soon. It made her tremendously sad, but she didn't want him to know it.

"Yeah, I haven't seen them in a while, so it will be good. They're very excited to meet you."

"Oh, really? You told them about me?" Peyton asked, now feeling extremely nervous about what she had just agreed to.

"Of course, I did. I knew they were most likely going to meet you this weekend, so I had to tell them about you. Plus, why wouldn't I? You have made me so much happier in the last couple of months than I have been in my entire life," flattered Noah as he brushed the side of her cheek. "You bet I took that opportunity to brag about you!"

"You are so sweet. How did I get so lucky?" Peyton cooed and stared dreamily into his eyes.

"I could ask the same thing," he smiled affectionately and bent over to kiss her on the lips. He leaned his forehead onto hers and whispered, "I better get going. I'll text you the address to the school, and here," he paused to pull a piece of paper out of his pocket, "is your ticket."

"Thank you." She stood up on her tiptoes and gave him a quick kiss. "Text me."

"I will," he promised and with one last kiss, he was off.

CHAPTER 20

Saturday came quickly, and Peyton was both relieved and nervous. The last couple of days, Noah wasn't able to come and see her because he had things going on at his school that he had to attend, and he was trying to spend time with his parents. Peyton could understand why he hadn't been around since he had invited her to his graduation ceremony, but it made her uneasy. She could only imagine the countless questions his parents must be asking, considering she was a widow at twenty-four. She hoped that he was preparing them well enough for when they finally met.

Besides feeling worried about meeting Noah's parents, she felt as if a weight had been lifted off her shoulders. She was, knocking on wood, happy. She was singing around the house, chatting with her parents cheerily, and texting Noah constantly. The last couple of days without seeing him didn't feel nearly as hard as the last few weeks. Maybe it was because they finally figured everything out and knew where they both stood. For the first time in a long time, Peyton felt confident in her relationship and knew that no matter what happened, Noah was always going to be there. Through the good, the bad, and the ugly—and it put her at ease in a way she hadn't felt since she had Derek in her life. She felt confident in opening up to Noah and expressing her feelings, and she didn't let wanting him scare her away but rather let it empower her. She wanted to be with him, just as much as he wanted to be with her. She wasn't ready to admit it out loud, but she was beginning to think the last few weeks apart actually helped their relationship in a positive way. Absence truly did make the heart grow fonder. She loved him, and she knew it.

Noah let Peyton know that the graduation was at nine in the morning, so she got up early to run, shower, and get ready. Her mom made sure to come into her room to help her pick out an outfit while Peyton curled her hair and applied makeup. She struggled with putting the makeup on because she was still hot from the run, so she kept fanning herself to try and cool down. Her mom picked out a flowy, flutter sleeve navy blue dress to try and bring out the blue in her eyes. She also found a pair of strappy heels that Peyton had forgotten she even owned and knew she wouldn't be able to talk herself out of wearing this time. After almost falling over in her heels a couple of times, she stood in front of her mom, waiting for a reaction.

"You look beautiful," her mom said and started tearing up.

Peyton rolled her eyes, "Oh, brother. What time is it?"

"It's 8:30. You better get going if you're going to make it in time," her mom pointed out.

"Holy crap, Mom, why didn't you tell me!" Peyton rushed out of the room as fast as she could in heels and grabbed her purse and keys on her way out to the car.

Her mom followed behind her and stopped once she got to the front porch. "I'll see you in a couple of hours!" she called and waved.

Peyton waved back then drove down the driveway. With the way Peyton was driving, it only took her fifteen minutes to get to the graduation ceremony. She started panicking because she realized she didn't know what his parents looked like, but luckily, she spotted Dr. Schoenborn. He was not hard to find in a crowd.

She walked over to her old therapist and greeted him, "Hey, Dr. Schoenborn."

"Peyton," he held out his hand and she shook it, "it's nice to see you again. We saved you a seat." He pointed in the direction where there were two empty seats next to a couple already sitting.

The couple looked at Peyton and smiled. Dr. Schoenborn went on, "Peyton, this is my sister Wendy and my brother-in-law, Clark. These are Noah's parents."

His parents stood up, and Noah's mom held out her hand, "Hi, Peyton, it's nice to meet you. Noah has told us a lot about you," she said in an airy sweet voice. She was short and petite with short pixie-cut brown hair and dark brown eyes.

"It's nice to meet you too," Peyton stuttered and held out her hand to Noah's dad. He was much taller than his wife, easily over six feet, with blonde hair that looked like it was slowly turning white and the same blue eyes as Noah's. "Hi, Clark."

"Hello, Peyton. Nice to meet you," he said in a gruff voice. It seemed as if Noah was a nice mix of both and came out a handsome, smart man.

They all sat down in their chairs with Peyton sitting in between Wendy and Dr. Schoenborn. It seemed as though Peyton had gotten there at the right time because the ceremony started not a minute after they sat down. Music began to play, and the graduates started walking between the aisles. Peyton saw Noah walk down, and he winked at her as he walked past, which naturally caused her to blush. All the graduates sat in their seats in front of everyone, and the long line of speakers began. The president of the school, the vice president, the dean of students, and the class president all spoke. Each speaker took between ten to twenty minutes for their speeches. They did a good job, but it was a long time to stay seated and pretend to be engaged as she had no idea what most of the people were talking about. She was grateful when the dean of students stood back up to read off the names of the graduates.

"Matthew Albert Harris," the dean's voice boomed through the microphone. "Noah Marcus Hart." Peyton watched Noah walk across the stage, accept his diploma, and shake hands with a long line of old men. He turned to look at his family and smiled. Next to her, his mom started snapping lots of pictures quickly before he walked across the rest of the stage. The rest of the naming ceremony went on for another ten minutes, followed by some quick closing remarks, and then it was over.

Noah waded through the crowd of graduates and families until he found his own.

"Hi, guys!" Noah greeted them.

"We're so proud of you!" His mother hugged him first.

"Thanks, Mom," he said. He pulled away and noticed tears in her eyes, "Thank you for being there for me and supporting me."

"Honey, it's been a pleasure being your mom," she gushed and kissed his cheek.

"I echo your mother's comments," his dad said.

"Glad to hear it," Noah said and he hugged his dad.

"You've done a wonderful job, Noah," Dr. Schoenborn offered his congratulations.

"Thanks, Uncle Walter. Thank you for all you've done for me," Noah expressed and gave him a quick hug.

"Anything for you, Noah," Dr. Schoenborn assured.

Noah turned to Peyton and smiled, "You look beautiful."

"You don't look so bad yourself, handsome," Peyton complimented, and Noah walked over and gave her a tight hug.

"Thank you for coming, sweetheart," he whispered in her ear.

"Anything for you," she whispered back.

"How do you feel? You're all done!" his mother grinned.

"I feel weird. I feel like I should be doing something, but I don't have to," Noah answered.

"Well, you'll be going to work soon enough. For now, just enjoy the little break you have," his dad suggested.

"Yes! Like going to your party!" his mom sang. "We should get going. Your cousins have been working hard to get everything together, and they're so excited for you."

"Let's go then! Do you mind if I ride with Peyton? That way I can show her how to get to Uncle Walter's," Noah asked and intertwined his hand with hers. Peyton looked at him and smiled.

"Sure, honey, we'll see you there! Oh, but don't change out of your cap and gown, because I want to take some pictures!" she said quickly.

"Okay mom."

His parents went in one direction to their car, Dr. Schoenborn went in a different direction, and Peyton and Noah walked hand in hand to her car.

"You look good in your gown and cap," Peyton observed out loud and smiled at him. "Congratulations on graduating."

Noah put his arm around her while they walked to her car and kissed the top of her head, "Thank you. It's been a long road, and I'm so glad I'm done. I'm especially happy that I got to graduate with a beautiful girl on my arm," he beamed.

"Thanks for inviting me here. It was very cool seeing you walk across the stage. You accomplished something that not a lot of people are capable of doing, and it's amazing. Do you want to drive?" she asked, offering him the keys. "It will be easier for you to just drive rather than me take directions. Sometimes I swear I still can't tell the difference between my lefts and rights," she admitted.

Noah laughed out loud and replied, "If you

don't mind me driving your car, sure I'll drive. My uncle's house can be kind of confusing to find."

They hopped into the car and drove about ten minutes through town heading in the opposite direction of Peyton's house, eventually driving through a thick grove of trees. Then, unexpectedly, the trees dispersed and revealed a beautiful lake with a gorgeous house nearby. It was a beautiful two-story craftsman style house that had to have been ten thousand square feet. It had three garages, a long driveway, and even a boat ramp by a lake, nestled off to the side of his property. It had all the bells and whistles that a pudgy stout man needed to live.

"Holy crap," Peyton mumbled under her breath.

"Yeah, it's not small, that's for sure," Noah chuckled. "He always wanted to live next to a lake so he could fish whenever he wanted and have a big garage for all his cars."

"He collects cars?" she reiterated.

"Yes. He loves cars and loves working on them. He considers it his hobby," Noah explained and parked the car in front of the garage. "You like parties?" he smiled his crooked smile, which sent Peyton's heart racing, and she shook her head.

"No, not particularly, but I'll suck it up for you," Peyton sighed and smirked.

"Thank you, it means a lot," he gave her a quick kiss, and they walked into the house to party it up.

The party lasted a couple of hours. Her parents showed up right on time with Chris and Gloria in tow and headed right for Noah and Peyton. Her parents were very eager to meet his parents and went on and on about how much they loved Noah. They immediately hit it off and started swapping stories about their children, and Peyton left the conversation quickly so that she didn't hear her parents embarrass her.

Chris found himself at the food table where there was an assortment of sandwiches, meatballs, chips, salads, and desserts. Peyton watched Gloria tug at his shirt and tell him to slow down, but once Chris was near food, there was no stopping him. Peyton knew this because he had done this constantly growing up. He refused to engage or talk with anyone unless they stopped by the food table, and then he would end up eating himself sick. Peyton was grateful that Chris didn't live at her parent's house anymore because it was nights like these where he would stay locked up in the bathroom.

Peyton met a lot of family members, but luckily, Noah refused to let go of her hand, so he was there for all the meet and greets. She finally met Dr. Schoenborn's wife, whose name she found out was Emily. She met their daughters, a couple of other aunts and uncles, lots of cousins, friends, and even Peyton's favorite person in the entire world, the bubbly blonde Barbie, Brittany. She charged up to hug Noah, which was extremely awkward seeing how Peyton was holding his hand, but Noah refused to let go, so he hugged her with only one arm. Luckily, she kept it short and sweet, and Noah shuffled away from her as quickly as he could, looking apologetically at Peyton. She just laughed it off so that he knew it was all good. Her mom kept eyeing Peyton and smiling at her as if she was acknowledging that Noah refused to be away from her the entire evening. It not only made her mom happy, but it made Peyton extremely happy. She felt like she fit right in with his family and, more importantly, with him.

Toward the end of the party, when people were slowly starting to leave, Noah pulled Peyton aside, "I would love to come to your house, but my parents are leaving tomorrow, so I should stay here with them," he explained.

"Oh, don't worry about it! You should be with your parents. Thank you for inviting me and my family. It's been a fun day," she assured him.

"Yes, it has been. And I got to spend almost the entire day with you," Noah hummed and embraced her.

"Yeah," Peyton realized. "I guess we did," she said, wrapping her arms around his waist.

"I'll talk to you tomorrow once I drop off my parents, okay?" he asked.

"Yep, that sounds good. I think my parents already left, so I'm going to go too. With a week left before the wedding, Gloria and my mom are slowly going crazy. They're probably going to need my help," Peyton speculated. "Not to mention, Gloria's parents are coming in a couple of days, so things are definitely going to start getting crazy."

"That's right, the wedding is next week. Are you excited?" Noah wondered and started walking her out to the car.

"I'm very happy for them. They seem to truly love each other, and I think Gloria is going to be good for him. She seems to keep him in line," Peyton giggled, remembering Gloria telling Chris to lay off the cookies.

"Good. They seem happy together."

"Yep," Peyton said. She pulled out her keys and unlocked the car. "Do you want to come with me?"

"With you where?" he teased and smiled. He was merely giving her a hard time.

She giggled and rolled her eyes, "You think you're funny, don't you."

"Oh, I know I'm funny," he laughed and continued to wait for her to repeat the question.

"Will you go to Chris and Gloria's wedding with me? You know, as my date?" She made sure to clarify and could feel the blush coming on, which made Noah laugh again.

"Yes, I would love to take you. It sure took you a

while to ask," he said and raised his eyebrows. "Were you wanting to ask someone else?"

"Yeah, there was another guy at the ceremony who looked exactly like you, and I wanted to ask him instead, but he was already busy next Saturday. So, I settled for you," Peyton joked and started giggling to herself.

"Sorry to disappoint you," Noah rolled his eyes. "You are trouble."

"That's not the first time I've heard that," Peyton informed him, and he tilted his head back and laughed.

"I'm sure," he smirked. "But really, I would love to go with you. Thank you for asking me," he kissed her on the cheek. "Alright, I better go."

"Well, I'll talk to you tomorrow. Have fun with your parents," she said and smiled at him.

"Thanks, Peyton," he leaned over and kissed her again. "Drive safely. Text me when you get home."

"Okay, love you," Peyton froze where she stood, and her eyes opened wide. "I mean, see ya later," she stammered. She had not meant to say that at all and couldn't believe it had slipped out of her mouth.

"What did you say?" Noah prodded.

"See ya later?" Peyton lied.

"No, not that, the other thing," Noah coaxed and walked around her car door so that she was standing face to face with him.

"Look, I didn't mean to say that. It just slipped. I'm sorry that I made it awkward," Peyton spluttered and tried to sit down in her car, but Noah took her hand and wrapped his arms around hers.

Noah chuckled and crookedly smiled at her, "Peyton," he said as he pulled her in close.

"Yes?" Peyton whined, feeling perplexed and embarrassed.

"I love you too," he breathed and kissed her, pressing her body into his. Noah was gently moving his mouth on hers, and she could feel one of his hands getting tangled up in her hair. She knew she loved him and, over the last few days, had wondered if he loved her too. Now she knew he did, and when she heard him say it, she felt so happy that she thought her heart was going to burst right out of her chest.

"Oh, Noah," purred Peyton, once Noah pulled away.

"Yes?" Noah quietly breathed.

"I really do love you. I've known it for a while now, I just was afraid of the timing. But every time I saw you and spent time with you, I fell more and more in love with you and missed you when you would leave," she expressed and wrapped her arms around his neck.

"I know," he began, "I knew you were worried about timing, which is why I tried not to make you feel any pressure. I tried to go as slow as I could, but the more I saw you, the more I wanted to be with you. The more I wanted to be with you, the more I realized I was falling in love with you, and baby, I fell hard."

This time Peyton pressed her lips against his, and they kissed more passionately than before. She let her hands play in his hair, and Noah kept his arms wrapped tightly around her waist, while pressing Peyton up against her car. By the time they finally pulled away from each other, they were quietly panting. She rested her head on his chest, which was gently rising up and down beneath her cheek.

"I really should go back in there. My parents are going to wonder where in the world I am although I really don't want to go," he sighed and put his hand on her cheek. "I will most definitely be calling you tomorrow."

"Good," Peyton hummed, "I'll be looking forward to it."

Noah kissed her quickly on the lips and finally took his arms back, "Bye, Peyton."

"See you later," she laughed, knowing that's what she had meant to say earlier, but she was grateful now that she hadn't.

She didn't know how she made it home. It felt like her head was in a complete fog, and all she thought about was Noah. Thankfully, she made it home safely where her mom was waiting at the dining room table ready to ask her why it had taken her so long to drive home. However, once she told her mom the reason, she started crying and hugging Peyton, saying over and over again, "I told you that you weren't going to be alone!" Peyton let her mom squeeze her and say that because, in all honesty, Peyton was just as relieved as she was.

CHAPTER 21

The next day, Peyton's phone rang, and she swore her heart skipped a beat. Noah had called just as he promised and asked if he could come over. Peyton warned him that by coming over, he was subjecting himself to wedding preparations, but he didn't care. For the next couple of weeks, Noah decided to take a little break before starting work, and he made it a point in saying that meant lots of Peyton and Noah time. Which, of course, Peyton had no problem with.

This became a pattern throughout the week. Noah would call sometime after breakfast asking to come over, Peyton would tell him "yes," and then he would come over and be put to work by her mom. Peyton felt bad that Noah was spending his free time fixing fences with her dad, painting, and helping the rental crew put together a huge white tent, but Noah didn't seem to mind. On the contrary, he seemed happy to do the work. He and Peyton would constantly catch each other's eye and smile at each other, and they had plenty of time to talk and laugh. And, at one point, Noah chased Peyton around with the hose.

They were cherishing all the time they were spending together. Not only did they love it, but Peyton's parents did too. Whenever Noah wasn't looking, they would look at Peyton and smile at her or give her a thumbs up. One time Noah kissed her while they were planting more flowers in the front yard, and Peyton saw her mother jumping up and down clapping. It was completely embarrassing but, at the same time, hilarious to watch her go nuts.

On Wednesday afternoon, Gloria's family—parents, brother, and sister—showed up, and everyone was told to be on their best behavior. Peyton spent the entire morning re-cleaning the house so that it was in tip-top shape while her mom ran around making sure the beds had clean sheets. To top it off, her mom wanted to make it feel like they were at a cute bed and breakfast, so she put little chocolates and an orange-colored rose like the ones in Gloria's bouquet on the pillows. Peyton would laugh at her mom every time she saw her run through the house. And then her mom proceeded to shout,

"Shut up!" and kept running in her intended direction. Her dad tried to calm her down, but it didn't do any good. She was a stressed mess, but once she heard the door knock, she immediately snapped into hostess mode and was a whole other person. This also made Peyton laugh, but she kept it to a quiet chuckle, so no one could hear her. Well, except for Noah. He had noticed her laughing fits and would shake his head and laugh at her.

Once Gloria's family arrived at the house, they visited for a while to become better acquainted, and then everyone had dinner. It was quite a full house with Gloria's parents, her brother, Eduardo, and her sister, Emilia as well as Chris, Gloria, her parents, Noah, and herself. The house felt like it had shrunk. Since the tables and chairs had arrived earlier that day, they all decided to eat in the white tent to discuss what they needed to do over the next couple of days. Peyton could tell being in the tent was making it very real for Chris, and he was getting nervous. Gloria must have picked up on his nervous energy because she walked over to him and started rubbing his back.

Peyton liked Gloria's parents. They were fun, lighthearted, and easy-going people. It was awkward at first because her parents didn't know a lot of English, but Gloria helped translate when she needed to, and things started to relax more when they could communicate easier.

The next day everyone went into wedding mode. The boys, including Noah, were sent to string lights in the white tent, and the girls were in charge of making flower bouquets. When Gloria wasn't paying any attention, Gloria's sister and Peyton were putting together Gloria's bachelorette party. Peyton's family didn't drink and, luckily, neither did Gloria, so it was going to be a relatively calm party. Emilia and Peyton decided to do a spa night at a local resort that included manicures, pedicures, facial masks, and massages. Then halfway through the night, they were having pizza and frozen yogurt delivered to the spa. Emilia had picked up a tiara and a bridal sash for Gloria and bridal party sashes for all the bridesmaids. Luckily, Gloria's parents were helping pay for the party, so it wasn't all coming out of Peyton's pocket. Gloria had five bridesmaids—Emilia, three friends from college, and Peyton— and the resort was no cheap thing, so she appreciated Gloria's parents chipping in. In all honesty, she didn't want to go to the bachelorette party. She only wanted to spend time with Noah, but she knew it meant a lot to her brother to spend time with his future wife, so she didn't complain about it.

Once the time for the party came around, Peyton said goodbye to Noah, who ended up being invited to Chris's bachelor party. Peyton had heard rumors that his party consisted of paintball, top golf, and go-carts. The ultimate bachelor party was what she heard some of Chris's friends say. Since Peyton didn't know any of the girls very well, besides Gloria, she was kind of the odd man out. The girls were nice and would ask her questions, some about her and Noah, but that was about it. They were gushing over Gloria and her wedding day, which was exactly how Peyton thought it should have been. All it meant for Peyton was that despite the squealing loud laughter and major giggling, she was able to relax and get lost in her thoughts. With all the wedding planning and preparation, she was constantly thinking about her wedding with Derek and if there was a possibility of her having another one...

The night before the wedding, she was sitting on the front porch steps with Derek, looking up at the stars. It was getting late, and her mom was kicking Derek out because he had been teasing her mother about trying to find the wedding dress. Peyton knew he didn't really want to find it, he just liked getting a rise out of her, which cracked Peyton up.

"I can't believe we're getting married tomorrow," Peyton swooned.

"Yeah, I can't either. It seems like just yesterday that we met, and now we're going to be stuck together forever. Wow, is it too late to back out?" he teased, and Peyton elbowed him in the ribs.

"Very funny," she said sarcastically.

"You know I'm kidding." He wrapped his arm around her. "I can't wait for tomorrow… to be over," chuckled Derek.

"Derek!" Peyton exclaimed.

"You know what I mean. Once the ceremony is over, we're off to Mexico, and then it's just you and me. I can't wait till we can just spend some time together, just us. Without my mom calling and nagging me about making sure my groomsmen get fitted for the tuxedos or your mom bugging you about where to set up the dessert table," he explained and kissed her on the forehead. "I'm just ready to be done with the wedding planning and for it to be back to just us hanging out and enjoying each other."

"I know what you mean. I didn't know there were so many things that went into a wedding. I've been tempted to tell everyone to forget it, we're eloping!" she admitted and started laughing. "My mom would have freaked."

"It's not too late!" Derek waved his arms up excitedly, "Let's go!"

"No way," Peyton decided, "we're already so close. And this is for our families just as much as it is for us. That wouldn't be fair to them. Plus, it will be fun."

"You're right, as usual," Derek noted. "It's a good thing I'm going to have you around. I don't know what I would do without you."

"I know exactly how you feel," she smiled and kissed him for the last time as his fiancé...

The rest of the night went exactly as Emilia and Peyton planned. During the manicures and pedicures, the pizza and frozen yogurt arrived, and they finished the night with facial masks and massages. It left them all so relaxed that all the loud laughter and squealing had finally stopped, and everyone went home, ready for bed. Once Peyton hit her pillow, she was out like a light.

The next morning, Peyton walked down the stairs and was surprised to see Noah and Chris sitting on the couch.

"What are you guys doing here?" asked Peyton.

"We were brought Gloria's brother home late last night. We were too tired to drive back to our houses, so we slept on the couch. Not to mention, Noah's car was here too." Chris told her.

"You slept on the couch? You both stayed overnight?" Peyton was surprised to hear that Noah had stayed over at her house without her knowing. She all of a sudden felt a little insecure and hoped she hadn't snored last night.

"Are you okay with that?" Noah chuckled and stood up to walk over and hug her.

"Oh, yes. It was smart of you both to just stay here knowing you guys were too exhausted to drive back home. What time did you guys come back home?"

"Two in the morning," Noah informed her and scratched his head.

Peyton laughed, "Well, no wonder you guys are so tired. Probably wasn't the smartest thing since mom probably has a huge list of things to do. Not to mention we have the rehearsal dinner tonight. Mom set up a reservation at Felipe's."

"Yeah, we should probably hurry home to shower, get a change of clothes, and then come back," Chris moaned. "Did Gloria have fun last night?"

"Yes, she was perfectly pampered and had a blast with the girls," she answered.

"It looks like it. I can't imagine the last time I saw you with nail polish on your nails," Chris observed out loud.

Peyton chuckled and looked down to see her toes, "Yeah, it's been a while. Well, I'll see you guys in a little bit. I need to find Mom."

"Bye, sweetheart," Noah kissed her on the cheek and followed Chris out the front door.

"See you in a bit, Sis," Chris waved and left.

Peyton waved back and walked to the front

windows to watch both cars leave right away. Once she saw the two cars gone, she ran to look for her mom outside in the back. She walked through the garden and found her by the tomato plants, weeding.

"Hey, Mom," she called over to her.

"Good morning, sweetheart. Were you surprised to find some boys downstairs? I sure was," she chuckled and kept pulling weeds.

"Yeah, that caught me off guard a little. But I guess I'm glad they were smart enough to know that they were too tired to drive home and just crashed here," she said bending over to help her mom pull weeds.

"Yep," her mom nodded, "I agree. Did the girls have fun last night?"

"Oh, yes. I've never heard so much giggling and squealing in my life," she said.

"I'm sure. They seemed very bubbly and loud when they came to the house," her mom observed. "But, I'm glad they had fun. Gloria deserves it. She seems so happy to have her family here with her. I'm sure it's hard for her to live so far away from them."

"Uh-huh, it made me think back to my bachelorette party, and the night before the wedding. You know when Derek kept trying to look for my wedding dress just to drive you crazy?" she recounted.

Her mom laughed, "Oh, yes. That boy was so

rotten. He loved driving me crazy, just like you do. You guys truly were a match made in heaven."

"He was pretty amazing," Peyton agreed. "I miss him."

"Sure you do," her mom patted her leg, "But can I tell you something?"

"Go for it," Peyton braced herself.

"I think people come into our lives at very specific, if not perfect, times when we need them. At that time in your life, I think Derek was perfect for you. But once he passed, something in you changed, not in a bad way. But I think, right now, if you were to ask me who is your perfect match, I would say Noah. You guys complement each other so well that it just amazes me," she divulged to Peyton.

"You know, Mom. I think that three months ago, if you had told me that, I would have gotten very upset. But now, having been with Noah, I think you're right," Peyton admitted.

"You've come a long way, my love," her mother praised. "I'm proud of you."

"Thanks, Mom. I think I need to do something," decided Peyton. "I think I need to fix things with Lucy."

"I knew you were going to say that," her mom smirked.

"How could you know I was going to say that?" she questioned and stood up from the dirt ground.

"I just know these things," she shrugged and stood up with Peyton.

"Well, while the boys are heading home to shower, I'm going to head to Lucy's," she told her mom.

"Are you ready for that?" her mom eyed warily.

"Yes," she affirmed, "It's something I feel I need to do, and I know I'm not going to be able to let it go."

"Well, you be safe driving out there then. Let me know how it goes," she kissed her on the cheek then went back to tending the garden.

"Oh, I will," Peyton promised and walked out of her mom's personal oasis.

CHAPTER 22

*P*eyton was parked outside of Derek's old house but couldn't find the will to get out of the car. She would look up at the house and stare at it for a while, and then stare at the steering wheel wondering what in the world she was doing. She wondered whether or not Lucy was even home, but then she looked around and saw her car parked in the driveway. She took a deep breath, stepped out of the car, walked to the door, and knocked.

She heard movement coming from the other side of the door, and then the door swung open to reveal Lucy.

"Peyton?" she gasped. "What are you doing here?"

"We need to talk," Peyton told her.

She huffed, "Okay, fine. Come in. Mom and Dad aren't here right now," Lucy informed her.

"I'm here to talk to you," she stated and followed Lucy to the couch. She started having many flashbacks to when she, Derek, and Lucy sat on that very couch and had lots of movie nights, laughs and fun.

"Okay. Talk," Lucy shot out, but Peyton didn't let it bug her.

"I have come here to apologize. I should have never ignored you the way I did or your parents for that matter. It's just that every time I thought about coming to see you guys or calling, I couldn't because you guys were constant reminders of Derek," Peyton explained woefully.

"I get that, Peyton, but don't you think you were that same reminder for us? But we still reached out and wanted to see you, and it was like you just disappeared. Once Derek was gone, so were you. It felt like we were mourning two people," she sniffed.

"I see that now, and I never intended to do that. I had to mourn my own way, and I just wanted to be alone to process and get over it. For the entire year, I didn't talk to anyone, and I barely left the house except for errands for my parents and to see my therapist. I promise you, I didn't mean to offend or hurt you at all. I was just trying to cope and go on one day at a time," she assured Lucy, but she still looked upset.

"What about that guy from the restaurant?" she snapped.

"Oh, you mean the one who was with me when you yelled at me in front of the entire restaurant? Which, by the way, was not okay!" fumed Peyton.

"Whatever," Lucy rolled her eyes.

"I met him at the therapist's office. He's the therapist's nephew, and he helped out at the front desk for a couple of weeks and asked me out," she replied to the previous question.

"Don't you think that's a little fast?" she snipped.

"Don't you think that's none of your business?" Peyton deflected. "Lucy, I loved your brother. I always have, and I always will," she sniffed, feeling tears well up in her eyes. "Believe me, I debated back and forth about whether or not I should even entertain the thought of dating another guy only a year after Derek. But my mom told me that there's a time to mourn, and then there's a time to move on, and Derek wouldn't have wanted me to be so unhappy," Peyton shrugged her shoulders, trying to form words between her tears. "I knew she was right. Don't you?" she stared intently at Lucy, who was struggling to talk herself.

"No, he wouldn't have," she shook her head, "He would have wanted all of us to be happy and having fun."

"That's what I think too," Peyton smiled and nodded her head. "I really am sorry."

"It's okay. I'm sorry too. I should have never berated you the way I did during your date. That was awful of me. I saw you with that guy and just snapped. Especially after not hearing from you in over a year, it lit a fire in me. But still, I shouldn't have done that, and I feel bad," she apologized and hung her head.

"It's okay. I understand." Peyton hugged her, and they both cried for a while. They blubbered and would try talking to each other, but then couldn't understand each other. Peyton knew this was what she needed to do. The last piece of the puzzle to make herself truly feel complete again. She hated the thought of hurting someone, especially her in-laws. She knew she had to face them and apologize.

After a few minutes of crying, they pulled away from each other and started laughing.

"Well, I hope I didn't completely ruin your date the other night," she lamented.

"You didn't. We worked through it, and it's all good now," Peyton assured and smiled.

"What's his name?" asked Lucy. "He looked very handsome. And then when I saw him stand up," she whistled. "The muscles on that man! I had already partially forgiven you when I saw him walk away," she laughed.

Peyton busted up laughing and nodded her head, "Yes, his name is Noah. He just graduated from dental school last week."

"Good looks and smarts? Wow, sounds like you got a catch. How did you get lucky with two amazing men? I can't even find one!" she teased.

"I don't know," Peyton shrugged. "I don't feel like I deserve either of them. Someone up there must be looking out for me."

"Probably Derek now," Lucy decided and became quiet.

"I think so too. He was pretty amazing. My brother is getting married tomorrow, and I was at his fiancé's bachelorette party last night, and all I could think about was my own wedding with Derek," she admitted to Lucy, who started laughing. "He undeniably loved to give our moms a hard time."

Lucy laughed, "Yes. Remember when he hid all the men's ties, and my mom was searching everywhere for them for like an hour, and he just started busting up laughing? She wanted to kill him. I think he did that just a few hours before the wedding, too, so she was super stressed trying to get all the details figured out while he was just looking for trouble."

Peyton busted up, "Oh my gosh, I completely forgot about that! That was so funny. Of course, I didn't hear about it until after because I was getting my hair and makeup done. I do remember your mom coming into my room asking me if I knew where they were, and when I told her I didn't know, her eyes went super wide, and she ran out of the room. Just her face alone cracked me up. Oh, Derek," Peyton shook her head, smiling at the memory.

"Oh, Derek, is right. He certainly knew how to put a smile on people's faces. Remember at your bachelorette party when we were all getting spray tans, and my cousin had asked for the wrong color tan, and she turned completely orange?" Lucy giggled and went on, "She was so upset, she spent most of the night scrubbing her body, but it was no use. She did her best to stay out of as many pictures as possible, but being in the bridal party we were luckily able to capture that mistake."

"That's right! She begged me to have the photographer edit the pictures because she was so embarrassed by the tan, but Derek said no way. It was too funny," Peyton chuckled.

"I missed this," Lucy said quietly.

"Me too. It's been nice to have a girl talk. I haven't had that in a long time," Peyton recalled.

"Yeah, me either."

"How about this? Once a month, we get together and have a girl's night and make sure to catch up on our life's events. That way we never lose touch, and we'll get to see each other," planned Peyton.

"I would love that! Let's do it," Lucy clapped her hands in excitement and smiled wide. "Thank you for coming by, Peyton. It means a lot."

"I should have done it a long time ago, but I'm glad I finally did," Peyton grinned, and Lucy smiled back. It was as if they had never missed a beat. They picked up right where they left off, and Peyton couldn't be happier.

Peyton stayed there for another hour talking to Lucy and catching up on her life. She had regretted not coming by sooner to see her because she had missed Lucy. Even though the last time she saw her, Lucy was yelling at her, she realized how much she missed their friendship. Peyton ended up inviting Lucy to the wedding, which she was excited to attend since she and Chris had graduated high school together. She left Lucy's house with a smile on her face and a sense of accomplishment. Some relationships were worth fighting for, and she was so glad she had found her way back to Lucy.

When Peyton pulled up the driveway, she noticed Noah's car parked. "Dang, he beat me," she mumbled under her breath and parked next to Noah's car. She walked through the door and found her mom in the kitchen, making lunch.

"You were gone a while," she pointed out, "It must have gone well."

"Yeah, it did. All is well again. We're going to try and have a girl's night once a month to keep in touch with each other," Peyton informed her

"I think that's a great idea, Peyton! You need some girl time. I don't know when was the last time you had a girl's night beside Gloria's bachelorette party. I'm so glad you two worked things out. You girls used to have a lot of fun," her mother approved of her idea.

"Thanks Mom. Um, where are the boys?" Peyton looked around, searching for Chris and Noah.

"They're out back with Gloria and her family setting tables for the reception. I need to call Maxwell's and make sure they're coming on time with all the food. Oh! I also need to call the bakery and make sure they're delivering the cake today, so we can put it in the fridge," she rambled off.

"Mom, why don't I do that? You go make sure the boys are making those tables pretty," Peyton offered and pulled out her phone to start looking up numbers. "Do you have the receipts, so I know what exactly you ordered?"

"Yes! They're over on the dining room table. Thank you so much, honey. I needed to take these sandwiches out to everyone anyway, and I keep getting distracted," she said, sounding relieved.

"No problem, that's why I'm here. Do you mind telling Noah where I am?" Peyton asked.

Her mom grinned, "Sure thing. He's been so good about helping. I just love that boy."

"Yeah, me too," Peyton smiled.

Her mom walked over to her and gave her a big bear hug. "It makes me so happy to see you happy! Especially after this past year, you deserve some happiness and someone to take care of you. And now, I think you may have it! It's just so great, Peyton. Alright, I'm going out back. Hopefully, I'll be back soon. Let me know if Maxwell's or the bakery give you a hard time," she said and then rushed out the back door to deliver the sandwiches.

Peyton went right to work and started calling the restaurant to make sure they were on schedule with the food catering. Luckily for them, they were on schedule and were planning to show up right on time a couple of hours before the wedding. Chris and Gloria wanted to feed everyone dinner, so they would walk down the aisle at five and then have the reception right afterward since Gloria's parents were paying hundreds of dollars for food. Peyton felt bad that her mom ended up planning the entire wedding, but since Gloria's parents lived in Mexico, it made it hard for them to help Gloria. Even though Peyton's mom planned and put together the wedding, she was grateful that Gloria's parents were willing to hand over a big check to cover all costs.

After calling the restaurant and double-checking

the order, she called the bakery to make sure they were finishing up the cake. While she was talking to the bakery, Noah walked in and smiled her favorite smile. Peyton thought he looked like a supermodel strutting in with his fitted jeans and his dental school logo t-shirt. He looked casual but pulled it off effortlessly. Peyton couldn't help but be attracted to him and could feel her face flushing when he walked in. The first thing he did was walk over to her and wrap his arms around her while she was still talking on the phone, which did not help her focus on the conversation. When Peyton was asking what time they were planning on delivering the cake, Noah started kissing her head, and Peyton was having a hard time keeping her train of thought.

Once she received confirmation that they were going to be dropping off the cake in a couple of hours, she was able to hang up the phone and focus on Noah.

"You did not make that easy for me," Peyton stated and slipped her phone in her pocket.

Noah chuckled, "Was I distracting you?"

"Yes," she confirmed, "Yes, you were."

Noah kissed her affectionately on the lips and kept his arms wrapped around her waist. Peyton only pulled away ever so slightly so that she could speak, "Now you're definitely distracting me," she whispered and kissed him again.

This time Noah pulled away, "I'm sorry, did you need to make another phone call?"

"Nope, I'm all done," she smiled and kissed him again. While they were kissing, someone came through the back door, which caused Peyton to jump away from Noah.

"Am I interrupting something?" Chris teased and started laughing.

"Is that a rhetorical question?" Peyton said sarcastically and walked into the kitchen for a drink of water.

"That's up to you, Sis. I just came back to grab some water for everybody. Mom and Gloria are redoing all the table decorations. She says us men have no taste," Chris chuckled and put his hands up, "Fine with me. I don't want to have any taste. I just want to marry my woman tomorrow!"

"Should I tell Gloria that you referred to her as 'woman'"? Peyton threatened and started laughing.

"You like seeing me get in trouble with her, don't you?"

"Yeah, I do actually," Peyton admitted. "Does Mom need me out there?"

Chris shrugged his shoulders, "Probably. I'm afraid to go back out there myself."

"Sissy," Peyton mumbled, and Chris threw a wad of paper at her.

Peyton walked back over to Noah, who was undoubtedly amused by the conversation between the two siblings. "There's never a dull moment when I come here," he admitted, and all three of them laughed.

Chris walked back out to see what he could do to help, which left Peyton and Noah alone in the house again. "Did I ever tell you how amazing I think you are? You've helped so much with the wedding even though you never needed to pitch in the way you did," she took his hand and smiled up at him. "You could be spending your days relaxing and doing whatever you want, but instead, you've been letting my mom put you to work. It's so nice of you to do all that for Chris and Gloria."

"You know, I didn't just do it for them," Noah hinted in his deep voice.

"Oh yeah?" flirted Peyton.

"Yes. Helping your family out has been no big deal, and I've been able to be with you all week too. To me, that's worth it," hummed Noah, giving her a quick kiss. "Is that okay with you?"

Peyton nodded, "I've loved having you here. It's been nice to see you every day and get to know you better and be with you."

"I feel the same way," he grinned.

"Good. Should we get back out there? I need to tell my mom that the cake is going to be delivered in a couple of hours." Peyton and Noah walked hand in hand out the door and toward the big white tent.

"Isn't there a rehearsal dinner tonight?" Noah asked.

"Yeah, there is. I think it's at six tonight, and it's actually at Felipe's," Peyton answered. She looked at Noah, who was smirking at her, and the light bulb finally went off in her head. She stopped walking and turned to face him, grabbing his arms, so he stopped walking too. "Oh my gosh, Noah, will you come with me and be my date tonight? Be my date all weekend?" pleaded Peyton.

"Yes. Yes, I will," he smiled crookedly and continued, "I wasn't trying to guilt you into asking me."

"No, I don't feel guilty. I wanted to ask you! I completely spaced, and this morning I went to go see Lucy..." Peyton trailed off as she noticed that Noah had a confused look on his face.

"Wait. Lucy from the restaurant?" he asked.

"Yeah. I went to her house this morning," Peyton clarified.

"Oh, really? How did that go? Is that why you weren't here when I arrived?" Noah questioned, and they started walking again to the tent.

"Yes," Peyton confirmed and started telling him about her morning with Lucy. He didn't say anything until she finished telling her story.

"Do you feel better now?" he asked thoughtfully.

Peyton nodded her head slowly, "Yeah, I do. It

was good that I went and finally mended that bridge. Ever since that night at Maxwell's, the thought of her being so upset with me has been eating at me. So, I went in hopes she could forgive me, and luckily, it all worked out."

"Good. I'm glad you guys figured it out," Noah put his arm around her and kissed the top of her head.

"Yeah, me too," Peyton smiled, and they walked inside the tent.

CHAPTER 23

*E*veryone kept decorating and adding last-minute touches until about five, and then Mom had everyone get ready for the rehearsal dinner. Peyton dressed in a black dress with red heels and pinned her hair up. She felt sort of ridiculous with how much she dressed up for a Mexican restaurant, but she knew if she came down the stairs in jeans and a t-shirt, her mom would have made her change anyway.

She started down the stairs only to see Noah waiting for her. His jaw dropped. She came further into view and felt her face flush. With Noah's eyes watching her, she had to focus extra hard on walking in her heels down the stairs. Once she got to the bottom, Noah wrapped his arm around her waist and kissed her.

"You look beautiful," he whispered in her ear and kissed her cheek.

"Thank you," Peyton looked up shyly, smiling at him.

"Get a room," Chris called.

"Or, don't," her dad piped up.

"We won't," Peyton clarified and shot a look at her annoying brother.

"Can we go now, please?" her mother begged, opening the door and gesturing for people to walk out. Everyone did as they were told and headed to the rehearsal dinner.

The dinner lasted about two hours, and it went by fast because everyone was having a blast. Gloria and her parents seemed right at home with the restaurant, and Peyton's family loved watching Gloria's family open up and getting to know them better. Her mom had rented out a large party room, where they all ate endless amounts of chips and salsa, continuously talking and laughing.

Peyton's family was able to meet more of Gloria's family who had flown in to celebrate the beautiful couple. Gloria had a few aunts and uncles come, which meant lots of cousins. Peyton forgot their names within the first five seconds of meeting them. Peyton's parents were loving all the excitement and laughter and talked a lot with Gloria's family.

Chris looked so happy—and so did Gloria.

Peyton could tell she was more in her comfort zone with her family around, and she seemed genuinely full of bliss and joy. Peyton believed that Chris was happy because Gloria was. He stayed by her side the entire time and made conversation with all of her family. There was a brief moment when Peyton felt some pride toward her brother and was proud of him. He had grown up so much over the last year, and she could tell he undeniably loved Gloria.

Peyton observed the same thing from Noah. He was so good about going with the flow and being friendly toward everyone, and it made him easy to love. She was falling so hard for the man, and she was glad he was with her at the dinner. Noah and Peyton sat next to each other the entire time, making sure some part of their body was always touching, whether it was a hand on the thigh, Noah's arm wrapped around Peyton's body, or holding hands. It kept Peyton's heart rate up, but she didn't mind. She had an amazing guy who loved to be around her, and she had never felt so special.

After everyone decided they had had enough chips and salsa, people started heading home to prepare for the next day, including Noah. As much as Peyton didn't want him to go, she knew it made sense for him to go home, so he didn't drive as far. Gloria's parents made her say goodnight to Chris, so she could get enough sleep for the next day, and

Chris came home with Peyton and her parents. Once Gloria's parents and Peyton's parents all went to bed, Chris and Peyton sat on the couch in a daze.

"I can't believe I'm getting married tomorrow," Chris stared blankly.

"Me either," Peyton chuckled.

"Do you think I'm ready?" he asked nervously.

"Oh yeah," Peyton nodded. "You two are perfect for each other," she assured him.

"She is pretty amazing, my little *mamacita*," he smiled and looked as if he was daydreaming, "Well, I better get to bed. See you in the morning," he started lying down on the couch and pulled a blanket over him.

"Night, bro," Peyton patted his leg and went to bed.

CHAPTER 24

The next morning, the house was in complete chaos. Gloria's mom left early to meet Gloria at the hair salon, and Peyton's mom was nagging at Chris to shower, but Chris kept eating bowl after bowl of cereal to combat his nerves. Her dad ironed his and Chris's shirts, and Peyton was in charge of putting flowers in the vases and finishing any last minute touches for the reception. Gloria wasn't showing up until right before the wedding in a limo that would also be taking Chris and Gloria to the airport for their flight to Hawaii. Her mom didn't want to risk Chris trying to sneak a peek at Gloria before she walked down the aisle. Which he would have totally done. All the bridesmaids, except Peyton, were getting ready with Gloria and were coming in the limo along with her. They invited Peyton to come along, but she knew her mom would want her around to help.

In no time, it was four o'clock, and the caterers were starting to arrive with the food. The groomsmen arrived to get dressed in their tuxes and ultimately got their stamp of approval from Peyton's mom. Peyton decided it was time to get dressed, too, in her bridesmaid's dress, which was a blush pink maxi dress. Thankfully, it didn't look too bad on her, but it was a little long on her, which forced her to wear heels.

Once she was dressed, she looked for her mom out back, where they were holding the ceremony. After the walk through the garden where flower petals lined the path, it opened up to about a hundred chairs set up with an archway covered in flowers at the end, where her mom happened to be. She was still trying to add more flowers so that very little of the metal showed on the arch.

"Mom, it looks beautiful. Stop messing with it," Peyton reckoned, and her mom turned to scold her, but then her eyes lit up once she saw her in the dress.

"Peyton, you look gorgeous!" she gushed. "That pink looks so pretty on you! Are you going to trip in that dress?" Her brows furrowed when she looked at Peyton's feet, "You're wearing heels, right?"

"Yes," Peyton raised her dress to reveal her sparkly heels. "See?"

"Oh boy, walk slow. You're walking with Noah, right?" she wondered.

Peyton shrugged her shoulders, "I think so? I would assume so." Chris found out at the rehearsal dinner that one of his buddies ended up with the stomach flu and wasn't going to be able to make it. So Chris asked Noah to be a last-minute replacement for a friend who was unable to make it to the wedding. Peyton was surprised, but so happy that Chris had thought to ask Noah.

"Maybe he should just carry you down the aisle then," her mom smirked and kept putting flowers on the arch. "Man, I'm so glad Gloria decided to change her colors from red and green, to blush pink and orange. It's so much prettier. Not to mention the dresses she picked for you girls is so flowy, and I love the three-quarter length bell sleeves on them! You'll be able to wear it for other occasions and not just for today."

"Yes, I agree. Uh, Mom? People are going to start showing up soon, and you haven't gotten dressed yet," Peyton pointed out and grabbed her hand. "Step away from the arch."

"Fine!" her mother gave up and stomped off toward the house.

Peyton followed her back inside the house to

find Noah sitting at the dining room table in his tux.

"Wow," Noah stood up, awestruck, "You look amazing."

"You're not so bad yourself," Peyton winked and kissed him on the cheek. "It's a good thing you had a pair of navy dress pants to match with the other boys. I like the pink tie too."

Noah smirked and leaned in close to her ear so only she could hear, "I'm never going to wear this tie again. Only today, for your brother."

Peyton had to restrain herself from barking out a laugh. Luckily her dad walked down the stairs in his tux, and Peyton had completely forgotten she was trying not to laugh. She whistled, "Look at you, Daddy!"

"Oh, brother," he rolled his eyes. "Guests are going to start showing up soon," he turned to look at Chris and all the groomsmen. "I need you boys to go stand out front by the walking path to help guide guests to their seats when they show up. If you get lost, follow the rose petals and the candles," he said sarcastically and winked at Peyton.

"Alright, men," Chris clapped his hands together, "Let's move out!"

Noah kissed Peyton's cheek, "See you in a little bit."

"Bye," she waved and looked at her dad, "You

really do look good, Daddy. I haven't seen you wear a tux since my wedding!"

"Well, it's not my favorite outfit to wear," he admitted. Just then, they heard someone walking down the stairs and saw her mom step down in a sparkly burgundy dress with her makeup perfectly done, accenting her hazel eyes, and her brown, curly hair pinned up in an elegant twist. "You look absolutely beautiful," her dad swooned and kissed his gorgeous wife.

"You don't look so bad yourself, stranger," she smiled, "Your tie is crooked though." She reached up to loosen the blush pink tie and straightened it out. "There," she chuckled, "Now you're perfect." Staring at her husband, her eyes looked as if they twinkled, and it made Peyton hope that someday, in about twenty years, she would have someone look at her the same way her mom looked at her dad.

"What time is it?" She looked around aimlessly for a clock.

Her dad looked at his watch and reported, "It's four twenty-five."

"Oh! I wonder if guests have started to arrive!" She ran over to the window as fast as she could in her four-inch heels, and peered through, "There are lots of cars already, and the boys are walking people back and forth! I hope Gloria and her bridesmaids are on time! Is her dad helping walk guests? I haven't seen him…" she trailed off.

"I believe so, honey. I don't believe there's anyone in the house except for us," he confirmed. "What time should the boys stop walking people?"

"At about four fifty-five. Then the guests will have to find their own seats. Gloria said she wanted to walk down the aisle at exactly five o'clock and not a minute later. The guests will have to figure out for themselves to follow the flower petals. I need them to stand in line so that when the brides-maids show up, they can hook arms and start walk-ing," her mom explained. "Peyton, will you help me grab the bouquets and do some last minute touch-ups, so we can hand them to the girls once they show up?"

"Sure thing," she answered quickly and headed to the fridge where the five bouquets of orange, pink, and yellow roses were. "Man, I did a good job making these things," she gloated.

"Yes, you did," her mom affirmed. "How are you doing with everything?"

"What do you mean?" she asked, puzzled.

"You know, with your little brother getting mar-ried," she explained quietly.

"Oh yeah. I mean I had a hard time at first, but I'm very happy for him. They seem good together," she responded and shrugged her shoulders, "I'm glad he's happy. Everyone deserves to be happy, right?"

Her mom smiled, "You're so right."

They finished pulling out the bouquets and adding any final touches until her dad called out, "Four fifty-five!"

All three of them walked outside to find the guys still waiting for guests until her mom put them in a specific order—Chris's childhood friend Evan, Chris's friend Brad, his other friend Nick, Gloria's brother Eduardo, and then Noah last. Peyton handed each of the groomsmen a bouquet to hold, while Chris and her parents walked to the backyard.

Within a few minutes, the limo pulled up, and out came Gloria, her mother, and the other bridesmaids. Gloria looked absolutely beautiful in her strapless mermaid gown, her hair half up with curls falling on her shoulders and her smoky eye paired with a pretty pink lip. All the bridesmaids had their hair curled, letting the curls loosely fall onto their shoulders. Peyton felt a little guilty with her hair loosely pinned up hair, with curls falling down either side of her face, but figured it was too late to fix her hair now. Then Gloria looked at her and smiled, so Peyton knew she was just fine. Her mom kissed her daughter and followed the trail of petals to the backyard, and then the bridesmaids were paired up with their groomsmen.

At exactly five o'clock, the music began playing "Canon in D," Evan walked with Gloria's friend Marisol first, and then Brad and Gloria's sister, Emilie, followed after about ten seconds. They were followed by Nick and Gloria's other friend Sofia. Next to walk were Gloria's brother, Eduardo, and her best friend Megan. And at the end were Noah and Peyton. She could hear Gloria's father getting a little emotional behind them, but she tried to stay focused on her walking, so she wouldn't trip on her dress.

"Did I tell you how beautiful you looked?" whispered Noah as they walked through the garden and saw the guests watching them walk down the aisle.

"You may have mentioned it," she breathed and continued to stare straight ahead.

"Well, you do," he chuckled, and Peyton giggled in response. They stopped once they got near the altar where he kissed her on the cheek before they each stood in their line.

They watched as Gloria walked through the garden arm in arm with her father, who was starting to shed a few tears. She looked as if she was lightly gliding above the grass as she walked toward Chris. Once they locked eyes, they couldn't stop staring at each other. They looked so head over heels in love that Peyton could feel her own eyes start to tear up.

Gloria's father kissed her gently on the cheek when they reached Chris, and then he sat down next to his wife. Peyton took the bouquet from Gloria who then joined hands with Chris, who had the biggest smile spread across his face—so big that it almost looked painful.

The ceremony was beautiful. The two exchanged vows that left the audience in tears. Peyton had no idea Chris could be so sentimental. Once the ceremony was over, everyone congregated in the white tent where the food would be served in a matter of minutes. Peyton made sure to look for Lucy and hugged her, letting her know she was happy to see her. Then Peyton got in trouble with her mother for wandering off when she was supposed to be standing in the receiving line.

"Somebody got in trouble," Chris sang and laughed.

"Hilarious," Peyton rolled her eyes and stood there like she was told. Luckily, her mom only made them stand until dinner was served, and then they were free to sit and eat. Following dinner was the cutting of the cake, which turned out to be hilarious because Chris was kind to Gloria and nicely fed her a piece of cake, but then Gloria shoved Chris's bite into his face. Everyone got a kick out of that and laughed. After the cake was cut and handed out to guests, the dancing began. This was the part where Peyton tried to make herself scarce, but Noah sought her out.

"Where are you going?" he chuckled and eyed her suspiciously.

"I was going to check on the caterers," Peyton lied and half-smiled at him.

"Oh, I'm sure. They look like they need a lot of help too," he pointed to the crew of workers covering the food and cleaning off the tables.

"Yeah, I guess not," mumbled Peyton.

"Peyton," he said thoughtfully, "will you dance with me?" He smiled his crooked smile at her, and his sparkly blue eyes twinkled at her, which naturally took her breath away.

"Sure," she smiled back and breathed. "Just as long as you're okay with getting your foot stepped on because I have two left feet."

He held out his hand, "I guess love hurts sometimes."

Peyton busted up laughing as he guided her onto the dance floor next to her parents. He pulled her close and they started swaying slowly back and forth. She looked around the room and dozens of eyes were staring in her direction. She had a lot of family and friends here, and she was sure that she was catching people off guard by dancing with a man other than Derek. She started feeling a little overwhelmed with the number of people staring at them and turned her focus to Noah.

"I think we have some fans," Noah teased and started quietly laughing.

"You noticed?" asked Peyton, worried she was taking the focus off of Chris and Gloria.

"I think the entire room is staring at us," Noah chuckled.

"Ugh, perfect," she groaned.

"Should we give them something to stare at?" he asked, looking a little too amused.

"What do you mean?" she wondered. Just as she asked, Noah spun her away from him—causing Peyton to almost trip over her own feet—then he spun her back in, dipped her, and bent over to kiss her. He pulled her back up into their original stance, and he had a big smile spread across his face.

Peyton, feeling her face completely flushed, was still dazed and tried to stammer out words, "Well, I think everyone is staring now." Noah laughed and held onto her for the next two songs and then let her sit down while a swarm of family and friends started asking questions.

Chris and Gloria only stuck around for another hour and left to get dressed in some street clothes for the airport. While they were changing, all the bridesmaids and Gloria's mom started handing out sparklers for everyone to light as the newlyweds walked to the limo. When they stepped out, they were completely surprised by all their family and friends waiting there to wave them off. Smiling and laughing, Chris and Gloria ran through the sparklers before hugging their parents goodbye and hopping into the limo to catch their flight to Hawaii.

The rest of the night consisted of taking down tables and chairs and cleaning up all the decorations. Luckily, a lot of people stuck around to help, so the cleanup didn't take long. Noah found Peyton after everything was cleaned up.

"Can I see you tomorrow?" he asked.

"Absolutely," she said thoughtfully. "You can help us eat all the leftovers. I'm hoping we don't have to cook for the next few days."

"Awesome," he kissed her, "I have some stuff to do most of the day tomorrow, but I'll be here around six, is that okay?"

Peyton was taken aback because she thought he would have come sooner but tried not to let it show and smiled, "Sounds good to me. Thanks for everything today."

"Anytime," he smiled and kissed her goodnight before he left.

CHAPTER 25

The next morning, Peyton and her mom slept in and ate cake for breakfast. Gloria's family had an early morning flight back to Mexico, and her dad had graciously offered to give them a ride to the airport. While they were gone, Peyton's mom received a text letting her know that Chris and Gloria made it to Hawaii and were laying out on a beach relaxing. This made Peyton incredibly jealous. She hadn't been to the beach in a long time.

Her dad came back home around eleven just before the rental company came by to pick up the tables and chairs and take down the big white tent. This took a couple of hours because they had to do some additional clean up from the night before, move the tables and chairs out to the company truck, and then work together to take the tent down carefully.

Peyton could tell her mom felt a whole lot better. It was probably an item checked off on her mental list of things to do. The next thing they did was strip the sheets off the two guest beds to be washed and start cleaning the house. They cleaned all the bathrooms, vacuumed the floors, swept and mopped, and wiped down all surfaces. Her mom was determined to make sure all the germs were taken care of from all the people that had been in her house all week.

By the time they were done cleaning the house, it was time for dinner. The fridge was full of chicken breast, steaks, guacamole, rice, salad, tamales, refried beans, salsa, tortillas and lots of dressings and sauces. Peyton felt as if it was a buffet because they reheated all the food and laid it out on the dining room table. Before Peyton knew it, it was six, and Noah was knocking at the door.

Peyton opened the door and saw Noah wearing dark wash jeans and a blue and white flannel shirt. It kind of made him look like a cowboy, a handsome cowboy.

"Hey," grinned Peyton.

"Hey," he grinned back and kissed her cheek.

"Are you hungry?" she asked him and waved to the food on the table, "We have lots, including cake and cookies for dessert."

"Sounds good, thanks."

"Hey, Noah, how are you doing?" her dad called.

"I'm doing good, and how was your day?" he inquired.

"It was busy with lots of cleaning and taking care of the last of the wedding things," her mom answered and handed Noah a plate.

"Thank you, and awesome! It looks great in here, but of course, it always looks good in here," Noah complimented and started scooping up refried beans on the plate.

"You're too kind," her mom gushed. "I couldn't have done the wedding without you, Noah. Your help did not go unnoticed. Thank you for being here every day to help set up and letting me boss you around."

"It was my pleasure. I was happy to help. Plus, I got to see a certain someone every day," he smirked, and Peyton started blushing.

"Well, regardless, it was very sweet of you to come whether or not it was for Chris or to see Peyton. You helped a lot, and it is greatly appreciated," her mom thanked him.

"Yes, thank you, Noah," her dad repeated and shoved a spoonful of rice into his mouth.

"Honey, eat some salad," her mom pushed the salad bowl toward him.

"I had some yesterday," her dad retorted. Peyton snorted, and her mom gave him a look.

After they were done eating, Peyton and Noah helped clear the table and clean the dishes, so they didn't leave it all for her mom to do.

"So, what are you guys planning for the night?" her mom wondered.

"I thought it might be nice to go on a walk," Noah suggested and grabbed Peyton's hand. "What do you think?"

"Sounds good to me. Especially after all that food I just ate," groaned Peyton and rubbed her stomach. "I didn't need to eat four tacos, plus more chips and salsa."

Noah chuckled, "Oh Peyton. Well, we'll see you guys in a little bit," he waved, and Peyton smiled.

"See you later." She put on her shoes and followed Noah out the door.

They started walking on the same path and headed to the back of the property where the river was.

"What did you do today?" asked Peyton.

"I had some errands to run, mostly," he said vaguely, but Peyton decided to not pester him.

"Where are we walking to?"

"I thought we could go to the river. We haven't been there in a while, and it might be nice to watch the sunset," he offered.

"Yeah, that sounds like a great idea. I bet I'm going to need to start cutting the brush back soon...," Peyton trailed off.

They found the fork in the path that led to the river, and once they turned onto the other path, Peyton started seeing pink rose petals lining the path.

"Hmm, I wonder if someone put these here by accident," wondered Peyton.

"Yeah, maybe," Noah shrugged his shoulders and kept walking. After about a hundred feet, she saw battery-powered candles flickering on the ground alongside the rose petals.

"Wait a minute, did you do this?" she asked, bewildered.

He tilted his head as if trying to hide a smile and said, "Maybe this was originally for Chris and Gloria, and your parents forgot about it."

"Right. I would have known about it. What is this?" The trail opened up to the river, and on the pier were dozens of the lighted candles with more rose petals. Peyton walked onto the pier and stared at all the candles and petals, "Noah..." she trailed.

Noah turned to face Peyton and took both of her hands, "Peyton, you are the most incredible, kind, and beautiful woman I have ever met."

"Thank you, but Noah..." she got interrupted again by Noah.

"You've been through so much. More than anyone should ever go through, but you have handled it so well. Not to mention, you're patient, hard-working, willing to help at a moment's notice, thoughtful, and caring. You are the woman of my dreams. I know I could never replace Derek, nor would I ever ask to, but I hope that you could give me the chance to be the man of your dreams and let me take care of you and love you the way you deserve," Noah expressed to her.

"Noah, you already are the man of my dreams," Peyton whispered and stroked the back of his hand with her thumb.

"I was hoping you would say that," Noah knelt on one knee and pulled out a ring box that held a gorgeous diamond ring—small diamonds intertwined around the band with a big diamond in the middle.

"Oh my…" breathed Peyton as she stared at the rock he was holding. "What are you doing?"

"Peyton, I love you. I love you more than I have ever loved anyone. I love being with you and spending time with you, I love holding your hand, and I absolutely love kissing you. When I'm not with you, I miss you like crazy. All I do is think about you and wonder when I'm going to see you again. That's about the time I text you and try to make plans with you. I don't want to spend another day, another moment, or another second without you in my life. I love you, and I promise that I will take care of you, be there for you, and love you forever. Peyton, will you marry me?" Noah asked with all the love and affection in the world.

Peyton looked at him and was in complete awe of him. He looked at her as if he was longing to grab her and kiss her. His eyes twinkled in the candlelight, and her favorite crooked smile was on his face. Peyton had barely noticed the sun going down, until she noticed shadows casting across Noah's face. She stared at his face and smiled. She loved him, with all her heart. She wanted to be with him, take care of him, and support him, and never lose him. She couldn't imagine him not being in her life anymore. In every situation, thought, or hope she had, he was always included.

"Yes, I would love to marry you!" Peyton promised. Noah took the ring out of the box and placed it on her ring finger. Peyton looked at the rock now on her finger and briefly forgot how to breathe.

Noah stood up, picked her up, and swung her around. Then he kissed her with a passion Peyton had never felt from him. They locked lips for a couple of minutes and then Noah gently put her back down. She definitely felt dizzy now but in a completely good way.

"I love you, Noah," swooned Peyton, and she kissed him again.

"I love you, too, my love. I cannot wait to spend the rest of forever with you," Noah purred and kissed her again.

All of the sudden, Peyton heard squealing coming from behind them and was rammed into by a body that started squeezing the two of them. Peyton was able to pull her head back just a little to see that it was her mother holding her phone in her hand, which made Peyton assume she had been taking pictures of the proposal.

"I am so happy for you two!" her mother exclaimed. "Oh, Peyton, I told you. I told you that you were never going to be alone. You're too precious to be left alone the rest of your life." She was smiling with tears streaming down her face, looking completely happy.

"Welcome to the family, son!" her dad said from behind Noah.

"Walter, he's always been a part of the family!" her mom said to him, hitting his chest.

"I know, but, oh, never mind. We're very happy for you!" he congratulated.

"Come on, Walter. Let's let them be alone! I need to make some phone calls!" she cheered and walked hand in hand back to the house with her husband.

Once they were out of sight, Noah was the first to speak, "Are you happy?"

Peyton nodded, "I think more than I've ever been. You have been the best thing that has ever happened in my life. You pulled me out of a dark place and have shown me a light I never want to leave again. I have you to thank for that."

Noah shook his head, "I didn't do anything, I just reminded you of your strength, and you did the rest. You are truly remarkable."

"Still, I couldn't have done it without you. And all the while you were finishing up dental school. You truly are amazing. I don't know what I did to deserve you," she admitted.

"I could say the same thing," he kissed her forehead. "But I'm sure glad I have you."

"Agreed," she smiled. At this point it was dark, and the candles were the only light. Nearby, she heard the crickets chirping and frogs croaking nearby, filling the air with their own sweet music.

"Should we go back? I need to call my parents and tell them you said yes!" he said excitedly.

"Yes, let's go back and eat more cake!" Peyton laughed.

Noah wrapped his arm around her, and they walked together, back to the house with some very excited parents ready to start calling all the relatives and make plans for their own wedding. She wouldn't have been surprised if her mom was already on the phone, spreading the joyous news. Peyton didn't mind though. Despite what she had gone through, she was given a second chance at love. A second chance to take care of someone and grow old together. A second chance to live a life full of happiness, laughter, and love.

EPILOGUE

7 YEARS LATER

*P*eyton woke up to the sound of her alarm at six o'clock. She turned to look at her husband, who was unaware of the annoying alarm sound and slept soundly. She smiled and rolled her eyes, wishing she could have slept as soundly, but she spent the night tossing and turning and running to the bathroom. She rolled out of bed, got dressed, and went outside for her walk. The temperature was cool for an August morning, but she knew it was going to be hot later. She walked only about a mile because her body started to ache, and the pressure of her belly was bugging her. She then decided to water her garden before the heat came.

Ever since she had had her own home, she loved having a garden. She sometimes compared her plants to her babies. She loved planting the seeds and watering and watching the sprouts slowly pop up through the ground. She felt as if it was some sort of accomplishment to grow something from a tiny seed and have it produce zucchini or peppers. This year, she tried strawberries, which had grown wild throughout her garden. After she watered, she went through and picked several strawberries, a couple of jalapeno peppers, some cherry tomatoes, and a big zucchini then carried them inside to wash.

Once inside, she decided to straighten the house before starting the rest of her day. She unloaded the dishwasher then loaded the previous night's dishes. She swept and mopped the floor even though she was sure it was going to be a mess by the end of the day. She vacuumed the living room and dusted all the surfaces. Her patterns hadn't completely changed since she had lived with her parents. She liked starting her day with a bit of exercise and chores so that she didn't have to worry about it for the rest of the day. She heard footsteps coming from upstairs and figured her husband was finally ready to start the day. When she looked at the clock, she saw that it was after seven o'clock.

"Noah! It's James's first day of school, and he's going to be late for the bus! Will you please make sure he's awake?" Peyton called up the stairs.

"I'll go check right now," Noah called. He heard

him open the door and tell their son that it was time to get dressed.

Peyton started pulling out a bowl and his favorite cereal so that the moment her son came downstairs, he was prepared to start eating right away.

"Is he ready?" she asked, trying not to nag.

"He's brushing his teeth now and is about to head downstairs," Noah called back down.

"He's barely going to have enough time to eat breakfast," Peyton added.

"I'm coming, Mom!" James came downstairs. He was the spitting image of Noah. He had dark brown hair that looked a little messy, but he pulled it off like his daddy. He also inherited his striking blue eyes but had Peyton's thick eyelashes. He was, simply, an adorable little boy.

"Would you like some cereal, bud?" she asked.

"Yes, please!" he answered. Peyton handed him his bowl of cereal with a spoon, and he started chowing down.

"Do I get some cereal too?" Noah asked while walking down the stairs wearing a pair of tan trousers and a blue long sleeve button dress shirt.

Peyton whistled, "Someone is definitely getting cereal."

Noah chuckled, "Good morning, beautiful," he kissed his wife and then her tummy, "How's little sis doing this morning? I heard you get up four different times last night to go to the bathroom."

"She's resting right on my bladder. I can't help it," Peyton complained. "I'm not getting any sleep. I'm surprised you heard me."

"I was a little nervous about James's first day of school and had a harder time sleeping," he explained.

"Yeah, I was too," she told him. "Are you excited for your first day of kindergarten?" she turned her attention to her son who had just taken a big bite of cereal.

"Yes! I can't wait to play with all the kids!" he said with a mouthful of food.

"You are going to have so much fun! Are you sure you want to ride the bus? Daddy or I can take you to school if you want," she offered and secretly hoped he would take her up on it.

James shook his head, "Nope, I want to ride the bus. It looks so cool!"

"It is cool, buddy," Noah chuckled

"Mommy, when is sister going to come?" James asked.

"In a couple of weeks, honey. Are you ready to go? The bus is going to be here in two minutes," Peyton handed James his backpack and handed Noah a banana and a granola bar.

"No cereal?" he teased.

"I didn't think you would want it since you

have to be at work in fifteen minutes!" Peyton deflected and started getting out another bowl, "Let me get you some cereal."

Noah started laughing and closed the cabinet, "I'm only kidding. You know just what I need. I am late, I have an early patient this morning that needs a couple of teeth pulled. Oh, honey, the bus is here!"

"James!" Peyton called, "Come on, let's go! Noah, get your phone ready, so we can take pictures!"

"Okay!" he answered.

The three of them ran outside toward the bus, and Noah pulled out his phone. Peyton and James first took pictures together, and then Noah took a turn.

"Mom, I'm nervous about going to school. What if no one likes me?" James wondered, almost on the verge of tears.

Peyton kneeled slowly, so she was looking at James straight on and smiled, "You just be your nice, kind self, and everything will be fine. Show them that fun, bubbly personality of yours, and you'll have friends in no time. I love you so much, James Derek Hart. I will see you this afternoon, okay?" She gave him a big hug, feeling tears well up in her eyes. Then, he ran over and hugged his dad.

"Love you, buddy. You're going to do great!"

Noah encouraged and kissed his son on the top of his head.

James ran to the bus and waved before he got on, "Bye, love you!" Then the doors shut, and he was gone.

"I can't believe our baby is going to kindergarten," Peyton sniffled, and Noah helped her off the ground.

"I can't either. It seems like yesterday we were changing his diaper or teaching him to walk," reminisced Noah.

"I know," Peyton cried. Noah rubbed her back and guided her back through the front door.

"It's alright, honey. I'm sorry you're sad, but I gotta go. That poor kid is probably waiting for me to yank his teeth out and is a nervous wreck," Noah reckoned.

"Now, you're leaving me too! I'm going to be all alone! What am I going to do all day?" Peyton wailed. Clearly, her pregnancy hormones were getting the best of her.

"I'm sorry, sweetheart. What you need to do is rest and try to take a nap. Just remember, I'll be back later and so will James. Every time I leave, I will always come back. You'll never be alone again," Noah kissed her and walked to his car. "I love you!" he called back.

"I love you too!" Peyton said back. Then she all of a sudden remembered, "Oh, don't forget, we're having dinner at my parent's house tonight! Chris and Gloria are in town, and James will get to play with Mario and Hector."

"Okay, honey. Bye!" he climbed into his car and drove away.

Peyton waved and smiled. She missed him the moment he left but knew that he would be back. Just as he said, she was never going to be alone again.

Dear reader,

We hope you enjoyed reading *The Second Chance.* Please take a moment to leave a review, even if it's a short one. Your opinion is important to us.

Discover more books by Morgan Utley at https://www.nextchapter.pub/authors/morgan-utley

Want to know when one of our books is free or discounted? Join the newsletter at http://eepurl.com/bqqB3H

Best regards,

Morgan Utley and the Next Chapter Team

AUTHOR BIOGRAPHY

Morgan Utley was born and raised outside the city of Portland in the lush green state of Oregon. Morgan is currently residing in Orem, Utah, where she is raising four handsome boys while supporting her husband through medical school. She considers her faith and family to be the most important parts of her life. If she isn't chasing her boys around, you can find her outside enjoying a run or in the kitchen baking something sweet. *The Second Chance* is Morgan's first novel.

The Second Chance
ISBN: 978-4-86750-529-8
Large Print

Published by
Next Chapter
1-60-20 Minami-Otsuka
170-0005 Toshima-Ku, Tokyo
+818035793528

6th June 2021

Lightning Source UK Ltd.
Milton Keynes UK
UKHW041836140621
385519UK00001B/147